Bryan Appleyard is an award-winning s???????? ???????? ?????
and columnist for the *Sunday Times*. He is the author of
several books, including *The Brain is Wider than the Sky*:
*Why Simple Solutions Don't Work in a Complex World, How
to Live Forever or Die Trying*: *On the New Immortality* and
Brave New Worlds: *Genetics and the Human Experience*. He
lives in London.

Praise for Bedford Park

'A witty and erudite historical novel, set mostly in London
in the late-Victorian and Edwardian eras ... It is also a
brilliantly lively, often very funny reconstruction of a lost
world of artistic endeavour and social idealism through
which Appleyard's American abroad wanders in a fruitless
search for his true self.'

Nick Rennison, *Sunday Times*

'Appleyard has created this novel, set in the West London
suburb of Bedford Park, around the lives of noted
Edwardians ... Beautifully written.'

Daily Mail

'Nothing in Bryan Appleyard's *Bedford Park* betrays the fact
that it is his first period novel: not its deft characterisations,
its virtuoso dialogue, its dry and economical wit, or its
choice of a narrator and material quite outside the author's
own experience ... Excellent fiction.'

Timothy Mo, *Spectator*

Also by Bryan Appleyard

The Culture Club: Crisis in the Arts

Richard Rogers: A Biography

The Pleasures of Peace: Art and Imagination in
Post-War Britain

Understanding the Present: Science and the Soul of
Modern Man

The First Church of the New Millennium: A Novel

Brave New Worlds: Genetics and the Human Experience

Aliens: Why They Are Here

How to Live Forever or Die Trying: On the New
Immortality

The Brain is Wider than the Sky: Why Simple Solutions
Don't Work in a Complex World

BEDFORD PARK

A Novel

BRYAN APPLEYARD

PHOENIX

A PHOENIX PAPERBACK

First published in ebook in Great Britain in 2013
by Weidenfeld & Nicolson

This paperback edition published in 2014
by Phoenix, an imprint of the Orion Publishing Group Ltd

1 3 5 7 9 10 8 6 4 2

A CIP catalogue record for this book is available from the British Library.

ISBN: 978 1 780 22838 9

Typeset by GroupFMG using BookCloud

Printed in Great Britain by Clays Ltd, St Ives plc

The Orion Publishing Group's policy is to use papers that are natural, renewable
and recyclable and made from wood grown in sustainable forests. The logging and
manufacturing processes are expected to conform to environmental regulations of
the country of origin.

The Orion Publishing Group Ltd
Orion House
5 Upper Saint Martin's Lane
London, WC2H 9EA

An Hachette UK Company

www.orionbooks.co.uk

For Christena

For Christmas

Or is it the illusory world
That falls from reality
As we look? Or are we
Like a thunderbolt hurled?

One or another
Is lost, since we fall apart
Endlessly, in one motion depart
From each other.

D. H. LAWRENCE, *'Tommies in the Train'*

Eastern Atlantic, 1912

I start on this last, the ninetieth, London notebook once the Mizen Head and the whole ragged claw of the Irish coast passes from view.

Cherbourg, Queenstown and then this nothing. A priest took to one of the tenders at Queenstown and, leaving Southampton, we sucked the New York free of her moorings. She missed us by four feet.
'The power,' the captain laughed, 'the power!'

'One speech! I am going all this way for one speech. But it must be done, it *must* be done!'

Stead speaks in exclamation marks, a common habit among the Englishmen I have known. As ever, he is delighting in the sacrifices demanded of him by his urgent destiny. His passion contrasts strangely with the gentle shafts of sunlight playing on the starched linen. Everything in this room is both pale and very bright; it is the brightness of the sea. Pale brightness in which I seem to float ... It was like this when I left Chicago.

'Of course, on the subject of universal peace no sacrifice can be too great. Everything wrong in the world is a divine call to use your life in righting it, ch, Cal?'

The linen-muted sounds of lunch hover above the iron-muted thunder of the engines, whose vibrations form concentric circles in my wine. This churning machine keeps us alive on the ocean where we don't belong, and so much decorative care to hide the effort involved! The cream gilded salon of this steamship is immensely long. Superficially, it is Jacobean in style or, at least, the ceiling is – strange for a modern ship, but the English, I discovered long ago, don't like things to look like what – or when – they are.

Something in Stead's last statement awakens me.

'Universal peace? I thought you were speaking on spiritualism.'

'Cal, for goodness' sake!' Stead cries with kindly exasperation. 'We have discussed this at length. I am to address the Men and Religion Forward Movement Congress at Carnegie Hall.'

I am sure he is right, we must have discussed this. Stead is two years older than me and looks that at least, thanks to his tumultuous beard and the ill-fitting and uncoordinated clothes of an absent-minded old man, but he acts and thinks as if he were at least twenty years younger. He is holding his own against the clawings of the years more effectively than I. My memory, in particular, is not what it was, but the notebooks preserve the essentials.

I ran into Dora in the street a few days before we sailed and failed to recognise her, the golden hair now dimmed somewhat but the eyes still blue and alert. She was, it seemed, someone who reminded me of Dora. I stared, empty eyed, lost.

'*Oh, Cal, are you quite with us?*'

'*Yes, yes, I am so sorry …*'

'*Dora.*'

'*Dora. I know. Forgive me. Please. Forgive me.*'

Then my old heart leapt like a frog as I gazed into her still-dear features. She has not changed. Age, in her, has just brushed the surface … a slight blurring.

'Forgive you? Oh, Cal. I am so sorry I could not ...'

'I get so distracted.'

'I know. You must look after yourself, you are very important to us.'

'Important ...?'

Important to them – think of that! I have attained importance but too late, too late! I am sixty-one and, already, I have become an old fool, begging forgiveness from women in the street whose names escape me, and this was a woman I loved ... passionately, I latterly realised. But she said 'important to us' – whom did she mean? Or perhaps the point was that I was not especially, singularly, important to her. She had, at the last, proved that beyond doubt.

'The Americans still have not come to terms with the matter of Russia; they are a modern people but they are not truly forward looking. They need a little more simple truth if they are to progress.'

Stead is summarising the contents of his lecture, apparently forgetting that I am one of these naive Americans. I need not listen; it is all very familiar.

The sleeve of this coat is worn – there is a distinct shine around the cuff. I have not noticed that before. It is not like me; I was known about town for my fastidiousness in these matters. I always like to feel finished when I leave the house or, today, stateroom. Perhaps it is like me as I am now, an old fool. Frank would say I always was. He has known me long enough – forty years! – and must have amassed a good deal of evidence for the prosecution. What difference does it make? Neither more nor less than Frank's seductions or Dora's worried look or Stead's speech. What difference does anything make? Voyaging to London and, then, twenty-four years later, voyaging home. What difference?

*

Frank.

Frank is a sentence: subject and predicate. Frank is the doer of what is done to the done to. Ugly, vulpine, potent and yet, here's a thing I have always found strange, repeatedly he falls ill. So do I. I am frail. I suffer sneezing fits, a swollen face, breathing difficulties. I was, from the first, written off, not a survivor, not fully born into this world, almost transparent in my almost absence. The Colonel's disappointment with me in later life was merely an extension of his disappointment at discovering he had a transparent son with an enfeebled constitution. It was not the Chicago way.

I accepted this. I assumed I was the sickly – nasty word that! – type. But when Frank is sick it is an afterthought, a footnote to his vigour. Being sick is an aspect of his masculinity. For me, it is effeminacy, a sign of my submission. I would lie down; Frank would buy machines, a pump to cleanse his stomach, a tube to cleanse his bowels, or he would engage in alarming diets and frantic exercise. I think this means he has faith, faith that he is more than his body, which is, to him, a thing in the world, one more obstacle to be overcome. I lack such faith; my body is me, its shortcomings mine. My body is a picture of my soul but Frank's impatient soul inhabits his thickened body. After our deaths, my body-soul will moulder while Frank, free of mere body, will be haranguing Stead at one of his séances.

'I watched him on Blackheath – what a moment that was! I loved him and, for a time, I think he loved me. Such greatness!'

Stead has moved on to Turkey and Gladstone. I remember his unconsummated 'affair' with Madame Novikoff. Frank thought Stead had looked up 'affair' in the wrong dictionary. It is not his failing that, in his innocence, he attracts passionate women, though Frank claims he is more animal than he could ever admit.

'Stead,' he once announced, 'exudes semen through his skin. Ectoplasmic. The women smell it. He doesn't give lectures, he gives emanations.'

Frank always says too much and I always remember the wrong things.

'He turned a mob baying for Russian blood into an army ready to march against the Ottomans. We shall never see his like again. He bestrode the nineteenth century like a colossus.'

Stead's high-mindedness is seasoned with his usual spice of yellow journalism. He sees himself bestriding the twentieth century; then, at other times, there is this gentleness ...

Absent-mindedly I reach for my notebook to record this thought. I fill a notebook about every three months and have done so ever since I arrived in London, ninety notebooks ago. They were to form the basis of a book, I used to tell myself. In some moods the book was to be called *Titans*, in others *Lost Titans* and, in yet others, *Last Titans*. In one much darker mood, I considered *Chaos* the most appropriate title, though neither this nor any of the others sounded like the book I wanted to write – should have written. My American friends preferred *London Swells* and Agent Pinker, as we knew him, advocated *Modern Madmen: The London Set*. I pointed out there was no such set and, by the standards recently set by Herr Doktor Freud, they could hardly be said to be *that* mad.

'None of that matters, you poor Yankee innocent, think headlines!' Pinker cried. 'Reviews! Making a splash of it! Do not be held back by the exact truth of the matter.'

The notebooks remain just that, notebooks, in their special little trunk in the cabin. They will be found one day, doubtless, and I shall be reborn long after my death as a great documenter of this peculiar moment, that monstrous city and that enchanted suburb.

For my pre-mortem existence, they were a waste of time. I shouldn't have been writing such things anyway. Fordie always told me that 'the only occupation fitting for a proper man in these centuries is the writing of novels'. I guess fiction is truer than all this modern noise and I failed to be fitting and proper. I should have stayed in Chicago with its fires and the pork bellies. They were true enough.

'Cal, my friend, are you all right?'

I had passed my hand over my brow and closed my eyes, interrupting Stead's monologue. I had been, somewhere beyond any conscious strategy, concealing the bad manners of reaching for my notebook. Stead's eyes, even when, as now, gazing at me in concern, seem fixed on something beyond as if seeing *through* me – their clarity and penetration forming a sharp contrast with the man's general dishevelment. This face, for a moment, bewilders and shames me. Stead, of all people, deserves my attention. Stead is not Frank.

In truth, I am not quite all right. I had ordered Fordie's recommended lunch for both of us from the alarmingly knowing steward. We have had the Colchester Natives and were awaiting the pâté and then the quail with grapes. The Ponte-Canet '06 already hangs heavy on my brow and the oysters, combined with memories of pork bellies and Frank's semen remark, have left me feeling faintly ill. The long salon pulses slowly …

'Forgive me, Stead, merely a wave of fatigue and perhaps the motion of the ship.'

I gesture vaguely in the direction of the Atlantic, which our vessel cleaves at twenty-three knots. 'Not less!' the captain had cried.

'But it is dead calm! I shall fetch a doctor.'

He twists awkwardly in his chair, straining the buttons of what seem to be several waistcoats, seeking the steward.

'No, no, it's nothing ... the wine ... Fatigue often strikes me these days. I lack your inner fires; mine, such as they were, appear to have gone out.'

The words express a familiar failing of mine. I have always favoured discomfort over action. It is a fault that has held me back from so much, from everything, this reluctance to make things better for myself. I suffer in silence, not out of heroism but indolence or, on this occasion, embarrassment. The idea of a doctor bearing a bag bustling to my side in the midst of this crowded room is intolerable – the eyes of people gauging the extent of my decline, the days, hours or minutes left to me. Happily, I am relieved of this anxiety. Stead relaxes and smiles, an action that rearranges his entire beard. He leans over and pats my knee.

'No, no, the truth is your mind had wandered. I'm sorry I was boring you, you have other things on your mind. You are going home. You are leaving England.'

At the words 'leaving England' I see myself in a painting, a noble figure standing on the deck, scarf blown back, a look of fierce courage and concentration on the task ahead. Leaving means this comfortable room, the grand staircase, the monumental furniture, the starched linen, all the accoutrements of a grand English house to ease my passing.

'Yes, leaving England where so much happened ...' I murmur vaguely.

Stead looks concerned again.

'I think we should abandon lunch and get you outside.'

He summons the steward, cancels the remainder of the lunch and leads me away. A few heads turn, nothing too intolerable. Outside, he finds me a port-side chair facing directly into the brilliant sun and, as I recline, he tosses a blanket over me.

'Have rest, Cal, my old friend. Your London years have left you exhausted. No wonder! Twenty-four years is long enough in the maw of the modern Minotaur. You are going home!'

He leaves me, his eyes fixed contentedly on the beyond.

My London years! I sailed to London to learn how to be modern and now I sail back, none the wiser. Yes, I am going home. England is just behind me, America far ahead. The day is cold, bright and clear – there is salt on my lips – droplets clutch at the railings. The ocean wants to claim all things, and will. The ship drives westward, washing me with time passing, with brightness and empty air. I half-close my eyes to blur the people that come and go; the hot, bright knives of the sea and sky cut and melt their bodies. They pay me no attention. How could they? I am only half here. This is what it is like to leave and be left, to become the departed. The pleasant emptiness of the air is all about me. It is emptying me. My feelings have become memories, my memories have become gossamer, ectoplasm, a faint shimmer of the past in the blue, the infinitely blue, clarity of the present. Now, ghostlike, I shall dream for a time – of a girl practising 'a tinker shuffle picked up in Donegal' and of Frank. Frank the killer.

Part One

Part One

Chapter One
Chicago

I

I fell in with the very young night clerk at the Fremont House Hotel, not one of Chicago's finest. More accurately, he *acquired* me; from the beginning, he was the senior partner in our friendship. He claimed to be nineteen, two years younger than me, though he was, I calculated, even younger, a mere boy, yet it was impossible to regard him as anything other than a man – and a man of the world at that.

Ugly, short and stocky with the ears of a bat, his hairline almost met his eyebrows and his skin was the colour of pork fat. He exuded, however, an irresistible magnetism, thanks to his powerful chest, general muscularity and a certain fierce, canine eagerness in the eyes. He also had a strikingly deep voice that, in moments of excitement, boomed authoritatively across the dark Fremont lobby. His presence could appal, threaten and command even as it charmed.

Erotically obsessed to an extraordinary degree, he demanded details of any sexual adventures I may have had and talked in unsettling detail of what he planned to do with some girl he had seen that very day in the, as he put it, 'opportunistic streets of Chicago'. I was not persuaded that some of the things he described *could* be done to or with girls, and, having been raised by a strict father, a stern

3

product of the Second Great Awakening and the Civil War, I was firmly convinced that they *should* not be done.

From every aspect, my upbringing told me that this Frank was a dangerous degenerate. His very identity was dubious. Though usually addressed as Frank, he also responded to Joe and sometimes to James Thomas. His provenance was uncertain. Though his country of origin was, I assumed, England, it could equally well have been Ireland or Argentina.

The Colonel, my father, had shouldered the burden of warning me against such people the moment my mother died. He was stricken with guilt – his adored Ellie had died alone and desperate, her hands clawing blindly at the brand-new emerald-green velvet drapes while he was distracted by stockyard affairs. In response, Colonel Kidd, a fierce, obsessive though ultimately uncertain man, determined to honour her in death in ways he had failed to do in life.

First, there was the buffalo robe. This was a primitively decorated, heavy and odoriferous object that Ellie, in a paroxysm of nostalgic guilt, had bought for a huge sum at the height of the fashion for the culture of the Plains Indians. The fashion and the guilt passed, the market collapsed and left us with this worthless but weighty garment decorated with tepees, ponies and mystical bird life. After her death, he had it removed from a cupboard and hung it in the dark hallway outside their bedroom, a monstrous, stiffly creased projection into the narrow space. After several months and many applications of some special oil, the creases finally fell out and the hallway became navigable again. The smell, however, remained, filling the house with the faint, sickening odour of death on the prairie.

Secondly, there was me, a less definite form of tribute than the robe. Unable to hang me in the hallway or smell

4

my presence, the Colonel resorted to religion. Never before having been especially observant, now he determined to outdo his late wife in religiosity. He attended church, prayed noisily night and morning and worked tirelessly to ensure the salvation of the soul of their only child.

His inner doubts only fanned the flames of his outer faith. Daily warnings were issued, listing the worldly threats to my character and spiritual condition. These were delivered with an increasing air of panic as I attained adulthood and acquired a tall, slender and, for some, perilously attractive form. I lacked, I knew well enough, presence.

'You see Cal over there,' said one acquaintance, 'but when you get there, there is no one there.'

I did, however, possess, I was often told, elegance. The risks of my appearance were compounded, my father concluded, by the fact that I had no idea of the effect on Chicago society of my own charms. I was an innocent at large in a guilty world.

Generally, 'loose' women were seen as the greatest threat to such a man. They extracted, said the Colonel – reasonably enough, I guess – vital fluids. There was the equally pressing problem of the 'Devil's Disciples', villainous men who would wish to lead me astray. They were always, in the Colonel's fancy, muscular, short and dark. Close examination of their eyes, some minister had told him, would provide conclusive proof of their moral status.

'Regard their eyes, son,' he would say, 'regard them with great care. You will see within the bright, blazing fires of hell.'

I had suffered from panics of my own since the death of my mother and, knowing their cause was not the forces of evil but bereavement pure and simple, I was unconvinced by the fury of Father's strictures, suspecting they were symptoms of some internal disorder brought on by grief rather than by an accurate analysis of the world beyond our home. That said, it was hard not to conclude that he had a point of some practical import. Chicago really was full of short, dark men with hellish fire in their eyes and loose women were commonplace. To make matters worse, the raging destruction of the Great Fire the previous year had provided respectable citizens like my father with hard evidence that this was indeed a city perched precariously on the very lips of the mouth of hell and that, beneath the dark waters of Lake Michigan, a sea in all but name, demonic forces fought for control of their land.

I conformed to his wishes, my will to do so further stiffened by the ultimate threat that undergirded my father's warnings – the withdrawal of my inheritance. The city was replete with visible evidence of the degradations of poverty; the broken, struggling figures of the poor disfigured the streets. They would grasp at my sleeve, demanding money but also something much more than that. Periodically they assembled in meeting houses and called for the death of the rich. The Colonel was rich thanks to the pork bellies piled in the Union Stock Yards. I knew he was an angry widower, perfectly capable of cutting me off without a cent if the loose women or the hell-eyes ever got the better of me, or, perhaps, if I attended one of those meetings. Then I too would become a sleeve-grasper or a revolutionary. On balance, therefore, I decided it was safest more or less to live up to his standards.

Occasionally, of course, I did toy with revolt, or, at least, with the forbidden. After the fire, I tentatively explored the blackened ruins on De Koven and Jefferson and savoured the damp, burnt stench as if it were the fumes of the strong liquor against which the Colonel also periodically fulminated. The ruins stood and leaned precariously, like

6

attempts at buildings that had not quite worked and had been abandoned. The city, almost a ghost town, seemed, in my ever dreaming mind, to be a presentiment of an era of destruction, perhaps planned by the poor in their meeting houses. First Chicago would sink into hell's mouth and then the world.

Pale girls were salvaging what they could from the debris, their skirts tucked up and their white, dirt-streaked legs visible. They looked at me as I passed, as if, I fancied, they were, rather unenthusiastically, offering something. The spectacle stirred me. I imagined – I still do – an encounter with one of these curiously ageless girls. I imagine taking her behind one of the still-standing walls and kissing her, the pressure of her lips on mine, the taste ... But I had not got it in me to do it, perhaps I had not the presence. The wall might collapse, I thought, stupidly, and such an act would, if discovered, have alarmed and angered the Colonel and set in train a series of events with unimaginable consequences. Such was my cowardice and such the moral and financial brink on which I feared I was destined to live out my days. Yet suddenly, there was this Frank at my back, pushing me to the edge.

The weak point in my moral defences was that they were not moral at all. They were constructions of psychological frailty and economic self-interest that, like the burned buildings, leaned precariously. It was so overwhelmingly in my pecuniary and social interests to conform to the Colonel's demands that I simply did not know what else I could do. My virtue was born of fear, rational calculation and ignorance of the wider world rather than of any serious acceptance of my father's convictions.

It was this passionless adherence to convention that made me fatally vulnerable to the charms of Frank, a boy/

man with clear signs of fire in his eyes, but also with a key in his hand, a key not to the rooms of the Fremont, not even to the more improbable delights of white-legged girls – or, at least, not to those alone – but to something even more enticing.

2

Our first meeting was in the form of a collision on busy Van Buren. I was a foot or more taller than him and lost in some reverie while his head was bowed in thought. He rammed me in the chest.

'Why, sir, watch where you are walking!' I cried.

He stared up at me, the hell-eyes immediately apparent.

'Sir, my apologies, sir. I was deeply engaged with my thoughts about Shakespeare ... important thoughts ... Good Lord!'

He reeled back, staring at my face and clutching his head with his right hand, his elbow jutting theatrically forward. He was all angles.

'The resemblance is quite amazing. Forgive me, sir, but you overpoweringly remind me of somebody. Jones, captain of cricket and the most appalling bully.'

I appeared to have encountered a lunatic with a strange accent and formidably ugly, menacing features who wished only to insult me. He was probably burning with resentment at the sight of my expensive clothes. I have a particular fondness for dove grey, a colour which could enrage certain citizens of Chicago who thought of themselves as too engaged with the hard facts of the world to bother with such fripperies, though they did, very self-consciously, wear black.

'Excuse me? You are calling me a bully. I would point out, sir, that it was you ...'

I should have simply walked on but something intriguing about this lunatic prevented me. Also I had felt a momentary clairvoyant shudder, a suspicion that something of great future significance was occurring. Fleetingly, I saw the scene from above – two stationary figures amid the crowd that flowed along Van Buren.

In spite of my protests, I found myself coolly considering this man. Covering his compact, compressed body, his clothes were taut, seeming barely to contain the flesh within. His face was certainly unattractive but also stern, purposeful. The word 'adventurer' came to mind, possibly also 'pirate'. There was also, strangely, a touch of femininity in his theatricality, in the way he was now standing, with both hands clapped to his head and a comically exaggerated expression of wonder.

'No, no, not you. Jones, captain of cricket at my dreadful Welsh school. Born bully. But I soon SETTLED HIM!'

The last two words boomed across the street, a small explosion. People were looking around. This snapped me out of my fascination, leaving me intolerably embarrassed. I walked on. He was not deterred. He passed me, then turned to walk quickly backwards, all the while staring at my face.

'In fact, now I examine your features more closely, I see the resemblance to Jones is entirely superficial. I have an eye for bullies and you are no bully. I encountered that Boss Bill Tweed soon after I landed in New York, saw through HIM at once.'

The crowd parted more easily now that I was accompanied by this creature. He radiated too much energy and there was too much hellfire in his eyes. The ordinary, honest folk parted before his noisy reversal.

'Frank is the name ...' He paused long enough to establish that I was not yet ready to respond in kind. '... I work at

9

the Fremont, but it will soon be time to MOVE ON! I think I should try the wild lands to the west to make my fortune. I am tied to menial tasks in this city. But I refuse to be poor. Do you hear me? I REFUSE!'

He addressed the last words to the street at large as if he had been challenged, called to account. Some people now stopped and stared. I laughed to cover yet further embarrassment.

'Who on earth are you?'

'Good question. I trust you have a little time on your hands. The answer is thrilling but not short and not, for the moment, conclusive. Frank Harris is the name.'

'Calhoun Kidd.'

'Excellent, come to my hotel at once.'

The Colonel would have seen damnation oozing from the very fabric of the Fremont – the beat-up old chairs, the fat men playing billiards and drinking, all enveloped in the thick stench of stale cigar smoke. The glow of heavily varnished mahogany had been obscured by a streaked, blackish, reptilian patina. The carpets clung to one's feet and the windows turned even bright sunlight into a dusty, grey haze. The lights were, of necessity, blazing all day, their glass globes forming multiple pale suns in this gloomy nether world.

Frank briskly navigated this place. Though an employee, he sat in the billiard room and ordered drinks from his strangely compliant colleagues. He drank only soda water, having sworn not to touch intoxicating liquor before the age of twenty-one.

'Men are made ill,' he explained, 'by too early consumption of alcohol. I defy the drunken temper of the age. I shall not touch the stuff until I am ready.'

He told me tall tales of his struggles with the 'little men and crooks' who worked in the hotel, about how, in particular, he had exposed a meat-buying scandal and taken on an iniquitous individual named Payne.

'I fixed HIM!'

How did he work there? His contempt for his colleagues was barely concealed and he plotted against them all. When pressed, he attributed his survival to his ruthless ability to 'discover their secrets'.

'As a child, I one day found my nurse in bed with a man. My father would have flung her out on the street if he had found out. I saw at once what power this gave me. Thereafter, I realised, I only had to say "I'll tell" to get exactly what I wanted. Secrets set you free.'

'But doesn't that mean you must be forever hated and feared by those around you, those you blackmail?'

I uttered that last word with some nervousness. It caused him no concern.

'In time, the hatred turns to respect and the fear to admiration. I am usually accepted as one of them, but somewhat better, of course. See how I am respected here.'

I thought the true explanation was the man's uncanny aura, his presence, a mix of confidence, worldly wisdom and physique, that and his astonishing power over and obsession with women. This last must have earned respect from his most begrudging colleagues. Ugly as he was, Frank could stop a woman in the street and begin a conversation by asking directions or demanding where she bought her superb hat. Confronted by his prey, his whole being became sinuous, serpentine, as if every part of his body was moving in time with every part of the woman's. His eyes fixed on hers and never moved. She was invariably charmed, seduced almost at once. I felt I had met a man who possessed the one thing I could not have, the erotic. To Frank, the erotic was the only possible theme of any encounter between any man and any woman below the age of forty. To me, it was an impossibility or an embarrassment.

The climax of every tale he told was always the same – the genius of Frank was demonstrated, his insights vindicated. Absurd though such claims must have been, I found them easy enough to believe. The complacency of the Fremont staff in never refusing his demands was hard evidence. But perhaps this was also because he was in the company of a very wealthy-looking young man in dove grey and we were always engaged in dazzling conversation.

We did, visibly, dazzle. Frank became so excited by his own ideas and words that a thin film of sweat would form on his compressed features. His entire body would rock violently back and forth. Occasionally, he had to leap to his feet while talking and march rapidly in circles as he continued his tirade. I, meanwhile, found myself transported, laughing and improvising wildly on Frank's themes of female psychology, adventure and opportunity. He made me feel brilliantly smart, the cleverest man in the Midwest.

Foremost among his ideas were a series of anathemas directed at the countries in which he had lived. Ireland was 'a damned backward place full of subhuman peasants'; England was 'a monster of oppression and vanity'; Wales was 'made for bullies by nature'; America, worst of all, was 'an ignorant hellhole', but was, at least, 'ripe for discovery'. His contempt for the first three countries seemed a little unfair as each had provided occasions for great Frank triumphs. In Ireland, at the age of eight, he swam twice round a large boat in a heavy sea at his father's command and to the amazement of onlookers. His father demanded a third circuit until a concerned admiral intervened. In England he was the victor in a fight with a bear. In Wales he defeated the bully Jones, whom I supposedly resembled, in a boxing match of extraordinary brutality.

Argentina came up occasionally, but, aside from a few mentions of gauchos, he was vaguer about his conquest of that nation. America, meanwhile, was yet to see its own Frank triumph, but he was sure it would happen in the west, where he promised to 'kill thousands of Indians'. He believed, I detected with a shiver, in violence.

I did not care. All that mattered to me was the freedom of his imagination, his belief in his own importance in the world and his apparent knowledge of the great hidden forces lurking beneath the surface of the present age. His fervour burned bright enough to forge fiction into fact.

I had none of these qualities; I detected no hidden forces. My understanding involved only a certain humility in the face of what Father would call 'the way it is'. For the Colonel, the world 'is what it is' and a man's job is to get on with it. He should strive to be rich, not that wealth represents any kind of mastery of 'the way it is', it merely provides the most effective defence against implacable reality. Another, less effective, defence was, of course, a good wife, a being that, to my mind, bore no relation to the pale, bare-legged girls in the burnt-out ruins. St Paul's immiserating sentiment – it is better to marry than burn – was repeatedly employed as a desperate justification of marriage. Why, I wondered in response, would one stop burning merely because one had married? Look at Frank; neither one woman nor a thousand would ever be enough to quench his flames.

He was an anti-mirror in that he reflected not what I was but precisely what I was not, Caliban to my Ariel. This Ariel wanted to be Caliban and Caliban plainly wanted at least to disguise himself in Ariel's dove-grey clothes. He wanted to be tall, slender Cal; I wanted to be that Frank who, the only boy at an all-girls school, dropped pencils in order to crawl around among those feminine legs and even to slide his hand up them to disgusted squeals of protest, or, just often enough, to giggles or significant silences.

'You don't ask, you don't get,' said Frank. So he got.

In conversation, I discovered with dizzy amazement the terms cunnilingus and fellatio and, with something approaching panic, the dark possibilities of buggery. Though I could not imagine women ever succumbing to such treatment, Frank assured me, that was *exactly* what they did; it was, he said, their sole purpose in life.

'It is one of the leading illusions of our age that women have no APPETITES. They are like us, driven by great, inborn urges. They talk about these things among themselves even as they are taught to fear the very same urges in men and, when questioned, to deny their very existence within their own bodies. This is the MADNESS of the age. Other people at other times have lived more balanced lives, balanced between the oppressions of human society and the demands of biology. In the coming age, the sex instinct will overthrow these lunatics.'

At such moments I fancied he saw himself as the new Messiah, racing towards Bethlehem to celebrate his own birth, the sign of the coming age.

If it were not for the straitened era in which I lived and the gloomy burden of this city, I could have simply seized any one of those waifs in the rubble. Perhaps there was somewhere else I could taste the lips of girls whenever I felt the need. Kissing was all I considered; I was not yet quite ready to imagine the feeling inspired by these more exotic activities. Frank was the man to take me by the hand and lead me via kissing to whatever else lay in wait for me.

'I once asked a very talented seducer named Connolly,' he said in his best didactic manner while lounging in one of the Fremont's battered, once maroon leather chairs, a cigar in his hand, 'how he did it. He told me, "When you can put a stiff penis in her hand and weep profusely the while, you're getting near any woman's heart. But don't forget the tears." I've never yet managed the tears.'

3

He had arrived in Chicago in flight from the Monster – his father. Using money from a school prize, he bought a steerage passage from Liverpool.

'I WANT A TICKET TO AMERICA!' he boomed, employing the potent disguise of his voice to counter the effects of his evident youth.

'Bless me,' said the man behind the glass, 'I thought it was a giant talking.'

'So we're both mistaken,' replied Frank. 'I thought you were a gentleman.'

His father was like the Colonel in his moral fierceness. Here was something we shared. Frank did not, like me, accept his father, though I did not despise mine as Frank did his.

'A get all, give nought, a stingy hound! You know what I said when I first turned into Fifth Avenue? I said, "No more fathers for me!"'

Another little flame sprang to life inside my breast.

Frank's decision to flee England was precipitated in part by a long-standing grievance against his father's stern lack of imagination, also by an erotic adventure that had been halted by a train wreck. He had been in a field, busily licking the thighs of a certain Mary, when he was interrupted by a huge explosion. They had rushed to the scene and found many dead.

'It was an omen. I knew at once it was meant as a sign for me. I laid my plans for Liverpool and New York.'

'How on earth could that be construed as an omen?'

'Sex and death. Appalling but necessary bedfellows. The dead were the warning. I do not intend to die, I shall be the first immortal – not in spirit, in body. Remember that in years to come. I am, myself, an omen.'

In Manhattan he was employed as a sand hog on the Brooklyn Bridge – 'Fiendishly dangerous but what man could say no to five dollars a day?' He told me of the compressed air in the caissons and the ritual of compression and decompression at every shift. One man cut the latter because he was late for his girl and was dead by the time Frank reached the surface. Such scenes, he claimed, gave him a profound sympathy for the plight of the working man and, in Chicago, he had even attended some of those meetings of the poor. Socialism, he told me, is the future. I wondered if this meant the Colonel and I would meet violent deaths.

In New York, he also worked, fatefully for me, as a shoe black. One day, while shining the shoes of a Mr Kendrick, Frank delivered a Latin epigram, inspiring Kendrick to take an interest in this plainly over-qualified polisher and offer him the job at the Fremont. He arrived in Chicago and, soon afterwards, collided with me.

'Kendrick was the right man at the right time. He was meant for me. New York had no opportunities, but I felt something in the air in Chicago, some stiff breeze blowing from the west.'

'Have you, by any chance, had such a feeling elsewhere?' I asked, innocently, as if doing no more than keeping up the conversation.

'London. That's a city that's got something. I've not spent enough time there yet, but I will, once I've done with America. I remember wet-haired women – it always rains in London – with skirts banded by the stains of the horse dung, but with damp eyes, damp lips ... Yes, there is much work to be done in London.'

I saw my own Chicago waifs in this description and shuddered, imagining rain-dampened lips and knowing eyes.

'So,' I said, 'you would recommend London?'

'London is a woman with wet shoes and glorious eyes lighting up her wet pale face. Of course, she is the centre of the world, is she not? Everything has happened there and, rest assured, everything WILL happen there. Perhaps to you also ...?'

4

For a few weeks, the conversations continued. My walk from my father's office to the Fremont was a journey from one world into another. At the office I still trod the treacherous moral brink, alert for the fires of hell or, almost equally damnable, my own dreaming indolence. I stepped out into dark, earnest streets of sober enterprise and fierce maintenance of order. As I walked, the streets brightened, the skies above the buildings grew clearer and more enticing, bright chaos intervened. All around me, people were engaged in some fabulous project to invent a new, more delicious balance of human society and biology. Finally, when I arrived at the Fremont, I was at the very threshold of the new world. Westward, for Frank, lay adventure; eastward, for me, lay discovery.

One day I arrived at the Fremont to find Frank in riotous conversation with three cattlemen – huge, slouched beasts whose voices filled the lobby even more effectively than his own. Dell, Ford and Reece looked and spoke like the West, the unformed land of Frank's dreams. Their engraved belt buckles dug into their swollen bellies and their boots filled the space beneath the table like an impassable pile of rocks. They also had the smell of the buffalo robe upon them and the same unconquerable stiffness in their manner.

'Two dollars in Texas,' said Reece.

'Twenty dollars in Chicago,' added Dell.

'We drive 'em north,' said Ford, known to the others as 'The Boss', 'and just watch the price rise.'

Frank, however, could not keep his mind on the cattle.

'You carry guns?'

'Sure,' said Dell, 'have to – Indians, rustlers, some fool thinking he owns some girl.'

'Girls … there are girls?'

The cattlemen roared and rearranged their boots.

'All you can eat,' said Dell.

'And more than you can handle,' said Reece.

Within days, Frank left the Fremont, prepared to light out for Kansas.

'Are you sure about this?' I asked. 'Those men seem very hardened types.'

'Well, Ford is a bully sure enough, I spotted that straight away. I am good at crushing bullies, remember? For all their talk, these are simple men, I can deal with them.'

I was stunned once again by the sheer confidence of this boy who was a man, but now I felt fearful for him. What if everything Frank had told me was a self-glorifying lie? What if the boy was a fantasist now doomed to die at the hands of some hardened realist on the range? What if the damp-eyed girls of London were a dream and the battered and bleeding face of Jones a fantasy? I felt my bright, chaotic future ebbing away.

'Are you absolutely, positively sure?' I said quietly, fixing Frank's fire-filled eyes.

The flames suddenly dimmed, doused by a moment of penetration and reflection, perhaps even affection. He clutched my arm, his voice suddenly soft, almost feminine.

'I know you doubt me, my friend. I know you also fear for me and that touches my heart. I tell you I have to do these things. It is in my nature. I am what I am ...'

He paused and it seemed, for a moment, that he had been apologising for his very soul. Then, recovering, he leaned forward, smiling.

'... and I do what I do. A fool who does foolish things maybe. Trust me, I shall return and we shall meet again. Then I will tell you such tales ... And I have work to do with you. I need to take you to those fires of hell of which your father seemed so afraid. You will find they are what you have been seeking.'

The next day Frank left me in Chicago.

5

For sixteen years, I tried to still the fires Frank had lit in me. I suffered quietly and alone from an oppressive sense that I was living a good life in a bad place. For a time, my reason quelled my discontent. The fires burned and bare-legged girls still picked through the debris left in their wake. The pork bellies and my father's rigid sanity kept them in check. I rose through the company and occasionally satisfied myself discreetly with some small affair. I found myself unable – or disinclined – to aspire to the city's finest beauties, contenting myself, instead, with the occasional servant or shop girl or, more ambitiously, with the plainer daughters of the gentry. Their gratitude relieved me of any burden of guilt, but none ever provided anything like the dazed wonder nor the blessed release which Frank had so often described. Their mechanical loving was awkward and clumsy. They all wanted to marry, but their lips never tasted quite right.

Perhaps this life would have been enough if the Colonel had possessed the presence of mind to deny me all access to books. As a child of the Great Awakening, of the brandished Bible, he believed unthinkingly in the intrinsic virtue of the printed word. There was a substantial library in our grand Lake Shore house and there was a bookshop near by run by a small, eager, scholarly man named Priddy, who seemed all too aware of my longing for escape.

'Europe,' he said, his nose twitching beneath the weight of his nippers, 'that's the thing. Every man should see Europe. It is an education this land cannot provide.'

Priddy had, fatefully, a large topographical section. Over the years, I bought almost every title he stocked on the cities of the world. It was London to which I kept returning. I would stare at maps for hours, imagining the delights that must be available in streets named Pall Mall, The Strand or Cheapside, in squares named Paternoster, Leicester, Russell or Belgrave and in districts named Chelsea, Notting Hill, Bedford Park or Dalston. I read Dickens in a state of baffled ecstasy, Blake in wonder and fear. Wordsworth's sonnet 'Composed on Westminster Bridge' – 'Earth has not anything to show more fair' – made me yearn to embrace London's 'mighty heart'. Hamlet made me want to meet a ghost.

As I entered my thirties, the fever showed no sign of abating. The work grew increasingly onerous, the occasional lovemaking more desultory and the Colonel ever more impatient with my failure to marry and start a household of my own.

'What are you now? Thirty-five, thirty-six! Goddamit, boy!'

The book-reading habit, he now felt, had gone much too far and it was surely time for me to get 'outside' myself by being subjected to the demanding disciplines of family life.

At the same time, he appeared to be softening. The features, once as rigid as the Rockies, had begun to ease. It was a physiognomic symptom of an inner relaxation, a letting go of the harsh religiosity to which he had clung as a defence against or denial of his wife's death. When, thanks to his spies, he finally stumbled upon evidence of the extent of my meagre promiscuity, his anger required obvious effort and was short lived.

This softening engendered a greater comfort in our relationship. We knew each other far better than any old married couple, though I still felt that, one day soon, I could – I must – simply leave. The softening made the event seem more imminent; it not only made us more comfortable together, it also made the Colonel seem less fearsome and, perversely perhaps, less vulnerable. As a more relaxed and tolerant man, I felt, he should be less afraid of the world. Perhaps, therefore, he could survive on his own.

6

Chicago in summer had become to me an oven, a prison. The air was noxious with the smell of asphalt, horse dung and the pork packing sheds. In winter it was no better, with the gales lashing in from the frozen lakes, the blizzards making the streets jagged with ice. And the killing – there had been too much killing. The police killed the anarchists and socialists, the anarchists and socialists killed the police. It all started with the suffocation of that Haymarket bomb. There were dead policemen on Desplaines then thousands of supposed culprits captured and tortured. Louis Lingg evading hanging by blowing himself up in prison, the entire ghastly sequence reported. Everything was reported – Lingg's moments of survival without a lower jaw, his tongue ripped out and yet still whispering through a foam of blood to his doctors! I did not need to *know* these facts and yet I did. Chicago, the mad oppressor with its legions of blood-crazed journalists, told me. It was the new way of things. Frank had always said there must be violence.

One hot July day, the weight of the years ahead and the tyranny of this city unbalanced all. I stepped into the iron and glass cave of the conservatory where the Colonel sat amid the palm and ferns, sweating, sipping lemonade and occasionally attempting to glance at the *Tribune* that lay spread on his lap. In his great, dark red vest and leather suspenders and lying amid a pile of grubby white cushions, he looked as disordered as ever. Mess followed him, every room he entered became crumpled and wrecked. This conservatory, its plants run wild, was his apotheosis. Mess was, for me, unendurable. Every room I occupied looked immaculate and uninhabited, untouched, all was folded and put away. The Colonel, in contrast, regarded disorder as a healthy sign of his presence, it was a celebration of his being in the world. Neatness was death to the Colonel; perhaps it was to me as well.

The heat and dampness in the conservatory were nearly intolerable. He claimed that they eased many of the afflictions of old age – he was still in his early fifties, but had eagerly embraced ageing in his mid-forties – in particular those ailments that involved the bones. I had to remove my coat before I sat down and was obliged continually to pat my face with a handkerchief.

My father rang for an extra glass and we settled into our usual talk of business and politics, though we both knew well enough that neither was the true subject of this meeting. The Colonel had long known that I must be up to something; my sudden, rather solemn appearance in the conservatory indicated the moment of revelation had come. It was, he knew full well, not news – say, a favourable marriage – that was expected to please him.

There was a sudden, ominous lull which the Colonel filled by plucking at a stiff strand that had sprung loose from his great wicker throne.

'Father ...'

'You intend to leave.'

He had his spies as well as his lively suspicions. He even knew, all those years ago, about Frank. The Colonel's men had pronounced him 'a harmless son of a bitch'.

'I should have known you would guess.'

'For how long?'

'Six months, a year maybe.'

The Colonel nodded slowly.

'I shall manage.'

'You have Kurt here in the house and at the office ...'

Kurt was his stern major-domo, the Colonel's Teutonic colonel.

'I shall manage. But will you?'

'I am only going to London.'

'I mean will you manage without a purpose to your life?'

'London is a kind of purpose, I guess. And, besides, I shall return to take up my position ...'

'You shall not.'

He was now prodding at one of the pots with his cane.

'You mean you will not have me?'

'No, I mean, having left, you will attempt to invent some new purpose that does not involve Chicago.'

'That is not my intention.'

'INTENTION!'

There was a dull detonation and a cloud of dust as he struck one of the cushions with his stick.

'Nothing, I concluded some time ago, is ever anybody's intention. The world is the way it is and we just fit in, deceiving ourselves with inventions and intentions.'

There was a clatter as he dropped the cane. He was now plucking more violently at the wicker strand.

'It wasn't my intention to sit here sweating so damned much. It wasn't yours to go to London. It happened to you as this ...' he waves his stick at the dense foliage '... has happened to me.'

'This is not what you used to say.'

'I used to say what I damn well felt I had to say after Ellie's death. That also happened to me. Whose intention was THAT?'

'So all that discipline ...'

'Did you no harm, did it? Probably set a fire inside you. You've been burning to know what else there is. I have seen.'

He turned away to pluck once more at the wicker.

'Aw, go on, go to London, you'll find there is nothing else to discover. Goddamned London is the same as goddamned Chicago. It even had a fire, I hear. Perhaps you will marry at last, though I don't hear good things about English women.'

'That is not my int ...'

I stopped myself.

'You needed your mother to keep you here. Never was something I could do. It's a wonder it took you so long.

You are neither impulsive nor decisive. You didn't have to be. Good God, you'll soon be forty.'

I looked at the Colonel's ruddy face, the beard he still daily groomed to an exact point. I felt no resentment nor even wonder at the revelation that this Colonel was not the Colonel I had known all these years, the Colonel who had seemed to hold me back from that awful brink. Now I saw that he had only done so in the expectation that I would fall. I could have leapt over the edge at any time. So many years had been wasted by my refusal to end my suffering. No more! I remembered Frank's cry on Fifth Avenue – 'No more fathers for me!' I once vowed I would utter the same cry in Trafalgar Square. Now I saw no need for such a savage repudiation. The shackles had burst apart – and so easily, in but a moment!

'We will part on good terms, then?'

'We will part. You are my son, but I am not your mother.'

We said nothing for a few minutes. Then he looked me in the eyes.

'One thing, take the buffalo robe.'

'The robe …'

'To remind you.'

I was about to ask of what it was supposed to remind me, but then realised it was, in his mind, everything – my mother, this land. The prospect of this great weight and this deathly odour following me to London was grim, but I knew I had no choice. Kurt took the object down from the wall of the dark hallway. It was laboriously refolded by two of his minions and then packed in a wooden trunk.

A few months later I sailed for England.

Chapter Two
London

I

Down in the east, the dark east, down among the docks where London gorges itself on the world, where the rising sun makes of the Thames a golden road lined with the angular, blackened works of men, they have no money to spend on newspapers. They find their news on the walls where people chalk up stories of the latest murders – dismembered corpses in Limehouse and strangled women in Southwark decorate the cold, greasy brickwork. Tales of lives cut off in darkness and agony line the alleyways down which the poor walk, seeking work. In Whitechapel one Jack has been murdering and mutilating whores; he is said, by some, to be a gentleman. To the west, romantic London feeds discreetly on this slaughter, the more gruesome or morally significant accounts being published in the dozens of newspapers and journals. Jack more than satisfies the westerners' hunger for speculation and outrage, not least because he might be one of them.

My first London notebook was half full within a few days of my arrival. Everything was a novelty to eyes that had only seen Chicago, to a heart that had never beaten in time to the whole world's pulse. For that was what London was – the whole world, not even the hub or heart of the world, but the thing itself.

Aware of it singular status, the city recorded every aspect of her existence. Presses rumbled day and night, reporting London to Londoners, to the world and to posterity. The city was an eye gazing in a mirror and there she found herself always new, always important. Whatever happened in London mattered *because* it happened in London; she blessed and immortalised every action. Lingg's bomb in Chicago was as nothing next to the most casual, most domestic killing in Camden Town or Poplar.

Journalism, whether sensational or sober, was the city's trade. Nothing seemed to be entirely real until it was reported and I, having nobody to report to, had no choice but to scribble in the hope that I would one day become real in the eye of London. Then, one day, I did.

Through the windows, it is impossible to see anything but pale ghosts. The steam and the grime turn the city into a shadow play ...

I was sitting writing in an ABC, an institution so exotic it was not mentioned in any of Priddy's guides. It was not far from my rooms and I had often noticed its windows – misted and inviting. Finally, I had succumbed. It was full, the air was dense with smoke, humid with steam and thickened by the low thunder of dispute and gossip. It was an atmosphere that countered the thin, dry cold of London beyond. There was also a piercing, comforting smell of burnt toast.

Unfortunately, to my great embarrassment, the tea room was so crowded that I had been forced to ask a round-faced man in a bowler hat and overcoat if I could share his table. The man was reading a book of verse very intently and did not at first react. I posed the question more loudly and he looked up in slow amazement, swiftly replaced by a flustered display of extravagant good manners.

'Why, of course, certainly!'

I drank tea and ate some obscure cake while continuing to write. The other man remained lost in his book. He read it with a certain grandeur, holding it high in front of his face as if to demonstrate his seriousness and erudition. After perhaps ten minutes, he snapped it shut, placed it delicately on the table and looked at me.

'Forgive me, sir, I was immersed in Swinburne.'

'Of course.'

'He intoxicates. I take him everywhere in case I need to free myself of …' he gestured at the crowded room 'of … all this.'

At a nearby table a thin young man with lank hair noticed and responded with a petulant, knowing smile.

'Do you read Swinburne by any chance?'

He held the book up to my face – *Songs before Sunrise*.

'Come forth, be born and live,' I quoted, 'Thou that hast help to give.'

Slowly, majestically, he rose to his feet and, taking off his hat, held out his hand. His eyes were wide, his mouth gaping. To my horror, the whole room looked round, alerted by the sudden scraping of his chair on the tiles.

'A Swinburnian by my soul! By my very soul! Let me shake your hand. Binks is the name.'

Having grasped my outstretched hand, Binks sank slowly back into his chair, his eyes fixed on me as if we were long-lost brothers, united by freakish coincidence.

'Kidd, Calhoun Kidd. I am known as Cal.'

'An American cousin! Fresh from the prairies by the sound of it. Wonderful! This, this was meant to happen. Poetry makes everything happen!'

His voice was strangely wheezy as if he had lung problems. His tone was so ripe – his words seemed almost to be sung – that, at first, I suspected sarcasm or irony.

'I shall call you Cal, if I may, but I insist you call me Binks. My first name is Brian and it has always been a terrible burden to me. Imagine if Swinburne had been called Brian rather than Algernon. The man would have died in obscurity.'

Seated again, Binks replaced his hat and, reopening his book, flicked the silk ribbon to save his place before closing it again. He then studied me for a moment as if undecided what to do next. His eyes would have been those of a child, but for a shadow of something – a certain slyness perhaps. I felt he was trying to decide if I was worthy of some confidence or qualified for some initiation. Finally, he made up his mind that I was indeed worthy and, with a curious shrug involving his entire torso, he produced a small cigarette case and a penny. He gave me the penny and one cigarette and asked me to inspect them both.

'What do you think?'

'Think? They both appear to be perfectly normal.'

'Excellent! Now, abracadabra, which, rendered into English, means "I create as I speak".'

Binks stretched his arms to draw the sleeves away from his pale, surprisingly delicate hands and then rested his elbows on the table.

'Observe very closely.'

Concentration crumpled his face. He placed one end of the cigarette against the surface of the penny, closed his eyes, drew in a long breath through clenched teeth and began murmuring some incantation and rocking slightly. I glanced round the room, but nobody had noticed his behaviour or, perhaps, this being London, deep trance was an unremarkable aspect of daily life in an ABC. Binks was now rotating the cigarette back and forth. He let out a great gasp. The cigarette had, somehow, drilled into the coin and was now visible from the other side. Binks, still murmuring with his eyes closed, now pushed it with his forefinger. Slowly its entire length passed through the coin; finally, it fell on to the table, leaving both cigarette and coin unmarked. Binks's body relaxed.

'A little demonstration for my new friend, my fellow Swinburnian. The trick comes from Turkey originally, brought here by an extraordinary woman.'

'I am baffled as to how you did it. You have a rare talent.'

'Not I! I am but a conduit, a channel, if you will – but, yes, rare in the sense that it is the only oddity I have. Binks is largely talent free. I do have some attainments, however. I heard, for example, that the great explorer C. M. Doughty had an astonishing capacity for standing on one leg – or, strictly speaking, one foot – for immensely long periods of time. Intrigued by this, I have trained myself to do the same for several hours. Four and a half is my record. My next task is to achieve the same feat with my eyes closed. This is far more difficult for some reason. My son, Lucian, joins me. He is coming on. I believe it is mentally and physically beneficial. Sophie, my daughter, alas, finds me in this, as in so much else, ridiculous.'

He looked comically abashed.

'I am sorry to hear that.'

'Don't be. We must quietly accept that women are a different species and get on with our lives as best we may. The one-leg standing apart, I am quite incompetent at any of the more popular forms of exercise. I was dragooned into playing cricket once by some of my friends in the City – I have many, you understand – they made me wicketkeeper. One ball came at me with quite amazing rapidity and, fearing for my hands, I attempted to catch it with the bowler I was wearing. The ball went clean through to the boundary, ruining the hat. I was not asked again. Perhaps as well, I cannot easily afford a new bowler every week.'

'Cricket ...' I tried vaguely to respond.

'Yes, yes, I know, you wouldn't understand. Let me get on. Since we are plainly destined to be friends, brought together by a poet and this great city, let me explain myself. I am a failure. Little more needs to be said. I live in the greatest city the world has ever seen amid the highest intellects the world has ever known and I am but an onlooker, a spectator. Genius passes me by daily and knows me not. And you?'

'I guess, in that case, I am a failure too. But I have just arrived and perhaps my ignorance protects me in some way from humiliation.'

'You know nobody here?'

'A few contacts and I know one Frank Harris but I have not yet ...'

'You know Harris?'

Binks smiled uneasily and sat back as if reconsidering our friendship.

'Why yes, I do. But I have not seen him for years. I believe he is in London.'

'He is but you must be careful, Cal. Forgive me for speaking thus of your friend, but he is a scoundrel, not to be trusted, but a man of great gifts, no doubt about that. He moves in very high places. A good friend of yours?'

His eyebrows were raised, the slyness was now much more pronounced.

'I knew him years ago in Chicago.'

'Chicago!' said Binks, apparently impressed.

I explained the history that led me to London, to this very ABC.

'Fate,' said Binks, as I concluded, 'it was meant to be. You came to the right place – both because you met me and because London is the right place, the centre of the world. You know Greenwich is the prime meridian of the world? Quite right too. Time itself begins and ends here. Welcome to Alpha and Omega.'

Binks again fixed my eyes as if ensuring I had understood the deep significance of his words. The thin young man rose and approached our table, looking around as he did so.

'Hello, Binks, got a new friend?' he drawled sarcastically.

From a distance his face had appeared merely vicious. But now I saw signs of cultivation and intelligence, though the viciousness remained. The accent was a refinement of cockney I had not previously heard.

'Calvert, I did not see you.'

'I bet you didn't. Try and see me next time. You might find it healthier. We have, you may recall, a good deal of outstanding business.'

'I have not forgotten.'

'I am delighted to hear it.'

With that, Calvert nodded at me and briefly fixed my eyes. I had the uneasy feeling he knew exactly who I was. Then he was gone.

'My apologies, Cal, a very unpleasant young man. Where were we?'

2

Binks, it turned out, was not really a failure but something of a success in the financial quarter known as the City, an area into which I had only really passed through on my way to the East. Binks now offered to show me the best of the old cellars in the City where business was done on marble-topped tables over pints of claret or champagne.

'The whole world's money flows though those cellars; with some little study you can detect its ebb and flow. It makes a sound, I always think, a kind of rushing as of underground streams.'

He was full of advice on where to eat, where to walk, who and who not to see at the theatre, what to read and what to think. He told me I had the qualifications to do what he had so disastrously failed to do – mingle with genius.

'My appearance, my manner, my intellect, who knows what it is? But the truth is I do not fit. I am, to them, a tradesman, it shines from my features. You, however, have everything that I lack. First and foremost, you are American. That puts you above the petty jealousies and prejudices of this town. An American is welcome everywhere. He is without class, he is exotic in an acceptable way, he has recently acquired a culture of his own, he has tales to tell of the primitive savagery that lies beneath the fine veneer of civilisation. Well, London is at your feet, Cal, at your feet, I say! The city is your oyster!'

However, it transpired, I had one shortcoming. I lived in the wrong place. There was only one place for a man who wished to mingle with genius in its most modern form. It was the western suburb where Binks himself lived – though his own failings meant that, even there, he was no more than a spectator. He could, however, easily reach the City by train and his wife and two children – 'one apple for each eye' – lived surrounded by fields and fresh air rather than fumes and stench.

'It's the healthiest place in the world, a village for the city. Annual death rate no more than six per thousand. It is the new way to live. And it is part built by one of our geniuses, Mr Norman Shaw. It is the most aesthetic suburb.'

Binks did occasionally sound like one of the snake-oil salesmen or holy rollers that preyed on the poor in Chicago; nevertheless, I was grateful for him, I needed this man as some sort of guide. By profession, he was, after all, a trader in stocks and bonds, the oil in the wheels of the Empire's distant engineering. He connected London to the world. He had more than a touch of the huckster, a quality in others which, experience had taught me, remedied a certain lack in my character.

We met again in one of the City cellars and then again for dinner at a restaurant in St James's. Binks ate prodigiously, explaining, when he noticed my startled gaze, that it was a City habit to gorge oneself; indeed, it was almost a City law. Men, to prove their manhood and their hearty grasp of world affairs, had to eat until they turned bright red, poured with sweat, broke wind prodigiously and could barely stand up.

'Of course, I don't go that far. But I do like to feel a weight of meat inside me. It is strengthening.'

To me, food had always been a pollution. We ought to be able to feed on air. It must have been the memory of the pork bellies – cities and their meat.

Binks introduced me to other City meat-eaters who slapped me on the back, called me a damned colonial and roared with laughter. These hearty, confident men treated the wheezy Binks with unusual respect, not as one of them but as someone far more important. Binks was dismissive.

'I am useful to them, that is all. I do them good turns and they do some for me. I am more, well, mobile than them. They must be granite; I can be water.'

He would usually do one of his tricks, notably plucking real grapes from a still life on the wall. The meat eaters roared and applauded.

'Good old, tricky Binks!'

In one of those cellars, Tipton, a man with a monocle jammed in his eye and a cigar in his mouth, took me aside, evidently intending to exclude Binks. He invited me to join him at a lunch the next day at a house in Kensington Gore; it would be, he promised, fixing me with his glinting glass and nodding knowingly, a 'most interesting experience'.

'Our host,' he added, 'is one of the most remarkable men in London.'

3

It was a small house immediately opposite the park. Tipton rapped on the door with the silver top of his cane and it was immediately flung open by a colossal bare-chested Nubian who held aloft a broad scimitar. Tipton tapped me on the shoulder and nodded knowingly once more. The Nubian, who seemed to fill the whole of the cluttered hallway, bowed deeply and led us into a dark salon hung with heavy, oriental drapes and thick with perfume. Sitting cross-legged in a circle on the heavy rugs were four young women dressed in loose gowns and three jacketless men, all eating caviar and drinking champagne. Laughing loudly, they toasted us as we entered. I glanced enquiringly at Tipton, hoping to establish which was our host. He nodded at a shadowed corner at the far edge of the circle. I could see nobody in the gloom, but a deep voice boomed out.

'Well, well, well, Calhoun Kidd, my old Chicago friend. You have COME at last!'

'Good Lord, Frank!'

He would, of course, be one of the most remarkable men in London. The women looked at me with distant curiosity and the men laughed. Frank. Who else could it possibly have been in this coincidental city? I had been willing this encounter while being reluctant to find a means of precipitating its occurrence. Though I had not seen him for sixteen years, there could be no doubting the identity of that compact form, those eyes that burned both brighter and darker than anything else in the room.

In the event, we could not talk privately. The lunch – some kind of African food involving much lamb – passed idly but noisily. Frank busily assailed his guests with gossip, extensive quotations from the poets, primarily Shakespeare, and with tales of his contests of wit with a man called Wilde. Frustrated, as we were leaving I took him aside and arranged to meet him the next day.

Strange that I should have, in some way, not even admitted to myself that finding Frank was the point of this journey. Having now found him, I see that I was reaching back to that young, good time. That Frank seems unchanged is all that I could have wanted. He is now one of the great recorders of this city, both the eye of London and what it sees.

Even in the muck and chaos of Fleet Street, even in this disordered mingle of people, horses and carriages, I spotted him from a distance, alerted by the sheer pugnacity of his gait. He was walking swiftly while reading some papers and, though he occasionally glanced up, he did not see me until I addressed him.

'Frank!'

'Cal!'

'It's so strange that I should have come, all unknowingly, to your house within days of my arrival.'

For him, however, there was no need to diminish that encounter with the title of mere coincidence.

'SynchroniCITY!' he cried, 'Tipton was merely the agent of destiny. But I prefer to see it as justice, a balancing of the scales. Think of all the futile, coincidental meetings of little people. Ours, a meeting of great souls, is necessary to cancel those out. I should have looked you up when I was in Chicago again a couple of years ago ...'

I felt a little stab that he had not done so. I had been put me in my place.

'... great story about damned anarchists and a bomb. Louis Lingg – managed to blow himself up in jail. Amazing. Anarchists are everywhere these days. You know, I do find myself seeing their point ... It may be the only way to push this society in the right direction, the direction of the twentieth century. A few corpses should not discourage us.'

He gestured sadly at the passing crowds, at the great blackened palaces of commerce that lined the street, all that was the nineteenth century.

'There's a novel in it, though I doubt it will be written by me. I am a writer of greatness, you know, Cal, but I lack great readers.'

I was ignorant of the life he had lived without me, but this was where we should be, here at the centre of the world, here in this street of journals.

'I don't doubt it, Frank.'

He grinned. He looked almost untouched by the years, still powerful and compact and still the burning eyes. But now he had a thick moustache, redolent of that German philosopher's, which gave him a truculent air; his clothes, meanwhile, were very expensive indeed. He also seemed, mysteriously, taller. I soon discovered that this was because of the remarkably high heels on his shoes. He was, predictably enough, at the feuding, scandal-tossed heart of London, a journalist, it was said, of genius who had edited the

37

Evening News, taking its circulation to new heights and its tone to new depths, and now of the *Fortnightly Review*, a serious, literary journal. This latter was an unexpected appointment which, he assured me, 'ruffled the feathers of some very stringy old birds'. All in all, he was the Frank I had known, intensified and exaggerated by success.

He had, the previous year, married a rich widow with a house on Park Lane. Rapturously he listed Emily Mary Clayton's virtues and accomplishments, though he grinned and winked even as he did so, suggesting this was not a romantic arrangement. She had introduced him to Conservative members of Parliament, promising to make of him an English Bismarck. Frank was, on the face of it, well placed to pursue such an ambition, and not just because of the Teutonic moustache. His rise through the ranks of the press and his ruthless pursuit of scandal and strong *ad hominem* opinions had made him both feared and respected. He had made publishable what had previously been unspeakable.

'The Prince of Wales once said to me that we should forget whatever is unpleasant in life. "On the contrary," I replied, "we should PUBLISH it!"'

He was almost at the very summit of London's primary trade – the reporting of herself. He was a modern man, a 'coming man' or the coming age.

The one thorn in his side – and it was a sharp one – was the editor of the *Pall Mall Gazette*, William Thomas Stead, who had, in the eyes of the world, risen even higher than Frank. A few years before we met he had published *The Maiden Tribute of Modern Babylon*, a series of articles exposing child prostitution, a trade that had been conducted to satisfy the base lusts of even the highest. Stead had been, briefly, imprisoned but he had emerged as a man of power and stature. Frank was offended by this, also by the fact that Stead was seen as a kind of inventor or engineer, a journalistic Brunel, because of the way he had first *made* the news and then reported it.

It was a matter of *will* and its various manifestations. Stead's will was outward looking, he aimed to change things and he did so; Frank's will – consisting, as it did, of 'primary urges' – was all inward, but his assumption was that this very inwardness was what made him so important as an outward being. In seeking his own gratifications, he would liberate the world.

'Trust me, Cal, the twentieth century will be either Stead or Harris, the hypocrite or the truth-teller. It cannot be both, though on one matter we are agreed – the mob will rule in violence.'

Already, relations with his wife had all but collapsed. Her list of accomplishments did not include a talent for the erotic and, in any case, her age –- she was in her fifties – meant Frank would not have been interested had Emily been Cleopatra herself.

'Primary urges,' he confessed, 'and unregulated desires have had no part in our encounter.'

He told tales of her sobbing copiously as she opened wounded letters from his former mistresses at the breakfast table. Apparently finding this conduct incredible, ill mannered, he made matters worse by extolling the various talents of these other woman as if to explain the necessity of their presence in his premarital life.

'Did you not think that was unwise in view of her ambitions for you?'

'Why? It was a perfectly sound arrangement as it stood. We were of equal value to each other. It was her damned friends – snobs who cared more for origins than genius. They kept trying to humiliate me and, of course, FAILING!'

I hardly needed to be told that marriage had proved no impediment to his erotic career. As we drank champagne together in an establishment that was, but for the clientele, strangely like the Fremont, his tales of now unquestionably real sexual conquests were even more alarmingly detailed and numerous than his youthful speculations. Before I took my first sip, he was describing the flower-like sex and lithe body of one Laura Clapton.

'The taste of her – dear God! The only woman I've truly loved. How could any man with blood in his veins be constant in London when your mantelpiece is overflowing with invitations and there are always half a dozen pretty girls to weaken your resolve?'

'Well, I finally came as you suggested,' I said, attempting to evade the more agitating aspects of Frank's conversation.

'You did the right thing. No more fathers for you. Welcome to the murky modern Babylon. That's what Stead called it and the fool meant it as a criticism! London is the centre of civilisation, the queen city of the world. London is our mother and I need to take you, as I recall, to the mouth of hell, which is the queen's own mouth.'

'You look well, barely changed by the years.'

'I know, I am absurdly fit. Though short, I have a forty-inch chest and fourteen-inch biceps. I box. You remember my defeat of the bully Jones? I have a great gift for the sport. Also I eat sparingly, drink in moderation and use a stomach pump daily. Dr Schweninger recommended it for black water fever, but I find daily use has a generally beneficial effect. I cannot abide the way people just accept the decline of their bodies. Very few people realise how completely it is within the power of a fairly strong man of any age to make himself perfectly healthy. We bring old age upon ourselves. Remember, I have no intention of dying. I shall see out both the nineteenth and twentieth centuries.'

'Oh come, even you, Frank, must resign yourself to bodily decay in the end.'

'I am not so sure. I have heard of scientists who believe we can cure this monstrous ageing affliction. Sour milk seems to be involved. It cleanses the bowels.'

I was, in spite of myself, drawn to the idea of this cleansing. I had always felt that food was a pollution, a darkening of my transparency.

'Is that true?'

'It might be. Remember, Cal, we live in an age of journalism, when anything might be true, anything at all.'

4

Grateful though I was for my meetings with Frank and Binks, I was determined not to throw myself entirely into this world of possible truths. First, I needed some truth of my own. An old pioneer impulse inspired me to prepare the way by familiarising myself with the lay of the land. On arrival, I had rented modest rooms in St James's. From this base, I took increasingly bold walks in an attempt to grasp the shape of this city. The maps and guides I studied in Chicago fell far short of the reality, though they had warned me that the streets seen from the heavens were patternless; there was no consoling American grid. Experienced at first hand, this absence of form seemed to promise some more refined cogency, known only to the inhabitants, as if London's creator wished to baffle and frustrate visitors.

'What we all dread most,' I read somewhere, 'is a maze with no centre. That is why atheism is only a nightmare.'

London was atheism in stone and flesh, a maze with no

centre. Perhaps she was an even more monstrous vision, not even a maze, for a maze implies some connection between her parts and some path recently trodden by others. Here every journey felt like a foray into uncharted territory, as if the city remade herself anew for every one of her inhabitants and visitors and remade herself again with every sunrise. Perhaps, as one guidebook said, it was the city's 'want of logic makes it so very human'. My first impressions were only disconnection at every point of the compass and the want of logic felt crushing, a door closed in the face of an idling Yankee.

Everywhere things were being altered, knocked down or rebuilt. Old houses were turned into shops by filling in the gardens with salerooms. Streets were constantly being refashioned amid garlands of lamps and signs, and great gaps suddenly appeared among the buildings as some new and better way was discovered of employing space. I wandered, bewildered and enervated, pausing at one ABC tea room after another, grateful for their little continuities. Sometimes I wandered into Soho to be leered at and beckoned by old hags or, occasionally, pale young girls. The latter made my lips dry and my pulse race. For a time I did not seize the proffered opportunities. Fear of disease, I told myself, was the explanation. But was it really because the chaos of this city inhibited me as effectively as the rigour of the Colonel's Chicago? Or perhaps it was love I sought, true, as they say, love. Or just a kiss.

I went to Soho, in search of ...
  'I just ...'
  'Just what, darling?'
  'I just want to kiss you.'
  'Kiss me where, sweetheart?'

'Your lips.'

'Same question again, Mr Yankee, where?'

'Oh ... your mouth, just your mouth.'

'So you've come all this way across the big sea, all the way from Shy-Cargo, and then all this way to Meard Street just to kiss a little English cutie on the lips. Shy cargo! Shy cargo on the high seas! That's just what you are! I must tell Deirdre that one. Well, sailor boy, I call that flattering, most flattering indeed.'

'I didn't come just for ...'

'Oh, don't spoil, it, dearie. Now you'd better come up so we can have some privacy for this kiss, this oh so special kiss.'

'I'm not sure. Why not here?'

'You like my lips, do you?'

'They are perfect. I knew at once I wanted to kiss them.'

'Let me wet them a little for you, then, lover. There. Want to come up now?'

'OK, if you insist.'

'"OK"! Funny way you talk. Careful of the stairs, lover, don't want you breaking your neck when you've come all this way especially like. In here, sorry it's not up to much. Bet the girls have smarter places in Shy-Cargo. But this business don't pay over here. Nothing pays in Soho any more.'

'How long have you been doing this?'

'Well, not long, dearie, obviously, I'm the youngest working girl round here and will be until the next little flower comes along.'

'Why do you do it?'

'There you go spoiling your big treat again. Never mind about why, dearie, let's get this extra special kiss over and then see if you want some more ... Sitting down, standing up, lying down? Let's lie down.'

'What's your name?'

'Now let me see, what would you like it to be?'

'I don't know – ah, Laura.'

'There, now I'm your Laura. Little sweet-lipped Laura. Mmmmm ... ain't I delicious?'

'They are the most lovely lips.'

'Now steady on, let's think about this. Are you sure you don't want more than just a little kiss? You feel as though you do. Want me to kiss you down there?'

'Just let's kiss, please.'

'Oh, all right, first things first.'

'There you are. Is that enough?'

'I suppose so. Now let's get this big kiss done with.'

'Let me just look for a moment.'

'One moment, then, quick. I've got work to do, you know.'

'Laura, my Laura.'

'Yeah, I'm your little Laura and you're getting your kiss. Now ... There, is that what you wanted?'

'I wasn't ready – just one more, please.'

'No, out now, you got what you paid for. Out!'

'But ...'

'Out! Out or I'll call my Edmond. He'll soon fix you. Out, you stupid Yankee. Just a kiss! I never heard the like. There's real men out there, you know, men who know what to do with a girl like me. Out! Be off with you! Go. Fuck off! Miserable sod.'

Then, finally, as if rescuing me from my wanderings, apparently casually, Binks invited me to his suburban home.

5

On a bright, cold morning towards the end of January I took a cab from St James's and, the low sun behind me in the east casting deep shadows, watched London – the great white houses of the rich and the dark slums of the poor – unfurl herself, luxuriant and dubious as any concubine. Endlessly, she seemed to issue her invitations – 'Stop here', 'Look at this', 'Make me an offer'. Then, as, beyond Hammersmith, the buildings thinned out and fields appeared, I felt a new species of excitement. I had not yet left London and, at the sight of the green landscape, all England seemed to be upon me. My heart was open to the fields. I breathed in the cold bright air of the morning. This was a beginning; this was why I had come – not for England itself, but to go just beyond the edge of London, to assure myself that there was, indeed, such an edge. On the maps the city seemed shaped like a great unblinking eye whose gaze followed you everywhere. Yet, I reasoned, it must be possible to look back from some small distance, to fix this eye. I imagined doing this from Binks's healthy suburb, a western outpost of the city, a frontier town, built to mark the annexation of yet further territory for London's bright rich and dark poor. I was heading west, as Frank had once headed west and as the city itself was now heading west.

Just as London seemed to be ceding sovereignty to the fields, I found myself in a landscape apparently fabricated from dreams. Old England was indeed upon me, but in new, strange forms. I was surrounded by red brick houses with steeply pitched red roofs and deep, dark porches supported by short, bulging wooden columns. High balconies with white wooden palings emerged at curious angles and all these crazily exaggerated confections were crowned by tall, sculpted brickwork chimneys that sprang up to clutter the sky.

The styles and habits of what appeared to be the early eighteenth century were made exotic by sharp, unweathered brickwork and shining, unblistered paint. But something about this place was intended to feel even older than that.

This was supposed to have grown over centuries. It was not a made or finished place, it was a becoming place. Everywhere young trees had been planted, though they were as yet too scrawny to soften the dazzling novelty of it all, a novelty that was intended to be a fantasy of time passing without disturbing the deep, changeless peace that lies beyond the city walls. A dream of England in the nightmare of London. The prime meridian ...

The hansom drew up outside one of the slightly less extravagant houses in Woodstock Road. Here, at number seven, Binks lived in a modest semi-detached, though even this had palisade railings and a large dormer window emerging in triumph from its roof. I paid off the cabby, earning the usual grunt of disappointment that always follows an excessive tip, and nervously approached the front door. I could hear an old woman's voice complaining about something from the neighbouring garden. Binks's garden was largely bare earth with the occasional shrub struggling to belong. The door was flung open when I was still three paces away. Binks was standing there and, in front of him, a short lady with a sharp, prettyish face and an extravagant mass of curled blonde hair, piled so high and so wide that it seemed it must be too much for her slender neck to bear.

'Cal! My dear friend! Welcome to our home and at once you must meet the Duchess herself, my dear wife Enid.'

Laughing, she curtsied briefly, smiled and raised her eyebrows in a way that I could only interpret as coquettish.

'Honoured, I'm sure. Binksy has told me so much about you, his fine American. I've never met an American.'

'And you too, Mrs Binks,' I said, doffing my dove-grey hat and failing to find a phrase for her that would do justice to that 'fine American'.

'And here is Sophie.'

Binks pushed forward a serious and very pretty girl of perhaps thirteen wearing a grey dress, white pinafore and black stockings. She curtsied, her large, heavily lashed eyes fixed blankly on my chest.

'And, last but not least, Master Lucian.'

A boy of about ten appeared in a tight blue serge suit and a seaman's cap. He removed the cap, placed it under his left arm and held out his hand; I stooped and shook it solemnly.

'Well, hello there, Lucian, I guess you've outdressed us all.'

Lucian stared at me wonderingly.

'Why do you guess that?'

Sophie sighed, rolled her eyes and clicked her tongue loudly.

'Come in, come in,' said Enid, 'it's not much but it's our home and we want to make you welcome here.'

'May I take your hat and coat?' said Sophie, her eyes still fixed some way below my chin.

Binks pushed past them all.

'No, no, not now, I told you, I want to take Cal to meet my special friends. They're expecting us. We'll be back soon enough for a spot of lunch.'

For a moment, Enid flashed her eyes angrily at Binks, but then, with an effort, she brightened.

'Of course, we'll be ready for you when you get back. Don't hurry. It's just cold cuts. Nothing special.'

Binks grasped my arm and led me back on to the street. He began to march me hurriedly northwards.

'I've told them I'd bring this fascinating new American, just arrived in town. Very interested they are.'

'Told whom?'

'The Yeatses. Big figures round here, art types. The father's a painter and so's one of the sons, the other's a

47

poet. There's two girls but I can't get the hang of them. The mother never appears, ill apparently. Mothers are always ill, have you noticed? But not my Enid, very healthy lady. I'm nothing to the Yeatses, of course, just trade. But you're my key to their door. I've told Enid if we get in with the Yeatses, we get in with the whole neighbourhood. She won't listen. They're Irish, you see, she doesn't like that. She had some experience or other ... But the Yeatses are important. I don't think they're geniuses or anything. I mean Willie, the poet, is no Swinburne and Jack, the painter, is no Burne-Jones, but they're art and that's the point of this place.'

Binks was growing very breathless. I noticed for the first time a distinct cockney twang in his accent. Enid, too, spoke with easterly overtones. I realised that I had never learned anything about this man's background.

We turned left into Blenheim Road and came at last to another semi-detached, but grander, or, at least, taller than Binks's. This one loomed rather than nestled. The bay windows on its first two floors supported a further overhanging bay with a double window and, above, a giant gable. It looked unstable, as if the higher windows aspired to be bound to the earth rather than raised perilously skyward. The effect was, to my eyes, medieval. Binks bustled up to the front door and knocked loudly. A maid answered; she appeared puzzled.

'Binks and Mr Calhoun Kidd for Mr John Yeats!'

'But we was expectin' ...'

Insolently, the maid stepped past Binks and looked up and down the road. He adopted a stern manner as well as her accent.

'You was expectin' us, now call up yer master. We'll be waitin' in the front room.'

I was struck by the horrible, unbearable thought that Binks had brought me here uninvited. But it was too late now, we were in the front room and Binks was grinning and rubbing his hands.

'Art! You can smell it!'

'Binks, are we supposed ...?'

Before I could complete the question, a tall, slender man with an immense beard and an aspect of monumental seriousness entered the room. He stared at us, plainly baffled.

'Mr Yeats! So kind of you to invite us. This is my American friend Mr Calhoun Kidd.'

Yeats acknowledged me with a fractional movement of the head.

'Did O'Leary send you?'

'O'Leary? No, no, you are forgetting, we met at the arts club and you invited me round. I said I would bring Cal.'

The fog shrouding Yeats's features thinned to a dense mist.

'Ah ...'

There was a long pause during which I fancied I could actually hear the shafts of sunlight striking the furniture.

'... Binks!' uttered Yeats finally but unenthusiastically. 'Binks! My sincerest apologies!'

'Think nothing of it, Mr Yeats.'

A small crowd now entered the room, led by two young women.

'Binks!' cried Yeats again, clinging on to this one certainty. 'Now these are our daughters, Lily and Lolly.'

Both had fiercely determined chins. They curtsied and stared at us, evidently disappointed.

'And this is my son Jack and this, my son Willie.'

Here were two more prominent chins. Jack's suggested the same determination as his sisters', but that of Willie was quite different. This was a worried, sensitive chin. He was tall, as tall as me, slightly stooped, and he emanated an air of almost catastrophic awkwardness which I took for shyness, an impression that was quickly dispelled when Willie pushed his way to the front of the crowd to examine me in more detail, as if I were an exhibit in a museum.

'This is my new friend Binks,' continued the father, 'and his new American friend, Mr Calhoun Kidd.'

'American,' said Willie, who was now standing directly in front of me, his face no more than a foot from mine, 'that is a rare and interesting thing.'

'It is?'

'Certainly ... America is the land of all our dreams.'

His mind at once seemed to wander and he turned to address his father.

'But weren't we expecting ...?'

'Yes,' said Lily and Lolly in chorus, suddenly mischievous, 'weren't we expecting ...?'

'We had been led to believe ...' said Jack.

'Yes, yes,' said their father with embarrassed impatience, 'that too is arranged. I may have forgotten to mention the visit of Mr Binks and his American friend. But it is of no account, we shall simply be a little more of a crowd ...'

There was a pause. The tension rose with each passing second. Time's force was palpable in the city of the prime meridian.

'But look,' I said finally, avoiding the eyes of Binks, 'this is plainly of the utmost inconvenience. We shall leave and perhaps meet another time.'

'That is not necessary,' said Willie before his father could speak, 'we could do with an American. I have a new poem I think the Americans would like.'

His father said nothing. I could stand it no longer. Ignoring Binks, I began to fight my way through the crowd of Yeatses to the front door.

'I really think we had better leave you. There has been a misunderstanding.'

The maid also seemed eager to be free of us. She delivered my hat and coat in an instant and with an air of profound disapproval. Binks was hanging back, but, with every step I took, his position became more untenable. At the door I turned to say goodbye to the Yeatses but I found they were, chins thrust, all staring straight past me. Lolly and Lily were even pushing me out of the way.

'She's here!'

I turned again to see a cab had drawn up. From it was emerging a tall woman who appeared to be wearing slippers. She said something to the driver before opening the gate to walk slowly and unsmilingly down the path to the front door. The inhabitants of the hallway had fallen silent. Suddenly, unaccountably, I saw myself as from a great height, a suffering point in this Bedford Park, just to the left of London. I saw the railways, the roads, the houses, palaces and parks. People. I saw the smoking blackness of the city, the green fields of Surrey, Kent, the river, a glowing band of silver, and then the land becoming the sea. I was at last returning London's gaze.

As she reached the threshold, Maud looked up at me and smiled.

Chapter Three
Bedford Park

I

Frank closed his eyes, made a steeple of his fingers and leaned perilously far back in his oaken chair. He held this position long enough for me to begin to feel that he had forgotten about my presence in his office and then there was a thunderous report as he flung himself forward and the chair legs struck the floor. His eyes now glaring at me, he picked up a copy of the *Fortnightly Review*.

'Stepniak!' he cried, brandishing the journal, his chin inches from the desk's surface, 'heard of him? Real name Kravchinsky. Revolutionary and assassin, stabbed the chief of police to death in the streets of St Petersburg and now a contributor to MY PAPER! He lives in your New Jerusalem as it happens. They love him there, they are inordinately fond of revolutionaries. They make them feel both privileged and concerned. What's the name of the place?'

'Bedford Park.'

Frank leaned back again, closed his eyes and satirically whispered the name to himself to indicate his intellectual mastery of the suburb's inhabitants. Exasperation and a desire to impose myself rose within me.

Days had passed since I had met Maud and, finally, I had resorted to Frank, a device I had resisted for fear she would turn out to have been one of his conquests and I would be subjected to a litany of intimate details that would simultaneously inflame me with anger, jealousy, lust and, at last, doubt. But I had nowhere else to go; I could scarcely have gone to the Yeatses; the embarrassment of that afternoon's intrusion still lingered. I needed more than just a means of contact, I needed advice on the matter of London women in general and Maud in particular.

'Somebody bring me a whisky and soda and one for my FRIEND!' Frank bawled.

The *Review*'s offices were a dark, indecipherable arrangement of wooden and glazed boxes in which lamps burned all day to stave off the gloom. Men and a few women worked intently at strange ribbons and sheaves of paper. One I had seen crying, a few were eating and many were laughing. Conversations I had overheard while waiting for Frank to 'get round to me', as he put it, suggested the inhabitants took an anthropological view of the world beyond these boxes, finding it a source of comedy, wonder and disdain. Their anthropology was humbled, however, by the will of Frank. Somewhere in some distant box, there was a shuffling panic in response to Frank's demand. The drinks were brought in by a stooped, concave individual, old before his years but, seemingly, happy, lost in some dream of distant places.

'Orr. Regional news,' explained Frank irrelevantly, 'poor sod.'

Orr sniffed, grinned, winked at me and left. I drained my drink and stiffened myself.

'Frank, I had no choice but to come to you. I assumed you would know of this woman. M-A-U-D-G-O-N-N-E.'

'Yes, yes, no need to spell it, here we employ churls to do that for us. Right, Maud Gonne: rich, crazy for Ireland, though not Irish herself. Bad sign that. Lives in Belgravia. Worse, possibly. Probably on her travels now, she never stays in one place for long. Spends time with the poor in Ireland. Seldom spotted, often discussed, frequently in terms not becoming of a gentleman.'

His whisky vanished beneath his moustache.

'Anything else?'

'Known more as a beauty than a politician. Stead says she is one of the most beautiful women in the world. He should know, he went to prison for buying one, well, a child actually, not that he'd know what to do with a beautiful woman. She likes poets and soldiers – Irish ones – and hates Americans.'

'What!'

'Sorry, that last one was an invention. Me journalist, remember? Anything *might* be true. Come on now, tell me. Why this Desdemona?'

'Desdemona! I have no intention of smothering her, Frank.'

'Intentions in these matters are changeable over time and relative to circumstance. One day smothering is out of the question, the next … Tell me why this Ophelia.'

'Ophelia! Worse still! I must explain – I have thought deeply about this.'

'What is the difference between deep thought and ordinary thought? I have often wondered. Mere duration perhaps or investment of the self. Nothing more. Did you talk much?'

'Talk? Yes, of Ireland. I realised within moments of meeting her that I had spent my entire life in a world of men. To me, women had been negative beings whose primary attribute was that they were not men.'

Maud was not negative, anything but that. She raged, keened, chanted and implored. She knew a world of certainties, intentions, purposes, a world beyond, beyond even the offices of the *Fortnightly* and certainly beyond the base concerns of the body. She drank the wind, ate shadows and made love to ideas. Young Yeats had been bewildered and, I guessed, as stricken as older Cal.

'An admirable attribute that, not being men. But what, then, are they, these women?'

Women, the neuter sex – the thought had barely been formed in my mind until then.

'I suppose their not being men was why my father was happy with his dead wife. It was, for him, her natural condition. Perhaps that's what all men want, a dead woman. Alive, they cancel us out. It may be what you want, Frank.'

'Partly dead, maybe.'

'It's our lusts that do this. I have been no better. Women were either there to marry or to satisfy my lusts. They were things, conveniences. Maud is no thing.'

'Maud is nothing. We are all nothing, though we can, if we are strong, will our way to be something. For men like you, there will always be a Maud eventually. That it is this particular M-A-U-D is neither here nor there.'

I suppressed my rage at this easy dispatching of me to this category – men like me.

'You will find me something about her? I need information.'

'Very well, I will find you information, but first I will tell you a story, a story about Maud. I knew a young man called Stiles, lived in Wimbledon with his fresh young wife, Louise, I believe, just slightly too good for him from the point of view of appearance, an ominous harbinger. They were well set up – money from her father – and he was casting around for a job appropriate to his circumstances. He ran into me – excitable young man, slightly stout for his age – asked about journalism and I told him to go to a do in Mayfair that very night and give me a write-up. He, in turn, ran into Maud.

'She spoke to him of love and assorted other ABSOLUTES ...' He spoke the last word with disgust '... barely noticed him probably but he, of course, took it personally. She convinced him that love justified death, poverty cruelty and so on. He had never thought of such things, never considered such possibilities and, having considered them, he convinced himself he was in love with Maud. She approved, of course, and cared nothing for him but told him the *very fact* of being in love was a wonderful thing even though nothing could come of it.

'Young Stiles agreed with the first but could not accept the second. He bought a revolver, killed his wife, having thoughtfully explained to her that he had to "go with love", and flung himself at Maud's feet. She congratulated him for having achieved a higher state of being, but, alas, he remained too far beneath her emotional and intellectual level for there to be any kind of intimacy. He then killed himself. See?'

'See? See what?'

'One, Maud, thought it right to believe in love for others but, for herself, she took a more practical view; the other, Stiles, was persuaded to believe that what he felt was love whereas, in reality, he had merely come to believe in belief. Either way love as an abstraction and an absolute did all the damage. Love is no absolute, it is a box with an open top; there is no top to hatred's box.'

The story was horrific, too horrific. After a few moments doubt entered my mind.

'It's not true, is it, that story?'

He shrugged and spread his palms.

'Anything *might* be true. It is certainly artistically true and a clear warning about her character. But all right, I trade

56

in information – well, that and art. And this strange place you met … this enchanted and widely advertised suburb?'

'I intend to move there at the first opportunity.'

Frank clutched his head and lunged forward again, his chin now all but touching the desk's surface.

'And leave St James's! Are you mad?'

'It is a place of art and genius. You should be there, Frank. These suburbs are the way of the future. They are clean, free of the murk of the city. The city will one day drown in dirt and plagues. Very low rates of disease in Bedford Park, and no murders.'

'None yet.'

'Mr Yeats was very particular on that point. He has concerns for the safety of his daughters.'

Frank snorted.

'But none for his sons? Give these Bedford Parkers time. People anywhere will find reasons enough in the closet box of hatred to kill each other. And I would like hard evidence that there are more geniuses per square foot than in Mayfair. Apart from anything else, don't they have gardens? That would reduce the density.'

'Gardens certainly. Maud walked on the lawn, making every worm a genius with the touch of her slipper.'

'Slipper? She was wearing slippers?'

'Yes, that troubled me also. Perhaps she dressed in a hurry, her mind on Ireland.'

'Oh dear. Ireland. Maud it is then. A pity, I had hoped to interest you in Dora Parsons. D-O-R-A-P-A-R-S-O-N-S. No, I have not touched her, too undead for me; too, I can barely speak it, *kind*. Well, actually, I think I was too alive for her. Perfect for you. Sensible – no Ireland about her. But now there is Ireland and Maud.'

'Yes, now there is Maud.'

Outside Frank's office, London burst upon my senses as it always did – coal and dung, voices and rumbles, the dirty white sky torn by the latest Gothic fantasies. I walked slowly past the Royal Academy, crossed Piccadilly and turned down St James's Street. A ragged boy ran past me, brushing my sleeve and leaving a sooty stain. I waved my stick in his direction, but he had vanished, a peculiar talent of London boys.

A few days later, having heard nothing from Frank, my mind became clear, certain and calm. I rose at once, descended to the streets, still peaceful as night and fresh as morning. I walked, revelling in all this clarity, and, after an hour or so, took a cab and ordered the reluctant driver westward.

St Michael and All Angels in Bedford Park is a new church. It looks more like the house of a man than a god. On the red roof are dormer windows and a little bell tower, while, along the line of the eaves, runs a white paling that could have been stolen from a nearby garden. This arbitrary detail annoys Willie Yeats. He says, contemptuously, that it is to stop the birds falling off. This is a church for a people who are reluctant to engage with the Last Things, an engagement deemed essential in Chicago. There will be no Second Great Awakening here, there was scarcely even a first. Here the daffodils around this bench lack any proper solemnity, though they dutifully toss their heads in sprightly dance. The presence of the living God is acknowledged, though not thought absolutely necessary. Heaven is not elsewhere, it lies all about us in Bedford Park.

Across the street were the giant gables, bow windows and strange portholes of the Tabard Inn. More gables marched off to the left, forming a crazy sawtooth pattern against the sky. The church suggested domestic peace under the benign gaze of a reticent gentleman god; the inn had an engorged, drunken air. It flailed and reeled. Like the fat wooden columns of the house porches, every detail of the building was inappropriately enlarged.

It is an act of will, of a passionate longing. These people believe the modern world is a place from which one must escape. Bedford Park is an aesthetic utopia, a dream of England as she might be. The suburb is a verdict on the crimes of the city.

I had read about Bedford Park – 'The healthiest place in the world (annual death rate under six per thousand). Close to Turnham Green Station. Trains every few minutes.' What was it, this imagined village? It was not really old, there was nothing looked quite like this in Queen Anne's day, even if the street names – Marlborough, Blenheim, Woodstock – were intended to take you back to the violent glories of her reign. No, this was new, utterly new. It was built in fear, fear of the centreless maze of London.

Closing my eyes, I saw Maud. Imagining the taste of her lips – they were dry, I moistened them – my stomach hollowed with longing and my breathing became shallow.

These moments punctuated my days. For all the power of the sensations, they remained locked within. Since meeting her, I had done nothing but rage against my own weakness. I told myself I was waiting for Frank's information before I acted even though I knew that weakness it was. All I had done was make excuses to meet Binks. I was too much of a coward to enquire of anybody where she lived – Belgravia was all I knew – and the shadow of my embarrassment at that awkward, fateful visit persisted.

I dimly hoped that Binks would take me back to see the Yeatses and, by some miracle, there she would be – as if she were to be offered rather than seized. Maud and my weakness had come to dominate my existence. The notebooks were a poor distraction and even the maze of London now appeared thin and futile. I could not, it seemed, find my way back to anything without first finding my way back to Maud.

My time in this city was passing in empty, endless dreams. Nothing ever happened. The possibility of Maud weakened every resolve. I could have gone back to Chicago; but then I would never see her again. I could pass the days with Frank and all his famous friends; but then I might have missed a chance to see Maud. I could have met other women; but even those I passed in the street whose eyes I caught were notable only by not being Maud. I could have filled my notebooks with what would, one day, be a stupendous account of this city and its marvellous inhabitants; but then I would not have had Maud to sing my praises. Maud was all meaning and purpose, though taking the step of doing something practical to find her seemed even more difficult than doing nothing and not finding her. I was, I knew, half in love with my own passivity.

'What is the matter with me?' I enquired of the blue, gable-torn sky.

Shame and self-loathing overcame me. I could simply decide to act and I would, as once I did when I chose to flee the oppressions of Chicago and the Colonel for my English Heaven. It had worked then, it must work now. Struck in the back by a rising wave of determination, I rose from my bench outside the church, thrust my notebook into the pocket of my coat and determined to speak frankly to Binks. It would be a start.

Enid Binks answered my uncharacteristically firm knock. Her giant hair arrangement was intact but strangely disordered. Her features seemed somehow coarsened and aged, as if five years had passed since I last saw her. Unease emanated from the hallway, as surely as did the smell of dust and the scent of polish. She looked blankly, unrecognising, at me.

'It's me – Cal Kidd, Mrs Binks … Enid.'

'I know. I know.'

In confusion, she passed her hand briefly before her face to push aside a strand of hair. Then her expression became one of suspicion. She thrust her head forward and half closed her eyes; it was an assessing gaze.

'Have you seen Binks? He wasn't meeting you, was he? He meets you a lot.'

'No. But I came here to see him. He told me to visit any time. What on earth is the matter, Enid?'

I was intimidated by her manner and, at once, my determination ebbed and cowardice gripped my soul. Binks was not here and this woman with her suspicions stood in my way, as if she were actually concealing Maud in the gloomy depths of her home.

'Oh, come in. I'm sorry, Mr Kidd, he's just vanished. Lordy, he can be such a nuisance! Always got something on the go.'

She pushed open the door and turned her back to me to walk down the dark hallway. I followed and noticed Lucian sitting at the top of the stairs, his bare boy's knees tucked under his chin.

'Hello, young man,' I said, affecting the correct brisk, masculine voice.

Sophie in a white apron appeared behind the boy, put her hands under his arms and raised him to his feet. She looked down at me, stern and judgemental.

'Ma told us to keep out of the way when she's in a bit of a state.'

'Oh, well, you must do what she says. That is always best.'

Sophie paused as if wishing to say more. Her eyes flashed at me. My second sentence had angered her in some way. Then she turned and slowly climbed the steps, deep in thought and pushing Lucian before her.

Mrs Binks was now sitting at the dining-room table, one hand rubbing fiercely at the polished surface, causing a shuddering sound and a grey smear.

'He has these plans, you see, never tells me what they're all about.'

Her lips continued to move after she had stopped speaking and she was trembling slightly.

'How long has he been gone?'

'There's always something, something he won't tell me about. Men have such secrets, it's their way ...'

'Surely the meeting has simply gone on longer than he expected.'

Once again she regarded me with suspicion.

'What did he want from you? Or what did you want from him? He doesn't just make friends, there's always a purpose. Brian Binks is a mixer and a plotter.'

'You are overwrought, Enid. I know of no purpose. He has just been kind enough ...'

'Always a purpose, I tell you! There was something behind us moving to this out-of-the-way place – not in the town, not in the country, where is it? Nowhere, that's where. It's not real, this Bedford Park. Maybe you don't know what he's got in store for you yet. He has plans, bad ones, I'll wager.'

At this she banged her hand on the table so hard that a vase on a lace mat swayed precariously. I heard a movement upstairs.

'Calm yourself, Enid. Tell me where he went and when and I shall go and find him.'

'He wasn't here when I woke up. He's just vanished. He said last night he had a meeting …'

'The meeting must have been round here, then. I shall go at once and seek him out. He can't have gone far.'

Mrs Binks snorted derisively, but said nothing further. I waited for some sort of assent to my project. None came and I rose uncertainly.

'I shall be right back.'

In the hallway, there was a scuffle from the stairs and I looked up to see Sophie once again dragging Lucian away. But the boy was more determined this time. He wanted to tell me something.

'Da said he had magic to do. That's what he went out to do. Magic!'

'He does tricks, conjuring tricks,' Sophie explained wearily. 'Lucian thinks it's what he does all the time. Come on, stupid.'

'He does magic, I know it!'

4

I marched out into the street, possessed by an unfamiliar sense of purpose. Nevertheless, out of habit, I walked past 3 Blenheim Road. My quest, I was sure, would make me seem all the more intriguing to the Yeats family. There were no signs of life in the house with the mad, overhanging gable. I paused to absorb this inevitable disappointment, forgetting, as I did so, my quest for Binks. I reached into my pocket for my notebook, but changed my mind the moment I realised I might look absurd or even suspicious standing outside the Yeatses' house taking notes. The street was quiet but, to my mind, full of eyes. I could have been taken for an anarchist or even a policeman, perhaps observing Irish radicals.

The thought brought me back to Binks. I was a detective today. Here, at last, was a role I could play, an obligation. Perhaps I would have found Maud by now if I had simply created the obligation to do so by telling someone my intention. The Colonel was contemptuous of intentions, but they were, surely, virtuous if they imposed obligations ... but enough of Maud. I walked on down The Avenue and begin to think earnestly in a detective-like way of the matter in hand. Where would be a good place to have a meeting?

A man was walking hurriedly towards me, his head down and his hands in the pockets of his very tight jacket.

'Excuse me, sir.'

The man stopped and stared at me and, at once, I regretted my boldness. This was one of the most alarming faces I had ever seen. There was an immense forehead surmounted by a thick bush of black hair. The eyes were tunnels beneath a low and threatening brow. A round, pockmarked nose bloomed like some poisonous fungus over a thick beard in the midst of which could be seen very red, very wet lips. It was as if there had been a small explosion just behind his face.

'I ...' I could barely get the words out, '... am looking for a man and wondered if you had, by any chance, seen him.'

'Have seen nobody, nobody.'

He spoke with massive impatience and a thick accent. The 'v' was pronounced as an 'f' and he seemed to have inserted a 'w' after the 'n' in 'nobody'. He walked on, almost knocking me over as he did so.

'Forgive me, but are you sure?' I called after him. 'He has a round face and bowler hat. He has been missing for some time.'

The man paused. Ever since his cricket tale, the Binks in my mind's eye had worn a bowler. But I could not be certain of the hat and I cursed myself for failing to ask Mrs Binks what her husband had been wearing. The man turned, took two steps back towards me and put his hands on his hips, an awkward movement in his tight jacket.

'People disappear,' he snapped, 'it is way of things. Even here in happy, happy Bedford Park! I have been known to disappear. But, look, I am still alive!'

He spread his arms to demonstrate the living truth of his presence and offered me what was intended to be a consolatory smile but was more like a demonic smirk. Was nobody normal in this city, was everybody a 'character'?

'I go now but we will meet again. I can tell. We have something … between us. Your name …?'

'Calhoun Kidd, they call me Cal everywhere.'

'Stepniak they call me here, Sergius Stepniak.'

The name caused me to shiver – inexplicably until I recalled hearing it on Frank's lips. This was the assassin and revolutionary, the killer of the police chief. Nervously I adopted a breezy tone in response.

'You are called something other than Stepniak elsewhere?'

Stepniak relaxed and smiled. He spread his arms again, this time as if offering an embrace.

'Mr Kidd, Cal, in Russia I am called many things, some good, most bad. It is necessary to have the right enemies and the right friends. But there will always be more enemies. I go. We will meet again soon. I hope you find friend.'

With that, he marched off. I had accepted an assassin into my life. London implicates. Shuddering briefly, I composed myself and walked on until I was back at the church. There was the Tabard, but, after my recent experience with Stepniak, I could not quite bring myself to go inside and enquire further of the local residents. Reasoning that Binks may have arranged his meeting in the open, I crossed the road and stepped on to the grass of Acton Green, a flat, triangular park dotted with trees down one side of which lay the embankment of the railway – 'trains every few minutes'.

The scent of early spring, of earth, air and grass, lifted my spirits – they could scarcely have sunk farther. My march gave way to a gentle stroll and a daydream of walking in the sunshine with Maud. We talked of life, literature and Chicago. I told her tales of the Lake Shore house, the fire, the stockyards and the Colonel. I told her, self-deprecatingly, of my absurd buffalo robe, but she was intrigued; it was the art of the people, she wanted me to unfold it for her. In her strong but soft voice, she explained the injustices of Ireland, her eyes burning with purpose and conviction. For Maud, I would have fought for Ireland. For now, however, I needed to find Binks in order to free myself to find Maud. Always there was one more obstacle to overcome.

On the Green there was nothing but a few dark figures walking quickly, hunched in that peculiar English way as if it was always raining. I turned to retrace my steps, but, as I did so, there was a kind of flicker, a shadow in the sun. A bird perhaps? No, something in the world had changed. The unease that flowed from the hallway of the Binks house had now flooded out into this park and I was swept by a wave of dread that seemed to leave a hollow in my body's core. The day remained bright, but had, somehow, been blackened as if charred by fire. The dreams of Maud entirely vanished from my mind.

I looked once again around the Green. It appeared unchanged; it was that same spring-scented place that, moments before, had filled me with thoughts of love. I must have been imagining things, it was a digestive failing; most things, according to the advertising signs around London, were. Still, I knew I was trying not to think about something, something seen, some darkness. There was a deliberate flaw in this scene as in a child's puzzle picture, a pony with three legs, an upside-down house, a clown's lurid smile amid the foliage.

It was none of these things. The flaw was in the thick grass and shrubbery of the railway embankment. Turning my head slowly as if pushing against a great weight, I looked towards the embankment. There was, indeed, a black shape, slightly humped, in the grass. I walked towards it and, with each step, it became ever more clearly a man lying down.

After an apparent eternity, I reached the embankment and the prone man. A bowler hat was placed, oddly, on his back and his coat and trousers were unnaturally rumpled as if he had fallen from a great height. His face was pressed into the ground and he was surrounded by a glinting, scented halo of crushed grass. Both his ankles and his wrists were visible, raw, bone white against the brilliant green.

'Binks!' I cried, affecting a bright tone in an attempt to brush aside the encroaching horror.

I tapped the shoulder, the brief contact with the fabric of the coat sending a premonitory shiver of disgust up the length of my arm. There was, of course, no reaction. I stood back, unable to act, to do the obvious thing, and stared upward at the featureless blue where there was a bird flying, incredibly high, or maybe not. How could one judge height in this nothingness? How could 'sky' be a word since it denoted nothing? All of London but a thin film of darkness beneath ...

Finally, closing my mind to all this, I bent down and tugged at the right shoulder. The slope of the ground caused the entire body to roll over slowly, horribly slowly, crushing the hat. The head followed, the face finally turning to featureless blue a moment after the body had come to rest. It was Binks and, as the body rolled, two objects fell out of the mouth. My first thought was that they were clumps of earth. My second thought was stark disbelief. They were eyes. The sockets were empty holes filled with blood and raw flesh. The clothes had been ripped apart, revealing the chest. This had been deeply slashed three times with a knife in the shape of an 'N' or a 'Z'. Binks's chest had become a stew of skin, fat, bones and blood. I thought, absurdly, that Binks's lung problems were at last over.

Blades of grass adhered to the surface of this stew, like a scattering of parsley. The livid beauty of the spectacle entranced me, this astonishing splash of colour representing nothing but itself, not a man, not a death. Then, at once, it represented the corpse of Binks. I took two steps back and, fearing I might faint, sat down. I wanted to vomit, but I could not. The nausea was locked within me, an indigestible mass filling my entire torso. My inner organs wanted release, to burst free of this body and leave me as nothing more than another corpse on this bright grass.

A pastoral calm had returned to a scene which, not long ago, must have been rent by terrible human violence. Struggling to gain some purchase on my feelings, I imagined what that high bird and, now, a rising lark must see – the daisy-strewn grass, the gently swaying trees, the little people in their black coats, bent forward slightly as they crossed to and fro across the pattern of the green. This vicious spectacle of desecration could easily be overlooked if you could only rise high enough. How I longed to be a bird, a lark singing, indifferent to everything!

Further emotions crowded out the reverie. Was it, somehow, my fault that Binks was dead? How was I to tell Enid? I found myself cursing the fact that I could no longer ask Binks to help me find Maud. The commonplace insensitivity of the thought gave me the strength to stand up, look around and then begin racing back to the Tabard.

5

I burst in to find myself in an interior of dark wood and green and cream paint. The bright sunshine had left me with great globes of colour drifting before my eyes. I paused until I could make out pictures made of tiles on the walls. I heard a laugh from the darkness within. This brought me to my senses.

'There's a man dead on the Green,' I cried, 'fetch someone at once!'

I slumped into a chair, gasping. Its arms were polished by years of contact with the thick woollen sleeves of the working men. I rested my elbows on my thighs and found myself fascinated by the grain of the dark, dead floorboards. Half a dozen men were staring at me; not one had moved.

'Dead,' said one, 'well, we all die, don't we, lads? Might as well be out there in the sunshine when you do.'

'A fine day to die,' said another. 'There've been a few dead 'uns found on that Green. There was that Mrs ... What was her name?'

'Lloyd. Or was it Betty Highsmith? One or the other.'

'For God's sake!' I cried. 'Yes, dead, but not just dead.

And it's not a fine day to be murdered. It never is! Horribly mutilated. A vile crime, I tell you.'

They stared at me, shocked by my vehemence.

'Brian Binks did not deserve this,' I muttered as if to myself.

'Binks has been murdered!' cried the first man.

The six men now looked at each other and then rushed out into the sunshine. A moment later, one came back.

'Where?'

'That way.'

I stepped out of the door and pointed him in the direction of the embankment. I wanted to go back inside, lie down on the floorboards and forget. Reluctantly, however, I turned to walk back to the Binks house. Enid would have to be told and I would have to tell her.

Sophie answered the door.

'Did you find my father?'

Again that stern face.

'Hello, Sophie, I must speak to your mother.'

She looked suspicious, exactly, for that moment, as her mother had earlier.

'You found him!'

The correct answer in her terms would have been 'yes', though, strictly, the truthful answer was 'no'. Binks was not out there. Binks had departed.

'Just let me see your mother.'

'Tell me! I've got a right to know. I am the eldest.'

The damp curl of her angry lips, the unimaginable, untouchable perfection of the flesh of the young – Frank talked about it all the time – and their anger. Sophie was already discounting her mother's primacy.

'I have to see your mother now! So please get out of my way.'

She raised her chin slightly as if preparing to hold her ground. Then, with the bitter reluctance of the usurped, she stepped aside and waved me to the back of the house.

The kitchens of these narrow, terraced houses projected out into the back gardens as if added as an afterthought or squeezed out of the body of the building by the sheer pressure of dark space. Mrs Binks was there, most of her blonde hair now falling untended over her shoulders as if she were already in mourning. She was standing and staring out of the window into the dishevelled garden. Hearing me, she glanced over her shoulder, saw my face and seemed to understand everything.

'We was going to do that garden properly. With shrubs.'

The 'was' hurt me. Her speech had become more cockney, as if she already knew that her Bedford Park identity had fallen away.

'Enid ...'

'He was always making some excuse.'

'Enid, I found Brian.'

'He always had something else to be getting on with.'

Could she go on with this tone of dismal reminiscence for ever?

'I'm afraid something terrible has happened. You must prepare yourself ...'

She did not move, she said nothing.

'He has been murdered, Enid, murdered.'

Her back tensed, making her clothes quiver. She clutched at the sink, pushing so hard against it that it seemed it must crack, and then, finally, she dropped to her knees. There was a long pause in which she appeared to have stopped breathing. Then there was an agonised inhalation followed by a terrible howl that brought Sophie running into the room.

'Ma!'

She looked accusingly at me.

'What's the matter with her? What did you do?'

I put my hands on Sophie's shoulders but she shrugged them off.

'Your father – something terrible has happened.'

'He's dead, Sophie!' cried Mrs Binks. 'Murdered!'

Sophie's gaze flicked back and forth between us as if trying to ascertain whether, first, this was a joke and then, secondly, whether I was the murderer. Lucian appeared in the doorway and moved hesitantly into the room. Sophie shrieked softly and rushed out, grabbing the boy as she went. Still kneeling, her hands above her head, still clutching the sink, Mrs Binks was talking as if to herself, talking with the now fully unleashed accent of her childhood.

'He had it coming. He was always up to sommat. Never told me nothing.'

'Enid, is there somebody …?'

'He said the money kept coming in, so why should he bother me? Well, he's bothered me now all right, bothered me good and proper.'

'He was a good fellow, Enid, thoughtful. He wanted the best for you.'

I had no idea, I realised even as I spoke, whether he was 'good' or not.

'Good! You know he mixed with queer folk, crooks, them anarchists and table tappers. He always said sommat amazing was going to happen. Now it has, sommat amazing.'

She looked out of the window.

'There'll be no shrubs for us. That garden will never get done up nice now. He kept all the money to hisself, just gave me what we needed, just a bit at a time. I don't know where he keeps the rest, if there is any. I just don't know. He never told me nothing.'

She started sobbing. I put my hands beneath her arms and helped her up. She looked at me, apparently amazed that there was somebody else in the room.

'There's tea if you want it ...'

She walked, sobbing, out of the room, leaving me standing there, wondering what I was supposed to do, what I was supposed to feel. My life had not prepared me for this. My mother had died when I was still a child. In Chicago everything – life and death – had happened at a distance. I was a spectator. In London everything and everybody touched everything and everybody else.

I suddenly remembered the billiard games at the Fremont. London was a billiard table with four million balls in play, each one causing every other to move and each move causing the whole game to change. Binks had been the embodiment of this colossal, intimate system of cause and effect. He flowed like water, he had said, like a river or canal, connecting things. Who could have killed him? Anybody, every murder in London has four million suspects.

Sophie entered the kitchen silently.

'Ma wants some tea.'

'Sophie, I am so very sorry. How is Lucian? How are you?'

'He's said nothing. He's with Ma now. They're just cuddling. I'm fine. I've got to be, haven't I?'

'You're a brave girl.'

'Oh, and you're a big, brave man for finding Da. It just happens, doesn't it? What's bravery got to do with it?'

'Of course I'm not brave, but you are brave for being so responsible and nice to your mother.'

'It's just my way ... Perhaps I'm cold and unfeeling. Perhaps I just do what I have to do.'

Her words suggested an unpleasant truth about this family. I didn't want Sophie to say anything else. I just stared vacantly at the wall as she pushed past me to make the tea in silence and then left me alone in the kitchen once more. She had given me a cup. I drank it quickly while staring out at the garden. The hot liquid soured my stomach. Time passed sluggishly, painfully. There was murmuring and occasional weeping. I could do nothing; I just had to be here, waiting. Again I thought of that lark, flying higher this time, far higher, high enough to see the whole city spread beneath me like a map, a map with the strange rhomboid of Bedford Park on its western edge. I saw the tentacles of the streets, tying the place together, connecting, like the Binks waterway, all things.

A loud triple knock on the front door caused me to freeze, wondering what to do. Then there were four, even louder knocks. Sensing their stern authority and embarrassed by the fact that the others were doing nothing, I rushed down the hallway and opened the door. A very short, thin-faced man with a huge moustache, more flamboyant even than Frank's, was standing there. Behind him were two immensely tall constables.

'You are not Mrs Enid Binks,' said the man triumphantly, his moustache bouncing gleefully with every syllable. The constables laughed.

'I am Inspector Grand.'

'I am Calhoun Kidd, a family friend, Inspector. I found the body. You had better come in.'

Grand edged past, staring up at me as he did so; I stared back. The hall being narrow and Grand being very short, he seemed to be peering vertically upwards into my nostrils.

'An American, that's interesting.'

'Is it really? Mrs Binks is in …'

Grand raised his hand.

'No, Mr Kidd, I shall discuss matters with you first.'

Not knowing where else to go, I led him into the kitchen. The two constables followed, filling the room. Grand produced a notebook, exactly, I noticed, like my own.

'Very well, then. How did you happen upon the corpse in question?'

I explained my friendship with Binks, my regular visits to the house, my appointment today, Mrs Binks's concern and, finally, my foray on to Acton Green.

'It was an accident really, I was searching at random.'

'But, in the event, very successfully. It was as if you knew exactly where to look.'

I stared at him in disbelief as he embarked on a series of ludicrous questions – questions about my own background, how I knew the exact place to look, my feelings for Mrs Binks, my knowledge of Binks's business affairs. At once I felt affronted, but also unappreciated; I had found the body, I had rushed to tell and console the family. To be suspected by this man with his absurd moustache, and, I now noticed, a very intrusive mole on the line of his collar, was intolerable

'Inspector, would it not be wise to be occupying yourself with searching for the murderer instead of discussing my history in this kitchen?'

Grand smiled and looked round – and up – at his constables, both of whom interrupted their examination of the furniture to smile back and nod knowingly.

'We live in a scientific age, Mr Kidd, the wonders of science are all about us. Science has taught us all the value of close observation of all the facts. It is in the nature of police work here in England – though perhaps not in your homeland – to treat every aspect of a case as potentially significant. I have known a case where the colour of a man's socks made all the difference in a search for the truth. The truth, Mr Kidd,' he paused to ensure I was taking in the full significance of his words, 'is what matters, is it not?'

He turned for confirmation to the constables, both of whom nodded.

'In this case, you found the corpse; we have to eliminate the possibility that you put it there. I have known several cases where the so-called finder of the corpse was, in fact, the murderer. For reasons best known to themselves, perpetrators frequently wish to draw attention to themselves. Our best criminologists – I am thinking of Forbes and Wilkerson – have noted this paradoxical behaviour. Or perhaps – who knows? – it is not a paradox. Thesis-antithesis-synthesis, as Herr Hegel might have put it. Perhaps we are in the midst of what another German called a transvaluation of values. The Germans are ahead of us in these matters. What do you think, Mr Kidd? What is your opinion on these substantive issues of our time?'

'Oh, for God's sake, Grand! You are wasting my time and your own!'

I took out my notebook, tore out a page and wrote my address.

'This is where I can be found. Messages can be left at the Reform. And now I must speak to Mrs Binks.'

I forced my way out of the kitchen and found the family in the living room.

'Enid …'

She looked up at me, shocked by the sudden intrusion. Sophie was kneeling by her, holding Lucian tightly and awkwardly on her lap.

'The police are here.'

She nodded.

'Do you wish me to stay?'

'I do,' said Lucian.

'No, Mr Kidd, go, go.'

I was at a loss. I looked at Sophie. I hesitated until Grand and his constables started to force their way in. Unable to bear any more of their supercilious attention, I left, my passing noted by an ironic bow from Grand.

'Thesis-antithesis, Mr Kidd,' he called after me in a threatening manner, 'and then synthesis!'

I fled into the fresh air and breathed deeply. My stomach was still knotted with anger at Grand and his idiotic scientific methods that somehow implicated me. I walked briskly, but then, after a couple of minutes, I felt a fool. I had forgotten to tell Grand about Stepniak, an encounter that might well have had some significance. It would also have distracted Grand from casting suspicion on me. I considered going back to report the meeting. No, never mind, let the fool find out for himself.

Enervated by events, I hailed a cab to take me to St James's. Back at my rooms, I lay on the bed, breathless and hot, and wondered about my next move.

The thought came to me that, through my weakness, Maud and the death of Binks, I was fully engaged with this city for the first time. I had come to earth at last. Through love and death, London had trapped me in her game of billiards, her great system of cause and effect.

I slept for a few hours and then woke, realising my next move was obvious. I sent a note to the offices of the *Fortnightly Review*, giving the pale boy a shilling to be extra quick.

6

A very young woman was in Frank's outer office, also waiting for his attention.

'Forgive me, you are Mr Kidd, are you not? The dove grey betrays you. Frank was very keen that we should meet. I am Dora Parsons.'

'Oh, ah, er, yes, he has spoken warmly of you, Miss Parsons.'

'And of you, Mr Kidd. I feel we know each other already.'

There was a long pause as I tried to forget Binks and deal with this sudden intimacy. Her eyes were warm, bright ...

'Forgive me, I am a little distracted. How do you know Frank?'

The question made her awkward. She turned away from me and primly straightened her clothes, pressing her skirt down against her hips.

'He did my father a good turn when he was editor of the *Evening News*. He kept him out of the news ... Not that I think it was news really. Just a silly lapse, nothing to interest the public.'

'A lapse. I understand.'

She turned to face me again, her eyes, unnervingly direct, fixed on mine.

'Frank seems to think we have much in common. Do you think that can be true?'

'True? I can't imagine that we do. But Frank is no literalist. His words seldom engage in dull correspondences. In his mind we probably share a metaphor. Or perhaps you like Swinburne?'

'No. I read widely, however, I am very fond of the Russians – Turgenev in particular. Do you like Turgenev?'

I could not answer, though I thought I probably did like Turgenev. I stared down at the faded Turkey carpet. After a few moments of this, she spoke.

'You seem very distracted indeed. Are you all right?'

'I'm sorry, Miss Parsons, I am very anxious to speak to Frank on a matter of some urgency.'

'Yes, he said you were coming but rushed out of his office after our tea, something about a head- or deadline. He told me to keep you entertained, though to avoid Irish matters at all costs. Why would that be?'

'I can't imagine. One of his leaps of fancy perhaps.'

'Are you sure you're all right? You look quite pale. Would you like a dab of cologne?'

'No, no – oh, perhaps. Thank you, that is very pleasant.'

I felt her breath on my cheek as she dabbed my forehead.

'Americans, on closer inspection, do actually look quite different from the English. Your skin has a distinct pallor and texture. It must be the wind, blowing so long over the land.'

'The wind blowing over the land? I had never thought of that. Certainly in the West the women's skin seems to wither … My skin … Have you ever seen a corpse, Miss Parsons?'

'Oh, quite a few in the streets. I remember one, a youth, a child almost. He was in rags, a gentleman was holding him in his arms.'

'There is such a change that takes place from life to death. I never realised … Perhaps the pallor and texture you see in me are a result of my recent proximity to death.'

'You are very upset, aren't you? Someone you knew …?'

'Yes, and the family. Very sudden.'

'Did Frank know them?'

'I assume so, Frank seems to know everybody in London.'

'Or he says he does.'

'You do not believe him?'

She smiled, her face, framed by golden hair, now suffused with the satisfaction of imparting some local wisdom to this troubled American.

'Of course not. Nobody does. Frank says many things but he has yet to utter the truth.'

Chapter Four
At Madame Blavatsky's

I

Frank did not return. Miss Parsons and I finally abandoned all hope. Leaving the office, we both turned right to walk down Piccadilly. My mind was still caught up with the horrors of Acton Green while my body was calmly strolling down the greatest thoroughfare in the world with the wrong woman. Her sinuous monologue – I could find no words – wove bright threads in the heavy, darkening air around me.

'Do you think we have a Turgenev? Is it Hardy? I sometimes wonder. Do you think this is an exciting time to be here, in London? In England? You, as a foreigner, should know. Oh, look at that sweet boy, where can he be running to?'

She did not depend on my answers to such questions, but simply talked on, perhaps out of simple kindness.

For some reason, I did not cross to St James's Street but continued with her to Hyde Park Corner, listening to her grow ever more excited about the improving conditions of the London poor. She worked among them for some charitable institution.

'Frank,' she said, 'disapproves. He says I am weakening the species and I should read Herr Nietzsche and Herbert Spencer.'

'Frank is preparing for the Coming Age ...' I responded vaguely.

We parted with no future meeting arranged. This was hardly necessary in London, the city of coincidences; our next meeting was certain but its date unknowable. I watched her small, taut, determined form being absorbed into the darkness of the crowd, the pale faces like petals, and unexpectedly felt that I had lost something.

This momentary grief soon mutated into irritation with Frank. Where had he gone? But also why was he trying to corrupt Miss Parsons with his philosophers? I quickly retraced my steps, resolving to pin him down in his office. Sure enough he was there, already clad in his evening finery, all stretched over his hard, compact frame. The improbably pouting chest and the slender legs made him look like a sketch in his own journal.

'Frank, where were you, for God's sake?'

'CAL! How are you getting on? Have you found your place in London society without any help from me? Has there been a little girly to pass the time before M-A-U-D falls into your arms?'

He emitted a shout of laughter so violent that it seemed deliberately designed to advertise its own falsity. His mood was exuberant, even by his standards, and, somehow, malevolent. London and its inhabitants had begun to take on an even darker aspect since the corpse of Binks.

'No, nothing, indolence, idleness. I can't seem to find my place in this town. I met Miss Parsons who was also waiting for you.'

'Ah-ha! Never mind about that indolence. The solution is at hand. Join me. There is an event, a do, a great gathering, everybody will be there, ALL SMART LONDON! My God, you haven't even met Wilde yet, have you? Nor Carlo.

Another pervert, but he'll do you a wonderful drawing. Ah, but you've met Yeats. That would give you a misleading impression of high seriousness.'

'Quite. But there is something else …'

'And on that matter, I have some awkward news. You have a rival for Miss M-A-U-D-G-O-N-N-E. Willie found his purpose in life at the same moment that you did. Irish, you see.'

'Willie is …'

'Irish, yes, and in love with Maud, exactly. Though to be frank – which, as you know, I always am – I suspect he had just decided that falling in love was necessary to his poetic development when the slippered houri happened to appear in the enchanted suburb.'

Nausea rose within me. Willie was young, Irish and a poet; I was a mere American and not yet a writer of any kind. Frank noted my fallen features.

'Come, let's go. This event will ensure you forget Maud for a few hours at least.'

'I am not dressed.'

He glanced me up and down, making me aware of the smutty daytime air of the city on my clothes.

'Forget it. You're American, you can get away with anything, even dove grey. They'll love you, whiff of the prairie, hint of the frontier. They'll think you're an Indian-killer. London loves killers.'

At this, Frank succeeded; I did forget Maud because I had remembered Binks.

'That's what I want to talk to you about – a killer. Binks has been murdered. I found him, or rather his body.'

Frank paused.

'Binks …'

'You know him?'

'A little … a little … You found him? Do you think the killer wanted you to find him?'

'Who? What on earth …?'

'Oh, nothing. Why did we not know of this? They must have concealed it from us. Damned police. RYDER!'

A yellowish, perspiring man in shirtsleeves with a pencil gripped between his teeth appeared in the room almost before Frank had pronounced the last syllable of his name.

'I want a special on the death of Binks, his murder by an unknown assassin, all London agog, the grieving widow, the sinister conspiracies, the incompetent investigation, the usual …'

'Binks?' said Ryder in wonderment, but then he left before anybody could explain – though, of course, nobody could.

Through a visible act of will, Frank regained his composure, shook his head and emitted a loud exhalation followed by a quick laugh.

'You said no murders in Bedford Park! Ha! Disenchantment! It is the way of our time.'

'You replied, "None yet." You didn't know something, did you?'

'Pah! Perhaps I do … We can talk about this on the way. Let's have a drink at the Savoy. You'll love it, it's supposed to be like American hotels, but I can tell you now it knocks spots off the Fremont. As my dear friend, the Prince, says, "We should forget what is unpleasant in life!"'

2

He laughed and nudged me in the ribs with such force that I staggered slightly. Rushing out of the office, he waved away lines of anxious people demanding his attention. Ryder once again materialised to clutch my arm.

'Who is Binks?' he asked, fixing my eyes with a desperate, glazed look. Frank at once detached him.

'Do it yourself, fools!' he cried. 'If it's a mother you want, you've come to the wrong man!'

Out in the street of muck and noise, Frank whirled about before seizing a hansom from the grasp of a distinguished old man in a shining top hat with a rose in the buttonhole of his coat.

'Old fool from *The Times*. A lean and slipper'd pantaloon. Not quick on his feet – ha! Like his newspaper. We could have walked, but I get recognised rather too much these days.'

He looked suspiciously out of the window and then rapped on the roof.

'Quicker! Stand not upon the order of your going, but go at once. We have WORK to do!'

His strange and suddenly Shakespearean excess of exuberance seemed to be something to do with this event, but, at the same time, I felt he was reacting so violently to remove the matter of Binks from his mind. Something in my news had struck home. He was all but vibrating in his seat and his fingers constantly flicked and brushed at his clothes, his hair, his moustache.

'Where did you find Binks?'

His tone was now systematic.

'I met him in an ABC.'

'No! I mean the corpse – which, very well, is not actually Binks ...'

'Not far from his home in Bedford Park.'

I paused, realising that telling the whole story would take some time.

'I'll explain at the Savoy.'

'In that case,' cried Frank, rapping again on the roof, 'quicker yet!'

After much rapping, trotting and cursing, the hansom made a sharp right turn into a narrow alleyway over which a shining metal-faced pediment announced the entrance to the hotel. Frank paid the driver and strode inside. Stumbling, I rushed after him. I just had time to register a monumental black and brown marble palace, glowing with patches of gold, before I found myself seated in a corner table in an extremely crowded bar.

'My table,' explained Frank. 'My office, they call it. They know a man of substance when they see one. You won't see Stead here, hasn't got the wardrobe for it apart from anything else.'

The place was full of men of substance and their women – Londoners, rulers of the world, inhabitants of the black and golden maze, billiard players.

'Are you drinking these days?' I enquired. So much was happening, I had failed to familiarise myself with Frank's ordinary life in London.

'I said I would drink when I was twenty-one and I did. I confess it got out of hand a few years back. Lord Folkestone pointed out to me that I was consuming five or six glasses of cognac after dinner. I hadn't noticed. I don't get hangovers and there were no noticeable signs of drunkenness. Of course, I stopped at once. Went without for two years. Now I observe strict moderation. We will have martinis.'

'What are martinis?'

'Mainly gin, drop of vermouth. It has a very brightening effect in the early evening. I believe it goes straight to the brain, a very pure drink, very direct. Like me. So tell me about the thing that is not Binks, the Binks body.'

I explained with care and at length, my narrative reaching a climax with the discovery of the body and then fading into the anticlimactic comedy of the arrival of Inspector Grand. Frank listened intently and, finally, took out a notebook and scribbled briefly.

'I'll get some of my boys to look into this Grand character. But Binks was involved in the occult, you say?'

'Among many other things.'

'Did you notice any patterns in the cuts on his chest?'

'I thought there was an "N" or a "Z". But it was just a horrible mess, I may have imagined that, and I had no desire to linger.'

'"N"! I'll get my boys to check that too. I think we'll find something.'

'What?'

'Occult symbols, strange letters. There have been cases. Dangerous business exploring the other side, you know, the spirit world.'

Frank drank the remains of his martini. I had only taken one sip and recoiled from the cold, oily sourness that seemed to coat my entire innards. But, in imitation of Frank, I now drained the glass in one go.

'Right!' cried Frank. 'ON!'

I followed Frank's headlong rush out of the bar, fearing I would faint from the arctic gale that now swept through my head.

'About Willie and Maud ...' I gasped.

Frank stopped so suddenly that I crashed into him. We were in the centre of the dark marble lobby.

'Ah yes, I had overlooked that. You find the Binks corpse when what you really sought was the living Gonne body. Well, Willie Yeats has been pursuing her like a puppy these last few months. She won't have anything to do with him in that way, meaning, of course, the only way that matters. She just likes having poets to tea once in a while, Irish ones best of all, I imagine. Other women swoon for Willie. Perhaps the sex act holds no charm for her. There are such women, I am told, though I have never encountered one myself, they just need drawing out. These are things, however, of which Willie knows nothing. Neither do you, come to that.'

'You told me of Stiles ... But how did he *find* her?'

'Sympathetic because of her love of the indomitable Irishry.'

'No, I mean *where*?'

'Why does that matter? Come on, we are late.'

Moments later, we were in another hansom with Frank, again, rapping on the roof. I noticed we seemed to be returning whence we came.

'Quicker! You know I think I've heard of this Binks. But I can't think in what context.'

Startled, I glanced at him. The words sounded as false as his earlier laughter and seemed to contradict his assertion that he knew him 'a little'.

After a few moments, the hansom decanted us at the Café Royal and Frank, keeping his eyes fixed on the ground, rushed inside. I found myself in a cave of gold and red. Didn't anybody in this town believe in windows? Frank, with a swagger, greeted the flunkies that swarmed about him. They knew him well but one or two regarded me disapprovingly. Frank saw this and slapped me on the back.

'I know, boys, not quite up to the mark sartorially tonight. But he is American!'

'Ah!' they cried almost in unison.

'Come, Cal, and encounter the best that is being thought and said.'

Frank led me up a flight of stairs and into a huge, heavily curtained room filled with cigar smoke and a fantastically loud hubbub of conversation and laughter.

'Drink?'

'Well, another of those martinis ...'

'No, you must move on to champagne. Two martinis for a novice might result in an incident.'

He pressed a glass into my hand, toasted me and drank his own in one go. I did the same. Frank seized two more glasses.

'Oscar!' he cried.

A man as tall as me but fatter and with long, flowing hair had appeared in front of us. He exuded an air of massive bonelessness. His face was like soft rubber.

'Frank, my Caliban, how nice to see you and how entirely expected!' He turned to me. 'Frank, you know, has been invited to all the great houses of England. Once.'

Frank shouted his false laugh again. I saw he needed to impress this man and that being seen among such people was the point of this outing.

'Oscar, I'd like you to meet Mr Calhoun Kidd. This, Cal, is the celebrated Mr Wilde!'

He affected to notice me for the first time, looking me up and down, plainly considering my day clothes.

'Why, I am very pleased to meet you, Mr Wilde. Frank has told me so much about you.'

'I'm sure he has. Thank God, you're American. I thought, for a moment,' he gestured at my day clothes, 'our civilisation had crumbled to dust and Frank had omitted to report the incident.'

He took my hand. His felt greasy and, at that moment, I noticed he had a single blackened tooth.

'Oscar! You know we'd get civilisation crumbling to dust on page two at least.'

'Mr Kidd, you are a very lucky man. It is the height of fashion to be an American in London just now.'

I found I could not fathom the man's tone. A smile played around his rubber mouth but, whether this was irony at work or simple amiability, I could not tell.

'Really? I hadn't noticed. I have felt more exotic than fashionable.'

'Then you have not been paying attention. Every unattached woman in this town – and many attached, now I think of it – wants to marry an American. I take it you are some kind of pork packer.'

'That was part of my father's business in Chicago.'

'America,' said Wilde, 'has come on so since it was discovered. Though, personally, I feel it has never really been discovered, merely detected. Rather like you in London, Mr Kidd.'

'Not entirely undiscovered,' said Frank. 'Cal here has met Yeats.'

'Indeed! Young Willie has thrilled us all, a marvellous boy but a little pedantic. He once criticised my use of the word "melancholy". He said I should have written "sad". But the man in question was not sad, he was melancholy. It is quite different. Is it not?'

He did not expect an answer so I did not provide one. His gaze wandered around the room. He gestured at a tall, pale, thin man with a large head and a straggly, reddish beard.

'Have you met Shaw?'

'I have not.'

'Oh, you must. He is an extraordinary man. He has no enemies but is intensely disliked by all his friends.'

Wilde was a man of London in full, a spinner of paradoxes.

'Mrs Besant,' said Frank, eager to add his own sophisticated analysis, 'says he has a perfect genius for aggravating

Remarkably sharp for her, a woman of dubious preoccupations. She is now in league with Madame Blavatsky, a hellish partnership.'

Wilde dipped his head, not listening but rather waiting for Frank to finish so that he could continue.

'Shaw is also, like me, an Irishman,' he said, 'but, unlike me and exactly like all the other Irish people you will meet, he employs his nationality as a weapon against the English.'

'Is everybody here Irish?'

'I fear so. We had high hopes of Frank, but, it transpires, he was born in Galway. Or so he says. He is a compulsive liar, as we all are. Frank, Have you read Mr Stead's *The Truth about Russia*? Quite fascinating.'

Wilde had evidently discovered, as had I, that mentioning Stead was a sure way to provoke or humble Frank. He paused before throwing another dart with an air of indifferent cruelty. 'And how is Mrs Harris?' Frank's wife of convenience was plainly a social embarrassment, a too obvious sign of his upstart identity.

'Mrs Harris is more than well, thanks, Oscar. But Galway is NOT something I care to be reminded of. Yes, I breathed that same sentimental mix of incense and alcohol as the rest of you Paddies. To be fair, the Irish are a most lovable people even if in my childhood they were somewhat trying. And as for Stead's ...'

'Ah, the drunken sea captain. Maritime ancestry can be so difficult, don't you find, Mr Kidd?'

'I don't know. My father was an army man.'

'Really? How dull. When did he find time to pack pork? Now you must come and meet Shaw.'

Wilde turned away and, as he did so, I grasped Frank's arm.

'Look, I really don't want to meet these strange and ridiculous people, these ... flabby and pale people. I only want to talk to you about Binks and to discover what you know of Maud.'

Wilde looked back at us, noted that we were not immediately following his lead, shrugged and walked off, his head flung back, suggesting a proud sulk. Frank stared at me as if noticing a facial peculiarity for the first time. The evening's performance had fallen away. He could now find more satisfaction in the cruelty of exposure.

'Maud Gonne,' he said slowly, 'while basking in the adoration of Willie and provoking your passions, has a lover, a Frenchman, one Millevoye.'

'In France!' I gasped.

'In France and there is one more thing, a little thing.'

'Little?'

'Very. She is pregnant by Monsieur Millevoye.'

I was utterly lost, for words and for all else. He studied my face with a degree of sympathy.

'Events, dear Cal, have at last begun to mould you, shaping you to the viciousness of the world. And Binks – I think I have a line that may lead us to his killer. Journalism, you see, it is the heart of the matter. Through it pass all things. We know what others do not dare to think. But ...' he drew me away from the crowd '... I must tell you my idea of getting to Binks's killer.'

Has my delay lost me Maud or was this Millevoye already in her life when we met? He must have been. The time had been long for me but was short in the world. I have become an American in London waging war on the French and the Irish and seeking a killer. I have entered the maze.

Two days later Frank and I were in an enormous room in one of the largest, darkest houses in Bedford Park. The walls and windows were entirely covered by heavy, dark red velvet curtains. Three lamps cast a yellowish haze at one end of the room, leaving the other end quite dark. There was a single large table at the illuminated end and perhaps thirty chairs arranged in a large oval shape around the walls. On each chair sat a woman. They all wore the same elaborate white dresses, but the folds, pleats and ribbons were artfully disarranged to suggest not regimentation but freedom of spirit. The women had their hands placed, palms downwards, on their laps and they emitted a low murmur that rose, periodically, into an almost thunderous chant. Their eyes were closed, but the lids occasionally flickered without ever fully opening. Here and there a sandalled foot projected from beneath a white skirt. Apart from the movements of their throats, the women were entirely motionless. The room was heavy with a damp, ecclesiastical odour of incense overlaid with jasmine, lavender and patchouli.

There were no seats allocated to visitors. Frank and I were standing behind the line of chairs about halfway down the room. I was swaying slightly. We had been in there for half an hour and the sound of the chanting had become a solid object, a heavy sphere rolling around inside my skull. It was as if I had plunged into a dark lake, the curtains having become waving fronds and the women curious water creatures. To quell this hallucination, I strained to decipher the murmur of the nearest woman. After some moments of fierce concentration, I heard something like, 'The self-born, the sweat-born, the boneless, the twofold …'

Frank's eyes were flitting about, assessing, as far as was possible, the bodies beneath the spiritual clothes, though in most cases he had to be content with nothing more than a foot. Occasionally he found a promising or at least visible outline, nudged me eagerly with his elbow and nodded in the woman's direction. After the third nudge, I found myself growing irritated. Was this all he ever was, this mechanism of incessant carnality? Surely here there was something of importance. The atmosphere of the room and the sounds of the murmuring and chanting had begun to have a distinct effect on my mind and I wished to concentrate.

'For God's sake, man, stop it!' I whispered loudly enough to cause perhaps a dozen feet to shuffle at once and several chairs to creak as bodily positions were adjusted in protest. 'I wish to understand this ceremony.'

Frank looked knowingly at me, smiled and nodded.

'Be careful where you tread,' he whispered back, 'the ground is treacherous in these parts. You are being drawn into a land from which few return. The chanting is a drug, a mesmeric device.'

I ignored this and allowed my mind to sink back into what was rapidly becoming a trance-like condition. The murmuring and the scents overcame me, I succumbed to a waking dream. I was flying in large circles above Acton Green. Over there lay London like a vast field planted with some dark and smoking crop. On all other sides, there was almost uninterrupted green, England untouched. I felt the air rushing against my face and roaring in my ears. Strangely, I also noticed that I knew perfectly well that I was in a velvet-draped room in Bedford Park. Both locations were equally real to me, but my reason told me that it was to the room I must return.

A buffeting wind over the Green suddenly unbalanced me. I clutched Frank's arm to steady myself and, at once, I was fully back in the enormous room.

'Good God!' I gasped. 'Good God! There is something here, something ...'

Several women opened their eyes, looked steadily at me, absorbing the character of a potential convert. I was now staggering and in danger of collapse.

'A chair!' cried Frank. 'A chair for this man!'

None of the women moved, but there was a thumping sound and a shuffling behind the curtain. A plain, wooden chair was suddenly thrust at us through a dark gap in the velvet. It was held by two perfectly white, apparently male hands. Frank grasped one of the wrists and pulled. The chair was dropped with a bang and a clatter and the hand tried to pull itself away from Frank. They struggled for a moment. Frank, the boxer, appeared to be winning. Then the other hand re-emerged from the curtains bearing a pin which it thrust deep into Frank's thumb. He yelped and relaxed his grip. Both hands at once vanished.

'Damn, damn, damnable!' he cried, while sucking at his wounded thumb.

The thumb still in his mouth, he pulled at the curtains, trying to find the gap, which had disappeared into the heavy, dust-laden folds. The ensuing dust clouds made us both cough. Eventually, he gave up and helped me into the chair. As he did so there were three loud raps, as of an iron bar on wood. The murmuring and chanting stopped. There was a long pause and then the curtains at the illuminated end of the room were flung apart by some invisible agency. A stern-looking woman with very short-cropped, tightly curled hair emerged in a black dress that, in the dim light of the lamps, made her face look ominously pale. She appeared to drift forward rather than walk. Reaching the table, she placed her fingertips on its surface and leaned forward to fix her audience with her gaze, an action that made her face much more distinct.

'Besant!' murmured Frank. 'There she is! I told you she was involved. Stead has something to do with this, I know it! He meddles in this nonsense.'

'The most extraordinary thing happened to me, Frank. I was flying.'

'Mesmerism, animal magnetism, self-inflicted. A well-documented phenomenon; do not take it too seriously or you will be lost to polite society.'

'Silence!' commanded Besant.

The curtains behind her parted again, though now they seemed to be pinned together at the base so that a kind of pointed oval shape, a mandorla, was formed. More curtains were revealed and these parted in the same way. Frank suppressed carnal laughter. There was a deep rumbling and creaking sound which slowly grew louder. I stood to see what was going on. A very fat, seated woman appeared between the curtains. Her chair was on casters and was being pushed forward by a minuscule and seemingly diseased maid. As they touched the first set of curtains, the pinning at the base sprang open to allow the chair through. The effort was making the maid gasp and wheeze and, by the time they had sprung open the front set of curtains, she seemed on the verge of expiring. The fat woman did not seem to notice.

Now that she was fully illuminated, I could see that the bulk of her body was wrapped in countless layers of silk and lace, much of it faded and stained. On her head, tightly curled hair was glued down by dully shining grease or oil. Beneath, the face was an astounding combination of disease and power. There were multiple folds beneath her chin and swollen areas above and below her eyes. The skin itself was dead white, tinged here and there with patches of grey, yellow and blue. It could have been the face of a corpse but for the eyes that stared and flicked about the room with a kind of alert savagery.

'Madame,' cried Besant, 'is born to us once more!'

'Who …?'

'Blavatsky,' hissed Frank, 'a fraud of the first order.'

An extended but inconclusive ritual followed, throughout which Frank snorted and laughed. I strained to understand Blavatsky's words but even those I could hear through Frank's interruptions made little sense. The women, however, were enraptured and, as time passed, I began to see why. The words were only a small part of what was happening, a musical accompaniment. The true substance of the service lay in the concentration and power that emanated from Blavatsky and in the stern authority of Besant.

It all ended suddenly; the white-clad women departed, leaving Frank, myself, Besant and Blavasky in the enormous room. The wheezing maid was summoned and we were beckoned to follow them into another room that reeked of stale smoke and cats. Besant turned Blavatsky to face me.

'You have met, I understand, our dear Stepniak.'

'Stepniak, yes! How on earth did you know? I only once ran into him in the street.'

Blavatsky sighed noisily, smiled, rolled a cigarette, lit it and looked at Besant. I could hear the muffled voices of the white-clad women from the hallway of the house. They must have been leaving.

'"On earth,"' she murmured, continuing to watch Besant, 'is an amusing term.'

Besant nodded thoughtfully. This all took some time. Blavatsky seemed to delight in prolonged pauses.

'What do you know of him?'

A further pause followed during which she smoked half her cigarette. Her loose method of construction caused smouldering flecks of paper to detach themselves and float upwards while black shards of tobacco fell on to her clothes.

'He killed the chief of the secret police in St Petersburg. This, of course, made him welcome in London. But it was a worthless gesture. Stepniak is a vulgar realist.'

'I know that he is a killer.'

'Yes, but a very respectable one as far as Bedford Park is concerned. The people here are very progressive. But now you think he killed Brian Binks …'

'Did he?'

'Possibly.'

'Possibly! Possibly! Is that it?' cried Frank.

'Possibly.'

'So that is all the Secret Doctrine, the grand edifice of Theosophy, can give us – possibly!'

Blavatsky was now wreathed in the fumes of her uniquely pungent black tobacco – I had never seen anybody produce so much smoke from one cigarette.

'Did he have a reason to kill Binks?' I asked.

'A reason … well, some would say half of London had a reason to kill Binks. He was fatally well connected.'

'He was a dilettante,' said Besant suddenly, her face fierce and monumentally judgemental, 'a man with no centre, the last thing we need in these troublous times.'

'I have a centre,' said Frank, twisting the words into lasciviousness, 'I am the man for troublous times.'

'Strange, then, that I did not see you at Trafalgar Square, Mr Harris. Were you there to aid the struggle of the match girls?'

'Ah, Bloody Sunday – blood on your hands, Mrs Besant, innocent blood … You're right, I should have been at the

97

side of the match girls. They were very ...' he paused as if in parody of Madame '... pretty.'

Besant rolled her eyes and clenched her fists in preparation for what may have been a physical assault on Frank, but Blavatsky raised the hand holding the cigarette to silence them both.

'You have a question, Mr Kidd?'

'To whom was Binks connected?'

'To everybody. He was a crossroads, a junction, or possibly a delta flowing into the sea. Yes, there was something of water about him.'

'I know he was a magician ...'

'A conjuror,' snapped Besant, 'he did tricks, not magic. He knew nothing of magic.'

Frank sneered lecherously.

'What magic do you know, Mrs Besant?'

'The higher planes of intellectual womanhood will lie for ever beyond you and your grubby kind, Mr Harris.'

'Mr Harris is a very *modern* man,' said Blavatsky. She then extinguished her cigarette in a small, oriental bowl and, in an instant, seemed mentally to remove herself from our presence. Her eyes closed and the folds of her face became deeper. Her breathing was more audible. There was a sickly, sweetish smell in the room I had not noticed before. It was stronger even than the cats and the tobacco.

'Stepniak ...'

'Hush, Mr Kidd, Madame will return shortly with news for you.'

'A maiden fair to see.

The pearl of minstrelsy.

A bud of blushing beauty ...'

Frank was singing quietly to himself. Besant gave him a withering look but he sang on.

'A suitor lowly born,
With hopeless passion torn,
And poor, beyond denying ...'

Blavatsky was breathing more rapidly and shuddering slightly. Besant rested a hand on her shoulder. Frank stopped singing and stood in front of Blavatsky, his hands in his trouser pockets. He leaned over so that his face was a few inches from hers and sniffed.

'She smells strange, rather rank in fact. A sort of rotting stench. Is she partly dead, perhaps? Is that an aspect of the spiritualist's trance condition?'

Besant had gone far beyond anger.

'We are not spiritualists. Tell me, Mr Harris, are you afraid of something? Are you afraid of, perhaps, a greater wisdom than your own?'

Frank turned to face her.

'I am very afraid of that, Miss Besant, more afraid than you can imagine. I have not yet encountered any such wisdom and certainly not here and not now. You are a very clever woman, Madame is a very clever woman, and, of course, I cannot discount the possibility that you have some insight and that, one day, I myself might wish to see the Golden Dawn or, indeed, Isis Unveiled. Anything might be true. But, here and now, I see you have nothing to tell me. We have a simple, a physical problem. How did Binks die? *You* didn't kill him, did you? He had connections with your movement. Mr Kidd is distraught. I brought him here to see if you could help us in real, physical ways ...'

'Physical ways! You are so primitive. You sound as though you wish to evade knowledge rather than acquire it.'

'Knowledge! Well, yes, I suppose the Hodgson report for the Society for Psychical Research did refer to Madame as a "gifted" impostor, meaning that she does have some form of knowledge. I'll give her that.'

'That report …!'

Besant was about to explode, but Blavatsky was stirring.

'The one,' she said slowly, 'becomes two on manifestation.'

There was a silence. I began to wonder if this statement was the last word and whether it was time for us to leave. She stirred again.

'Our world is made of dualities. Binks is one thing; Miss Gonne another.'

A shiver ran through my body. There had been no mention of Maud. Besant had raised her chin and was looking at me through hooded eyes. Even Blavatsky had fixed me with a gaze that seemed to creep from under her brows.

'Miss Gonne?' I said, my voice trembling. 'What has she to do with this?'

'Perhaps,' said Frank, 'Mrs Besant can enlighten us. You too are, I gather, a great supporter of the Irish cause, an answerer of the Irish question, so to speak.'

'Indeed, Mr Kidd,' she said, ignoring Frank, 'three-quarters of my blood and all my heart are Irish. This city is not mine, it is the fortress of the occupier. Miss Gonne is not one of us …' she looked at Blavatsky for confirmation '… she is not transcendentally inclined in the preferred manner. She is, in fact, redeemed only by her fidelity to the cause of Ireland.'

'That may be so, but, I repeat, what has she to do with this?'

'All things are connected,' said Blavatsky. 'I understand in this case you, Mr Kidd, are the connection. Love and death, you have been subjected to both. Some might say you were lucky to be so much in the midst of the life of this world. Willie Yeats …'

'Yes …?'

'He joins the two, Binks and Miss Gonne. He can be a very angry young man.'

'What!'

I grasped Frank by the arm.

'Did you tell her about any of this?'

'I swear I did not. Bedford Park appears to be a very small place, though I would not wish to paint it. To be here is to know all things.'

'How very true,' said Blavatsky suavely.

'Then what,' I cried, 'in God's name, is the connection? Are you suggesting this angry young Yeats killed Binks?'

'The place is the connection, the place, study the place. Things converge here ... Things ... converge. Here.'

With that, Blavatsky signalled to Besant. The diseased maid reappeared and she was wheeled from the room. Besant remained, staring at some distant point.

I clutched my head in frustration.

'Great God, Frank! What are these people talking about?'

'A maiden fair to see.

'The pearl of minstrelsy.

'A bud of blushing beauty ...'

4

'My dear, dear father, you were right. I shall stay in London longer than I intended. You said you expected this, but, in case you were not serious, I am sorry to disappoint you ... I trust Kurt is caring for you. I remain always

    Your loving son,

    Cal.

'SON STOP DO WHAT YOU THINK YOU MUST STOP FATHER STOP.'

A letter arrived at my rooms. There was no note inside, only a newspaper cutting. The headline said, 'Wimbledon Man Kills His Wife for Love of Another', and beneath was a picture of a Stiles, a young man, slightly stout for his age. Anything might be true.

Part Two

Part Two

Chapter Five
Hilda Harper's 'At Home'

This scene looks cold but, in the air, there is a heavy sugges-
tion of later warmth. Beneath an iron sky, the Thames lies
still as if in waiting. Black ships stand and lean on the
great, grey nothingness of air and water, the cries of the gulls
are solitary, muted and reluctant while, to the east, the sun
brightens the sky to a paler grey. Lamps burn along the shore
from where rise muffled sounds of human activity; people are
uncertain of this day's arrival, it feels stillborn. There has
been a mighty disconnection. The river, the great artery that
joins London to the world, is severed, its flow has ceased. It
happens every day and men toil daily to mend the breach in
obedience to the law that states that, without the Thames,
anarchy is unleashed.

London Notebook Number 37 was almost full. In a few
days I would be able to reward myself with a new one.

These old houses were built for a slightly better class of person
than the ones who generally inhabit such blighted landscapes.
They have front gardens, most tended, and doorways with
porticos, though the columns are starved and thin, unlike the
overfed ones of Bedford Park. This street is clean and free of
scavenging dogs and emaciated cats. But the same grime covers

all. The walls are dark and a finger run along a leaf seeking nature's contact is marked with an oily shadow. The air tastes of something, a combination of coal smoke, iron and old, hard wood. Silence hangs in the air in the way it does after a mighty sound, an explosion or thunderclap, or as if the place had, just moments ago, been abandoned. The East is different.

I wrote no more; instead I waited and watched for another hour as the sky brightened and the Thames came to life. I saw two small steamers pull away from a wharf, their wakes slowly separating. Finally, reluctantly, I rose.

2

Halfway down the street, I heard a voice. Somebody was singing, but the words were inaudible and the tune indefinable. It was an old woman's voice. As I discovered the gate I sought, I realised that she was singing in this very front garden. It was, however, untended, overgrown with damp vegetation and the singer was quite invisible. The gate screamed in protest as I pushed it open, a shocking noise in all this stillness, but the singing continued, uninterrupted by the intrusion. I pushed forward through the leaves and boughs. Heavy drops fell on to my clothes from the disturbed fronds and a spider's web glued itself to my face. As I passed, the fronds sprang back, cutting off my exit.

> *Oh dearie, dearie me*
> *The old man's gone to sea*
> *And 'ere I lie*
> *And wonder why …*

The words of the song had become audible but the singer remained invisible.

As I emerged from the foliage, I saw a bicycle with a large basket over the front wheel leaning against the porch. There were pieces of rusting metal lying about and a broken easel, smeared with paint. Rot had attacked the door frame and, in the circular stained-glass windows on either side, odd fragments of glass had been replaced by pale wood, streaked with damp.

A brief wave of anguish made me tug too hard at the bell; a foot of wire emerged but there was no sound. I pulled again and managed to produce a series of flat, tired rings. The singing stopped; I heard a rustling behind me and to my left. I turned and saw aged eyes and grey hair amid the leaves. They vanished at once; the woman seemed to have crouched down and to be holding her breath. I took a pace towards her but, at that moment, the door opened.

'Enid,' I said, flustered, 'it is good to see you again.'

For a moment she did not react, as if she had failed to see or hear me. Then, finally, 'Mr Kidd.' She curtsied briefly.

It was not good to see her. Enid Binks had been treated unkindly by the years since her husband's death. Feathery lines surrounded her lips, which were in turn bracketed by deeper grooves. Her eyes had retreated into her skull, rendering permanent her suspicious gaze, and her hair had thinned and hardened into pale wires that sprang from beneath her white 'at home' bonnet. The shortness that had once been an aspect of her coquetry had become pitiable, an effect intensified by the way she held her body – slightly stooped in an attitude of defeat. But, slowly absorbing my presence and the memories it entailed, she drew herself up and raised her chin.

'I had your letter. We was expecting you.'

Unwelcomingly, she turned and I followed her into a dismal, faded interior into which, from the back of the house, the dim light of the morning struggled to intrude.

She turned left into the parlour and ushered me towards a dusty tapestry chair full of broken springs. Pottery ornaments – horses, birds, ships, a camel – lined the mantelpiece. Pinned to the wall above was a blurred charcoal drawing of bathers by a dark river which at once struck me as in some way exceptional amid this decor. She noticed my interest.

'Lucian done it. He's become a bit of an artist. Better than nothing, I suppose.'

'It's actually rather curious. He should keep at it.'

I had tried to inject a note of breezy optimism into my voice but she just shrugged.

'He might, but where's the money in that? I don't want to fill his head with ideas. That's what did for Binks.'

'And Sophie?'

'She went wild. I don't know what she do. She's up town a lot. She has friends there. She models for artists and takes in sewing and stuff, or so she says. These days I daren't ask.'

There was a shuffling and mumbling in the hall.

> *And 'ere I lie*
> *And wonder why ...*

The eyes and grey hair I had seen in the garden appeared at the door. The rest of the body was massive and made yet more massive by what seemed to be an ancient black ball gown trimmed with torn fragments of black lace that projected in all directions like dark sparks. The effect was that of a bomb caught in the act of exploding. The dress was streaked with grey mud from the garden. Leaves and cobwebs adhered to the the skirt. Atop this confection, the face was grinning furiously and, from the mouth, emerged a quiet hum.

'My mother,' said Enid hurriedly, apologetically. 'She came here to look after me when we moved, now look at her. Lost her mind.'

'I have indeed. I have indeed. Mind completely mislaid.'

I rose to greet her but Enid waved me back down.

'Don't bother. She hasn't the faintest idea what's going on, hardly knows who she is. Brain softening, they say. Nothing to be done.'

The mother smiled at me and winked, apparently in furtive contradiction of her daughter's diagnosis. She then began to shuffle slowly round the room, picking up the camel from the mantelpiece as she passed in an offhand manner that suggested this was a routine matter.

'How are you finding our old place, then?'

There was a touch of sarcasm and accusation in Enid's voice, as if by taking their Bedford Park home I had rubbed salt in her deep wounds. Again I aimed for a breezy response.

'Wonderful. I am so grateful you passed it on to me. I have made a few changes.'

'It's different for a man on his own. You don't want the same things.'

'The parlour is now where I work – well, write anyway. It is very convenient.'

Her perambulation had brought the mother to my chair. She tapped me on the shoulder with the camel.

'That's you done,' she said with sudden, businesslike briskness, and moved on, attaining, finally, the door.

'On the matter of Brian … I am sure you have heard …' I said, embarrassed by the contact of the camel.

'I have heard.'

'That the case was officially closed? Grand convinced himself that it was Stepniak so that is that.'

'Killed by a train, weren't he, this man?'

'On the level crossing. A strange and violent end to a strange and violent life.'

It was also, I mused, an anarchic end to an anarchist's life. 'I suppose it could have been Stepni— what's his name ...?'

'... ak.'

'Stepniak. Could have been. But it could have been somebody who never got killed by a train ... It all seems a bit convenient for the bobbies.'

She directed at me a look I did not fully understand.

'Grand says the mark made on the body was an "N", meaning "necator", killer. He suggested this is how Stepniak saw himself. He seemed very pleased with this discovery, along with my meeting with the man in the street just before I found Brian. He considered it conclusive.'

'Well, it could have been a "Z" and it would have been just the thing for a clever killer to do to get Stepniak hanged for something he didn't do. There were others ...'

'Others? Who?'

'Oh, it don't matter now. It really don't. How is your friend Mr Harris?'

'He is well, the same as ever.'

We seemed to run out of conversation. She sat back and plucked with both hands at the edges of her stained apron. Moments passed. I could think of nothing to say. I had no real reason to be here except for an obscure sense of obligation. Ever since the death of Stepniak, the apparent resolution of the case had made me feel I ought to visit Enid. This 'ought' had never been accompanied by any practical consideration. We knew each other well enough after Binks's death. I did what I could to help and had seized upon her need to leave Bedford Park as an opportunity for me to move in. I 'took the house off her hands', as we both put it at the time. I had to live in the enchanted suburb. I should have moved to Belgravia, of course, to be near Maud. The white façades of Belgravia were secretive, as were the bowers of Woodstock Road; but the former seemed utterly impenetrable, the latter suggested some possibility of admission and, after admission, privacy. In any case, Maud seemed to inhabit the entire world rather than any specific location.

'Even when she's here,' Frank had said, 'she cannot be said to be here.'

We had met, but each time was as if it was the first time. In spite of which I had proposed marriage – more than once. Maud had laughed each time.

Since I 'took the house off her hands', I had not seen Enid Binks. This left us with nothing recent or urgent in common about which to communicate. So still we did not speak and I was becoming oppressively aware of small noises in the room – great leaves brushing the windows, the creak of the springs in my chair. Finally, though feeling the matter was distasteful, I decided to ask her once more about the 'other' whom she suspected.

'Enid ...'

A large young man entered the room, hands in his pockets and his shoulders hunched. His feet were bare but partially covered by crumpled trousers that had almost fallen down. His head was twisted away from me at an angle suggestive of some deformity, but, more probably, it was because he did not want to engage with me or even because he was entirely unaware of my presence.

'Lucian, dear, you remember Mr Kidd ...'

He turned awkwardly, not by moving his head but by twisting his entire body. I rose and extended my hand.

'Lucian, it is good to see you again after all these years.'

Awkwardly, he straightened up and stared at me. The features were entirely closed, betraying nothing but a determined, troubled inwardness. With some effort I could just about detect the physiognomic vestiges of that boy on the stairs. But all had been intensified.

'I very much admire your drawing. I was saying to your mother, you should keep it up.'

He jerked his head in the direction of the mantelpiece, apparently angrily, as if I had been shown something shameful. He said nothing and the silence resumed, now thickened further by his presence.

'Is art something you would want to do with your life?'

'Wrong city,' he murmured, 'nothing good being done here. I'd need to be in Paris.'

'Paris! But there's nothing there, Lucian. Everything and everybody you could want is in London.'

His face opened a little, in wonder, and his body eased, freeing his head from his shoulders.

'Nothing! What are you talking about?'

Suddenly alert, Enid stood up and put her hand on Lucian's arm.

'Now, Lucian, dear, would you like to make Mr Kidd a nice cup of tea?'

He pushed her hand away.

'Nothing in Paris! What do you know? You're just an American.'

'Well, I think I …'

Tears welled from his eyes and his fists clenched. Suddenly Enid was whimpering and wringing her hands with anxiety.

'Mr Kidd, he sometimes …'

'Everything is in Paris, artists doing things you and your kind – you and that horrible friend of yours – wouldn't understand.'

Horrible friend – could he mean Frank? *How* would he know of Frank? He came close and thrust his face at mine. I smelt his sweat and his rank, angry, young breath.

'The world isn't like you think it is, Mr Kidd, not a bit like. There is magic in Paris.'

Enid was now pulling at his arm.

'Lucian, please ...'

'What is the world like, then, Lucian?' I asked, attempting to maintain a certain pedagogic distance from this boy, who seemed on the verge of violence.

Enid signalled to me with her eyes – do not provoke him was the message. His cheeks were lined with tears. But my question did seem to have a calming – or, at least, demoralising – effect. His body slumped slightly.

'I don't know but I know it's like something else, not like newspapers or silly plays or diamond jubilees or Bedford Park or ... or anything like that. I know it.'

He was now sobbing slightly and he finally yielded to the renewed pressure of Enid's hand. She led him into another room and closed the door and then approached me and now put her hand – pleadingly – on my arm, her son's appearance having drained some of her previous power over me.

'I'm so sorry, Mr Kidd, since his pa died he always gets funny when there's a man in the house,'

'Then I had better leave.'

'It would be best.'

I paused as I reached the door.

'There's one thing – you said somebody else could have been the murderer.'

'Oh, it were nothing, nothing, I must see to Lucian.'

She closed the door in my face and I found myself alone on the porch with the bicycle, facing once more the humid depths of the garden. I was relieved to be out of the house, but at the same time enervated by the sense of something unresolved, something important. Enid was in no mood to be pressed; I might have to return to this place. I stepped into the greenery and at once a hand clutched my wrist. The mother emerged, the wild, explosive shreds of her dress now speckled with water drops. She smiled and stared fiercely upwards into my eyes.

'Anything might be true, you know, anything!'

3

Agitated by the sterile tensions and muted threats of these encounters, I returned to Bedford Park, burying myself in the silence of my house. After an hour or two of lying down and pacing about the place, I decided something must be done to shake me out of this mood. I scanned the florid handwriting of the invitation notes on my mantelpiece. There were half a dozen; there were *always* half a dozen. I had been 'accepted' and that placed upon me the burden of a permanent obligation to be seen to belong. The suburb was a laboratory in which experiments were conducted to test the state of the world beyond. It was, however, sealed off to avoid infection, and each experiment was wholly of the mind, a *Gedankenexperiment*. The outsider might see nothing more than groups of people talking and making arrangements; insiders knew this talk and these arrangements were the most important explorations of the world as it was. I chose, therefore, to lose myself by accepting an invitation to one of Hilda Harper's 'at homes'.

'Richard Prince,' she was saying as I was shown in.

'Exactly, Richard Prince!' cried Peter. 'For an actor they march, for this puppet they take to the streets! Terriss was simply stabbed by another actor, a lunatic ... his name ... a nothing, a nobody. The newspapers screech about this. The people mourn.'

Peter registered my presence and, at once, deployed it for rhetorical effect. He gestured at me.

'It's like the death of your Lincoln, except here in London he is just an actor.'

Mrs Harper smiled complacently. She liked to hear such things said in her house. Always eager to be topical, she felt the horrors of the news ought to be softened by discussion. Fine featured with a long, graceful neck only tentatively lined by age, she wore clothes involving much figured velvet as an emblem of her attachment to new ideas.

'This theatrical nonsense corrupts the citizens,' continued Peter from within his immense shovel-shaped flare of beard and whiskers, 'it fills their heads with lies. Free agreement on serious matters between citizens, nothing more is needed, but it cannot be had if they only care for actors. Do they not see the need for the enfranchisement of man from the bonds of the state, not just from capitalism? It is the vision, the golden vision, and still they see nothing but puppets.'

His eyes were directed at me as he spoke.

'There is also,' said the well-versed Mrs Harper, 'is there not, a golden dawn?'

'Yes, yes, there is, the Order of the Golden Dawn. But that is more puppetry. This is not the time for such mysticism. It is the time for the multitudes to overthrow the tyranny.'

'But surely,' Mr Horsfall interjected, 'there is also time for the gentler things, the fabrics of Morris, the wonder of Blake and Wordsworth, the prose of Pater, the meanest flower that blows, the great spiritualists ...'

Horsfall was a large man with an anxious face and preternaturally soft hands. His broad definition of 'the gentler things' was almost wholly explained by the fact that he had designs on Mrs Harper, whose husband, a financier, was often away on business, leaving her alone in 2 Newton Grove, a grand mansion almost overlooking the Green. Horsfall wanted to be seen to be in favour of all possible aesthetic enthusiasms, as Mrs Harper was known to dabble widely in artistic matters and Horsfall lived only a few doors away with a 'difficult' wife. The 'fabrics of Morris' was a strategic touch; the walls and curtains of Newton Grove were all hung with his designs. The affair seemed such an obvious idea, but, sadly, Mrs Harper had her own vague designs on – or, rather, fantasies about – Jack, the younger, painting Yeats son. Romantic futility aged Mr Horsfall even as it rejuvenated Mrs Harper.

'Luxuries! All very well here in comfortable Bedford Park, not so good in Hackney or even Acton – the poor are just next door, Mr Spiritualist.'

Peter often named people by what he took to be their primary attribute. Many times I had been 'Mr American' when he was being routinely offensive about my country.

'America is just the country,' he had said, 'that shows how all the written guarantees in the world for freedom are no protection against tyranny and oppression of the worst kind. There the politician has come to be looked on as the very scum of society. Better a French prison than an American grave!'

His words had angered but also pained me, reminding me, as they did, of the bomber Lingg and all the threatening extremes of Chicago. Peter was, for all that, a comfortable person, one of London's many domesticated extremists, as harmless as he was charming. Unlike his compatriot Stepniak, he had not, to my knowledge, killed anybody.

Mrs Harper rose to adjust a portrait of her painted by a friend or enemy – these days they amount to much the same thing – of poor Wilde's who had been in prison and was now in France. The painting showed her head in profile emerging mystically from various shades of brown and off-white. Hanging above the mantelpiece, it was the enigmatic focal point of the room.

'We must sweep away every vestige of tyranny,' insisted Peter, 'tear the fetters asunder, open to mankind a new and wider scope of joyous existence!'

Mrs Harper put her hand on her breast and gasped.

'Calm yourself, Hilda,' said Dora, 'I don't think he means now.'

'Why not now? What is wrong with now?'

Dora sighed.

'Well, apart from anything else, we are having tea.'

Mrs Harper gazed ever more intently at the portrait.

'Tea, tea!' wailed Peter.

Dora smiled mischievously at me. Youthful, sensible, brisk, competent, wise, busy – it amazed me that she bothered to spend time with us. I was here because I was not sensible and I could not rid myself of the feeling – the fear, perhaps – that, collectively, these people were significant in ways of which they themselves were entirely unaware. But Dora was always satirical, spinning gilded threads of irony about our aspirations, threads that were, fortunately, invisible to most.

'You're quiet, Cal,' she said gently.

She wore a broad, blue sash around her waist from which her skirt flared about her hips. Her clothes often suggested something less sensible than her conversation.

'Yes, Mr American,' said Peter, 'what do you have to say about the revolution?'

'Perhaps it is already happening and we just haven't noticed.'

Peter snorted and waved an arm in mock despair.

'What do you mean by that, Cal?' asked Dora.

I had meant nothing, of course, it was just the first thought that had come into my head. But it was, I knew, another shot in Dora's long campaign to make more of me, to draw something new and strange from my soul's depths.

'I think,' said Mrs Harper, her nose in the air and her eyes still on her portrait, 'it is a very American thought. You like to think of yourselves as revolutionists, don't you, Mr Kidd?'

'No – well, I don't. I guess I don't think revolutionaries are strictly necessary. Revolutions happen of their own accord and they don't need to be bloody. Our own, of course, was. But now we have the automobile and the telephone ...'

'Pah! Toys!'

Mrs Harper turned at last from the portrait to nod approvingly at Peter.

'Just so,' she said, 'they remove us from the life of honest craftsmanship, of things well made. You should have met Morris, Mr Kidd, he would have told you a thing or two about automobiles and telephones.'

Dora smiled at me again and confidingly put her hand over her mouth as if to disguise laughter. In the corner of the room, almost concealed by a Morris curtain smothered in maroon tendrils, sat a cross-legged, thin, dark man. He had said nothing but he stared intently at everybody in the room, his pale face livid in the shadows. Mrs Harper had whispered to me that she thought he was a poet, but she wasn't sure. I suspected, judging by his gaunt, passionate air, he was a follower of Peter's.

'I did meet Morris,' I said, 'in the houseboat in Chiswick. Very impressive. But I prefer Ruskin – "How things bind and blend themselves together!"'

Horsfall stiffened.

'Impressive, Morris! There you fall short, Cal. The man was a genius ...' He waved his hand at the walls and then paused, aware that his enthusiasm might sound a touch exclusive for Mrs Harper. 'But, of course, Ruskin is a master of a different stripe.'

'Games and toys,' Peter groaned, 'toys and games.'

The doorbell rang and, after some considerable murmuring in the hall, the Tremletts were ushered in by Izzy, Mrs Harper's grimly sceptical maid.

'Mr and Mrs Tremlett,' she announced, her voice a slow, ironic drawl.

'Thank you, Isadora,' said Mrs Harper, affecting weariness as a defence against the superior wit of the lower orders.

'We're so sorry we're so late,' said Mrs Tremlett in a respectful stage whisper. She glanced at Mr Tremlett to indicate it was a problem of his, probably embarrassing and medical, possibly erotic, that had delayed them.

'Yes indeed, yes indeed,' murmured Mr Tremlett, adding, unconvincingly and with a sigh, 'wouldn't have missed it for the world, not for the world.'

Mr Tremlett, a tall, stooped man with a prodigiously long chin, was immensely knowledgeable about butterflies and had often made it known that he preferred the rustic hut in his garden to Bedford Park society. The spherical Mrs Tremlett, however, with her advanced hairstyle, was a belonger who was very reluctant to be seen out unaccompanied. As a result, she was annoyingly subject to the whims of her husband.

'We were discussing Morris and Ruskin,' explained Mr Horsfall, 'great men both, don't you agree, Hilda?'

Mrs Harper recoiled slightly at the use of her Christian name. She had no desire to be dragooned by Horsfall so she did not reply, taking, instead, a sudden interest in an aspidistra that was threatening to block the exit to the kitchen completely. Tremlett was as much of a problem as Horsfall. I suspected she had always felt threatened by his obvious independence of the society over which she presided.

'Ruskin for me,' said Mr Tremlett, but at once his face betrayed irritation with himself for having intervened so positively.

I glanced over at Peter, expecting a reaction, but he appeared to have gone to sleep. Izzy reappeared with fresh tea. Her eyebrows rose at the sight of Mrs Harper's concern with the aspidistra; she plainly feared more pointless work, another attempt to make the house just right. Her mistress was forever changing things in pursuit of a fatally undefined and ever receding ideal of domestic beauty. The thin man moved but only to recross his legs.

'I love Ruskin,' said Dora, feeling, I would guess, protective of Mr Tremlett. She would admire the very independence Mrs Harper feared. He looked at her, evidently surprised; he was not used to having his tastes endorsed by a woman.

'*The Stones of Venice*?' he asked tentatively.

'*Modern Painters*,' she replied. Tremlett glowed, having sung, briefly, in tune with a striking young woman.

'*Fors Clavigera*,' said Mr Horsfall, 'his deep concern for the working man.'

Mrs Harper murmured her reluctant agreement for lack of anything better to do. The phrase 'working man' woke Peter with a jolt.

'Ruskin! Mad, mad, mad!'

'Well, admittedly, since *Praeterita* ...' began Mr Horsfall.

'Do you not think, Peter,' Dora said coolly, 'that your own people are a good deal madder than Ruskin? You don't think your anarchist friend Monsieur Bourdin was entirely sane when he blew himself up in Greenwich Park, do you? Was that the Observatory he was after? Did he wish to kill time? Or that Monsieur Henry was in possession of all his faculties when he attacked the Café Terminus? Or that ...'

Peter was sobered and reluctant to engage with this evidently assertive and knowledgeable woman.

'I see your point, Miss Parsons, and I am not myself a believer in such nonsensical violence. But surely you see that the injustices of the world cry out against the sickening power of capital.'

'They do, they do!' affirmed Mr Horsfall. 'Do they not, Mr Kidd?'

'They always will. Injustices are real enough but they are a moving target, not to be hit by blind revolutionary fervour. It all started with Lingg and his bombs in Chicago, my home town. America has exported her native aptitude for violence.'

Mr Tremlett eyed me as if for the first time. I felt a sudden need to impress him. I remembered Lucian's words about art and magic in Paris.

'Perhaps it is to the art of Paris we should turn ...'

Peter looked at me with what may have been startled respect.

'That is so true, Cal,' said Dora softly. Her tone was satisfied and triumphant; she had drawn me out, or so she thought.

I was struck by a sudden thought of Maud, still haunting me and teasing poor Willie.

'The world,' she had once said, 'will one day thank me for not marrying Willie. He makes poetry out of his longing and unhappiness.'

What do *I* make out of *what*?

'Turn to Paris ...?' murmured Mr Tremlett.

'There they are remaking the world,' said Peter, 'but, alas, only in paint.'

Like Wilde, Maud was in Paris, there she had Millevoye and two children. She still had Ireland and had now annexed Alsace-Lorraine, another cause. Also there was her travelling menagerie, her animal companions. A life too full.

Mrs Harper now seated herself on a small wooden chair next to the sofa wholly occupied by Peter.

'How, exactly, are they remaking the world?'

'By starting from the beginning,' said Peter.

Willie had agreed with Maud. He was, he confessed, inspired by her rejections. But if she had accepted him? What then? Willie Yeats, the comfortable mediocrity.

Peter was now deep into a monologue about French painters of whom I had never heard. Mrs Tremlett was leaning forward and Mr Horsfall had stationed himself behind Mrs Harper.

'... the actual object, devoid of old meanings, of art's *ancien régime* ...'

I was not inspired by Maud's rejections. How could I be? I had barely been rejected. Only poets deserved that. Americans were given a mere laughing glance.

'... the common experience of the common things. *En plein air*! Light plays on us all. You are right, Mr American, the French artists are showing us the way.'

Mr Horsfall clapped his hands together, bit his lower lip in ecstasy and leaned closer to Mrs Harper. The room was enduring a paroxysm, a sublimation, an apotheosis.

'And all we have,' said Dora, laughing, 'is the *Daily Mail*.'

There was a crash and a muted cry. Mrs Harper had risen suddenly and, in doing so, had knocked over Mr Horsfall, who, in turn, had brought down the aspidistra. He struggled to rise from amid the soil, leaves and terracotta shards. Mrs Harper paid no attention. Her eyes, blazing with anger, were fixed on Dora. She took a deep breath.

'I will not – do you hear me? – NOT have that ... that ... that rag named in this house!'

I rose, feeling I ought to do something, either defend Dora from possible violence or help Mr Horsfall to his feet.

'That sneering, low, vile, gossip-laden ... that petulant panderer to all that is worst about this nation ...'

Mr Horsfall was now clutching the back of the sofa.

'Hilda, calm yourself,' he gasped.

'Driving us back into the dark ages, into limitless vulgarity ...'

Peter was surveying with satisfaction the chaos behind the sofa. Izzy had entered and her initial expression of mild surprise had been replaced by one of ironic resignation.

'An insult to everything that we in this room, this place, stand for ...'

Dora appeared to have taken the view that this outpouring no longer involved her and had gone to the aid of Mr Horsfall. Mrs Harper did, indeed, seem to have been elevated to a higher plane.

'We try to raise the working people up, to present them with the best that can be thought, seen, felt and said, and along comes this huckster, this Harmsworth, to drive them back into the intellectual and aesthetic squalor from whence they came.'

'He is a man inordinately fascinated by hats,' said Mr Tremlett, with a helpful air, 'he wants to reform hats.'

Once again he immediately winced at his own folly in intervening.

Mr Horsfall was now standing and Dora was brushing the soil from his lapels. He had evidently forgotten such matters, however. His eyes were fixed in wonder and adoration on Mrs Harper, who, now at the very summit of her peroration, seemed to glow with a cold, unearthly light.

'Hats be damned! If we, here, in Bedford Park, do not rise up and refute – no, destroy – this horrible emanation, if we do not drive back these forces of darkness, then England is doomed to a century of corruption and decay. A man who killed – yes, I say, killed – this Harmsworth would be doing no more than his common duty.'

The expression on Mr Horsfall's face changed to one of anxiety; plainly he feared Mrs Harper would test his devotion by asking him to dispose of Harmsworth. Dora, meanwhile, looked suddenly angry.

'Oh, Hilda, don't be ridiculous.'

'What did you say?'

Everybody started speaking and moving at once. Even Peter had risen to soothe Mrs Harper. Mrs Tremlett bustled over to the rear of the sofa to help Izzy clear up. Her husband stood, uncertain of what to do and affecting an air of amused indifference. There was a sudden and, in the context of this domestic storm, shocking whisper just behind me.

'*Et in Arcadia ego*, Mr Kidd.'

I spun round to see the thin man.

'Calvert's the name. We met years ago in an ABC. You were with Binks, your first encounter, I believe.'

Mrs Harper was stalking out of the room, clutching her head.

'Get rid of these people, Isadora, get rid of them all.'

Binks's phrase 'outstanding business' floated into my head and, at once, I was in that ABC.

'Yes, I do remember. Mr Calvert. How … nice to meet you again. What are you doing here?'

'Just observing.'

Izzy was ushering us to the door.

'What HH wants, HH bloody gets,' she muttered.

'You live here in Bedford Park?'

Calvert laughed.

'No, no, no, not for me. Anyway, we shall meet again soon, Mr Kidd, I must arise and go now. Business, you know, always business.'

And with that he was gone.

4

I have tried my best with 7 Woodstock Road – once the Binks, now the Kidd house – but the darkness has defeated me. I painted, I decorated, I polished, I introduced mirrors and the palest of pale rugs and hangings but still, somehow, the gloom remains. London's fear of windows has attained final and subtle expression in Bedford Park – the houses have windows, many magnificent ones, but they do not function as windows. A shaft of sunlight finding its way into any of these interiors does not brighten but, rather, enhances the absence of illumination. Meanwhile, the buffalo robe scents the place, prompting wrinkled noses but seldom comments from my visitors.

Nevertheless, in answer to the question asked of me daily – 'Have you settled in?' – I always reply, truthfully, 'Yes.' I have embraced the English ethic of 'cosy', which, no matter what extremities of radicalism or advanced thought are being discussed, always ensures that the sofas are corpulent, the hangings heavy, the lights dimmed by hanging beads or ancient parchment and the fires banked. I saw the point of it at once – the maze of London, perhaps its sheer greatness, has to be kept out of the home.

'*Et in Arcadia ego!* A man of a little learning, this Calvert. And you've met him before – he was watching Binks?

Deeper and deeper. And oh, that Dora brought up the *Daily Mail*! Hilda Harper evidently fears the Coming Age, the age of the masses.'

Frank was reclining on one of my 'cosy' sofas. He had taken to speaking much of 'the Coming Age' of which he was, it seemed, the harbinger.

'What is that smell? I have been meaning to ask.'

'Frank, you were talking about Calvert.'

'Twists and turns, twists and turns, tangled webs. London, you see. I know Calvert.'

'What!'

I do not know why I should have been surprised. Though having fled the *Fortnightly*, Frank had kept his post at the centre of things by buying the *Saturday Review* then making a name for himself with his outrageous commentary on the South African war. He had returned from Africa with a damaged digestion, a loathing of the Empire and a fierce determination to make as much money as possible. While still at the *Fortnightly*, he had also taken to writing short fiction. This had become a sensitive subject since reviews of his stories had been mixed in the extreme. His old enemy Stead, who, having made his name exposing Turkish atrocities against the Bulgarians and the scandal of child prostitution, had, latterly, embarked on adventures in spiritualism, had been particularly caustic.

'If,' he had written, 'Mr Harris has nothing better in his wallet than the narrative of the growth of and adulterous passion of a Baptist minister for the wife of one of his deacons, the world has not lost much by the fact that the editor of the *Fortnightly* has hitherto refrained from any attempt to make a name among contemporary writers.'

For some time after that, it was even more impossible to bring up the subject of Stead but also, in a curious way, impossible not to. Stead and Frank had much in common – notably yellow journalism – and, increasingly, the latter's excoriations of the former were always tinged with indulgence, even affection. Perhaps he felt a new kinship. Stead's spiritualism, which had extended to published conversations with the dead, had earned him more ridicule than had been directed at Frank. Perhaps also he sensed what I had known for some time, that they were two faces of the same coin, both prophets of the Coming Age.

Also, though Frank would rage at the injustice of his treatment at the hands of the critics, there was within him a certain weakness on the matter, a concealed lack of confidence, a fear, perhaps, of ultimate defeat and rejection. If he were to be so defeated, so rejected, then, like any man, he would one day merely die and be forgotten, an intolerable prospect to a man who felt himself surrounded by the greatness and immortal genius of London.

Matters were made worse by the fact that the fame he craved had begun to take monstrous forms. In a petty satire on suburban life called *Diary of a Nobody*, he had been lampooned as Hardfur Huttle, a man of monstrous insensitivity. Much worse was *The Adventures of John Johns*, an entire novel about Frank's marriage to Emily Mary Clayton, his infidelities and his use of women to gain power. The book, written by one of my countrymen named Carrel, had proved alarmingly successful and was read by all as biography rather than fiction. Even Wilde had professed admiration at the way Carrel had captured Frank. Successful and powerful as he might be, the hope that anybody would ever accuse him of greatness was fading. But, somehow, he bounded on.

'Calvert, done business with him,' he explained, 'looked after some tricky negotiations. Terminated them with quite a bang. He reads the Russians. He could easily have been

Raskolnikov in another life. Tortured but now very much in control, if you catch my meaning.'

'Tortured? How?'

'He tried to kill himself, but was rescued by a doctorish man named Tebb. Difficult to pull off drowning satisfactorily. A woman was involved, I think, but, of course, he always said it was despair at the condition of the world. Both good reasons.'

'How on earth do you know the name of the man who rescued him?'

'Journalism. There must have been a story attached – I can't remember it but no matter. Calvert's present role – as some sort of legal thing – is, of course, one more expression of suicidal despair. So Hilda Harper hates Harmsworth, how hilarious. Nothing wrong with the *Daily Mail* – kissing and fighting – I could have done it better, but Harmsworth hates Harris.'

'Frank, look me in the eye. I have two questions. First, what does Calvert want with me?'

'I don't know, ask him. What does anybody want with anybody? There are always reasons to speak to people in this city. Everything is connected, remember? Everything is connected and nothing matters. Is that what so and so said? This renders the question "why does X wish to speak to me?" meaningless. Motives are necessarily unfathomable. Full fathom five thy father lies ... Deeper and deeper.'

'So you cannot or will not answer question number one. Let me try question number two. Did you visit Enid Binks?'

'Why do you ask?'

'The mother said something – "anything might be true" – only you say that.'

'Circumstantial – anybody might say that, it is an insight

in tune with the Coming Age. SynchroniCITY. But, yes, I did visit the Binks household.'

'Why?'

'Sophie, a lovely creature, I found her some work.'

'What! She is a child, Frank.'

'Not any more, though I perhaps wish she was – those short dresses, those aprons, those black stockings.'

'You have corrupted her!'

'Cal, you never will understand, no matter how often I try to explain. I have awoken her, a delicious experience. In fact I have even introduced her to the Prince of Wales. He had her on his lap. There was an unfortunate … prematurity.'

'Good Lord! And what of Binks? Do you believe Stepniak did it?'

'Why should I believe otherwise?'

'The evidence is thin in the extreme. Blavatasky once implied that Willie was involved …'

He rose from the sofa, evidently frustrated by the conversation.

'Cal, for God's sake, this hardly matters. You cannot live your life in the endless pursuit of Binks's killer and Maud Gonne's body. It is, well, boring. He is dead and she is, well, gone. Let me introduce you to the new, awoken Sophie.'

'I love Maud and I am implicated in some way I cannot define in the murder of Binks. I feel some connection. Apart from anything else, he died so soon after meeting me.'

'Oh, really! It was hardly your fault. Parnell and Bismarck fell soon after you arrived. Blavatsky died, Tennyson died – what a fuss over that! Pater died, Carnot died. Oscar was imprisoned. Maud had her children. James's play opened and closed. Are they all your fault? Calhoun Kidd, the fatal American! Be realistic, Cal. Events are events, nothing more, nothing less. Everything is connected and nothing matters.'

'Something must matter.'

'No, nothing at all. But what is that smell?'

'Pah!' I cried, and jumped to my feet. 'You say everything is connected but what are the connections? The list you make is one of disconnection. There is no ... no ... story!'

Frank swept his hand through his hair, turning the brilliantined strands into vertical spikes.

'Story!' He flung one arm into the air. 'Story! There is no story to any of this. Things just happen, that is the simple truth. Oh, of course, we WANT stories and that is what newspapers are for. They pretend the world is made of stories. It works! We believe them! We make money by telling them a lie so huge they cannot even see it. Instead they grope at it like blind men feeling about the legs of an elephant.'

'So what, then, are these connections?'

'Just that, nothing more. They are threads lying in the mud which journalism picks up and knots together. You must learn this, Cal, you must learn that your story is an illusion. Calvert, Binks, they just happen. The mistake is to see the threads as causality. There is no such thing. How could there be in such a world?'

'Then how can there be a Coming Age? What you describe is indecipherable chaos.'

'Ah, that is a different matter.'

I stared at him for a long time, my mind blank but for great gales of confusion that blew every possible sentence out of my head.

'The smell is my father's buffalo robe.'

Frank collapsed back into the sofa, clutching himself and laughing.

'Of course, the robe ...!'

Later that night I wrote to Maud telling her I had abandoned all demands except that of friendship.

Chapter Six
Dora

I

Two small steamers were heading upstream, their paths slowly diverging, otherwise the river lay empty and still beneath the late morning sun. Along the Embankment below the Adelphi a few hansoms tapped and rattled. It was Sunday and London's bass rumble of voices and vehicles was muffled and distant. High in the plane trees pigeons were piping their contentment, occasionally struggling and flapping in irritation as a branch, disturbed by the light westerly, gave way beneath them. A boy raced out of Northumberland Avenue and then past us towards the City – a thief perhaps, but there were no pursuers. Dora stopped and stared after him.

'London boys! What do they do? There is always some urgent mission.'

'It is what boys everywhere do. They must always be altering the world in some way.'

'Is that what you were like?'

'It is what I wanted to be like and what my father wished of me.'

I felt her eyes on me as I closed my own the better to sense the touch of the air on my face, to conceal the pain I still felt at the thought of failing my father and to hide my suspicion that I was also failing Dora.

'You were not like that?'

I allowed myself a few seconds of empty air, empty thought, before I reopened my eyes to look into the brightness of Dora.

'I don't know what I was like. Does anybody? But I was a boy who lacked world-altering projects.'

'You did your father's bidding?'

'Of course. I meant without projects of my own. I always had my father's projects. I was a pane of glass through which you could see my father's face almost entirely undistorted until ...'

'Until Frank?'

It was a truth I had known but never stated so baldly. Frank changed me utterly. Dora demanded the facts – in this, it struck me, she was Frank's worst enemy.

'Until Frank. Except, I suppose, for the few pallid dalliances before Frank. He misted the glass.'

'Were they very pallid?'

'Very. And you?'

'My mother tried to make me join the fishing fleet to find a man in India. Her timing was poor. I thought I was in love and would not leave. Then, soon afterwards, somebody said something about the man and, in an instant, I realised I was infatuated with a fool. It was such a small thing ...'

'What was it?'

I feared I might have many such small things to dispel whatever illusions she had about me.

'He collected pipes.'

'Pipes!'

I began to laugh, at the absurdity but also with relief. I had no faults so ... banal.

She frowned for a moment as if cross with me and then joined in the laughter, her head thrown back.

'Yes, all kinds of pipes! There was nothing casual about his collecting. It was a large part of his life. Oh, Cal!'

She spun around, her arms outstretched, like a child. I looked at her and gasped, my lips suddenly dry. She was wholly here, in the world as I had never been and, perhaps, as Maud with her politics was not. Dora's body formed an inexplicable unity, compactness, a rightness that called on me to hold her. I was staring into the golden brightness of a life lived in this moment.

She grasped my arm and looked mischievously into my face.

'Have you ever seen anything funnier than the Fall of Horsfall as we must now call it?'

'Never. Nothing in the whole history of human comedy could have prepared us for that moment.'

Wildly laughing, she buried her face in my sleeve. With disgust, I observed myself stupidly fretting about the possibility of her make-up disfiguring the dove grey. This was my failing. Why could not I free myself into the present moment, into this present brightness, this glory? Perhaps, with Dora, I could.

'This way,' she said, suddenly brisk and purposeful.

We crossed the road and, skirting the somnolent bulk of Charing Cross, made our way to Villiers Street.

'Do not judge my little place in town,' she said with an expression of mock anxiety as we climbed the stairs, 'I cannot match your suburban palace.'

The little place was full of books and journals arranged in piles on tables. Here and there were imperial curiosities – an African mask, an Indian god. Her father was a man of some imperial prominence; he dealt in cultural matters and had made his daughter acquisitive, not for valuables as such but for information. Her desire to know was liberal and unselfish; she thought facts should be faced for what they were in the world. I wondered what scandal involving her father Frank had concealed; I wondered if there had been a price.

The windows were covered with lace, giving the light a dusty aspect. In here she shone even brighter as she flung off her short jacket, cried 'Tea!' and vanished into the kitchen. She would never have a maid, being, as she insisted, a modern woman.

'Or sherry? It's later than I thought.'

Her head had appeared around the door, playful and excited.

'Sherry, then.'

We sat on the sofa. I suddenly felt large and awkward, unable to find the right place for my legs. She lay back, her body offered, lit a cigarette and feigned a forensic air.

'So, Calhoun Kidd, why are your affairs so pallid?'

'I guess it is either the way I am or I have never found the right person. I don't think the women themselves have all been pallid.'

'Maybe they have. But, plainly, you saw no deathly pallor in Maud …'

'No, I thought Maud was to be the solution. It is not to be. I wrote to her saying I would trouble her no more.'

'Did you? Wasn't that a touch unnecessary, even self-indulgent? You broke off an affair that did not exist.'

'I suppose I meant I would not propose to her again.'

'That may have been a great disappointment to the lady. Her mind is, of course, on more urgent matters, but I'm sure she likes the odd proposal of marriage to keep her going.'

She laughed, having put Maud in her place. Then she curled up confidingly, her face thrust forward.

'Were you faithful to Maud?'

'I was. The moment I saw her the thought of any other woman did not seem, somehow, credible.'

'Perhaps you were looking for an excuse to be faithful to a shadow, to relieve yourself of the burden of women – rather like Willie, who was looking for a hopeless passion to further his art.'

'I don't know about Willie. He is, they say, a genius and they live by different rules, though I don't know why they should. I would have thought it was the task of a genius to be more, not less, like the rest of us.'

'So you felt nothing for any woman once you had seen Maud?'

'I felt agitation or perhaps irritation. There would be a flicker of feeling that I had to dispose of at once.'

'Just a flicker? Are you sure?'

'Yes ... until that day at the Harpers.'

'What! You went for Hilda?'

'You know that's not what I mean.'

She dipped her head and seemed to study the fabric of the sofa. She plucked a stray thread and then rose and started pacing around the room. Her hips swayed beneath her skirt. I was lost in desire.

'But you still love Maud whatever you might say about troubling her no more.'

Either she was undecided or this was just a game, a gambit to wring from me the right form of words.

'Maud was a dream and I have woken. Perhaps like you I have discovered my love was, well, not a fool, but not what I thought she was.'

'You mean she collects pipes!'

We laughed together, though now uneasily. Finally, she stopped and looked at me. Then she took two slow paces and knelt at my feet. I could not suppress a gasp.

'Are you quite sure you're awake now, Cal? I'm not sure you are. Perhaps I am the dream and Maud the reality. Or this whole London adventure of yours ...'

Her lips ... I looked away in an attempt to compose a serious response to her serious words. 'This whole London adventure' was a summary that made me very uneasy.

'I don't know what to say. If all that I now am is a dream – and, I confess, much of the time I feel that it is – then I am trapped. I cannot be taken seriously here and I certainly would not be taken seriously by my father in Chicago. I am adrift and my vessel does not seem to be watertight.'

Dora smiled and placed a hand on my knee.

'Oh, Cal, you are such a hopeless case.'

I could see nothing, nothing but her face, haloed in the golden filaments of her hair. I leaned forward to kiss her, believing that there was some way I was not actually doing this, that it might still be effaced from memory. She turned away, avoiding my lips, and shook her head, but not to me, to herself.

'You would go running at Maud's first twitch on the thread, returning to your true faith.'

I leaned back, my mind reeling with a desire that I knew would deform any argument I might devise. Speech at this point could be no more than an instrument of seduction, but, surely, that was what she wanted it to be so that she could feel seduced.

'I do not think I would. She is so remote from all that I am or want to be. The politics seem so trivial and I cannot imagine being with a women who travels with birds and monkeys. Now those are *her* pipes.'

She laughed, as I intended, and looked back at me, as I intended. Her face seemed illuminated by the bright threads of her dancing mind. She looked down, playful now, and rested her cheek on my leg.

'I have no menagerie but I have my strange projects, my good causes. These might be remote from you also.'

'But you help the poor! That is innocence itself. You are practical – food, clothing, houses – Maud is all theory and Willie is all dreams. He can follow her into the Empyrean.'

I would have followed Dora into the heart of light. She raised herself so that her face was close to mine.

'Then you had better kiss me, Calhoun Kidd.'

I found I was trembling as my lips touched hers, then pressed, then deeper, deeper. This was all I could do or wanted to do. I did not even touch her with my hands. She had her arms around my neck. We kissed longer and longer, deeper and deeper. I seemed to be trembling still. She made little noises which, finally, I realised were not pleasure but impatience. She took my hand and placed it on her breast.

2

Later, much later, she rose from her bed and, suddenly brisk, began to dress.

'I have my meeting, Cal.'

'Dora, I ...'

'Not now, I have my meeting.'

'I love you, Dora.'

She must have known this. She paused, smiled.

'I know, I know. I am glad.'

We parted on the street, she turning towards Trafalgar Square and I back to the Embankment. The sun, the London sun, warmed my face. Dora is mine. There was, I noticed, a mark of make-up on my sleeve.

*

A few days later, London avenged my love. Maud re-entered my life. It was a fine day on The Avenue; the very light seemed to dance. With the passing of the years, Bedford Park had become more comfortably worn and lived in. The trees and shrubs were established and the houses seemed more embedded in the local earth. Birds sang as if the place had been returned to nature. In spite of all of these consolations, Hilda Harper appeared pale and distracted as she turned the corner.

'Are you all right, Mrs Harper?'

'Quite well, Mr Kidd.'

'You will be at Mr Round's meeting tonight? I am looking forward to it.'

'Yes, I shall be there. And Miss Parsons …?'

Her eyes turned to the sky, seeking a purer element, as she spoke Dora's name, the name of the woman who had mentioned the *Daily Mail*.

'She is coming also.'

Her eyes, now alert, glistening and victorious, returned to mine. I had walked into a trap.

'That will be nice. Miss Gonne will also be there. She is over from Paris.'

I controlled a sickening wave of fear and embarrassment.

'That will be nice.'

'It will, won't it?'

A ripple of joy ran through her body.

'I trust Miss Parsons will not mention that, that … organ again.'

'I'm sure she wouldn't be so insensitive, knowing your feelings on the matter. Until later, then, Mrs Harper.'

'Until later, Mr Kidd.'

I continued south down Woodstock Road, attempting to preoccupy myself with architecture and nature. I reached, at last, my favourite bench in the garden of St Michael and All Angels and took out Notebook 39.

I just met Mrs Harper.

It was impossible. Life, at this point, was too full and too urgent for the painstaking assembly of details required by the written word, by the cold distance of reportage. Thought was too swift. The possible presence of Maud had disturbed me, as, plainly, intended by Mrs Harper. She knew of our connection and of my new connection with Dora. The triangle would be complete at Mr Round's. Maud would be her vengeance on Dora and the *Daily Mail*.

What truly disturbed me? Perhaps the prospect of Maud unnerving, unmanning, me as she had so often done before. What if the sight of her should tarnish the shimmering golden vision of Dora? This could not happen. Dora bound my reason and my impulse with a force too strong, even for Maud. Dora was not only, in herself, an alternative, but also a possibility. In slipping the bonds of Maud, I had felt as I had when I slipped the bonds of my father. I could, thereafter, do anything. The carefully reasoned restraints had suddenly become profoundly irrational, as if the laws of nature themselves had been exposed as simple-minded delusions. The taste of Dora was the taste of the world unfettered. Her life in the present was the life of facts, free of theory, of expectation and drab causes. Dora's facts were without antecedents, ever new, ever of themselves.

A train passes, a fly sits poised between my thumb and forefinger, the leaves rustle, a cry comes from the park, a maid hurries to the shops at Turnham Green, cloud thickens to the south, a wren draws an invisible catenary from bush to bush, an old

man stands immobile before the Tabard, the lichen on the stones
suggests a pattern, as does the disturbance of the grass by the
wind, Wilde languishes, Whitman and Tennyson are dead, the
anarchists conspire, Maud will be there this evening as will
my Dora. And what of Willie? Perhaps he will accompany
Maud. So be it. Intrusions, obstructions in the flow, a forked
branch in the river forming a brief tent of water. One moment
follows another, the present flows. The world is exactly as we
find it and no more.

3

'Mr Kidd, how unexpected to see you here.'

'Mr Tremlett!'

He was standing directly behind me, looking down, his head and neck forming what appeared to be a perfect right angle to his body.

'May I join you?'

'Of course. Please.'

He lowered himself slowly on to the bench as if distracted from the task by an attempt to remember something. He arranged his coat and his legs in a neat, ritualistic manner.

'I visit this church often just to sit quietly,' he said once all was in place. 'It is a very harmonious place.'

'I'm afraid I seldom go inside. It is this bench I like. Did you enjoy the other evening?'

'Oh, Mrs Harper's soirée. Yes, most interesting. My wife is very attached to these events. I am somewhat sceptical of their significance, but I enjoy them when I am persuaded to go.'

'They take you away from your butterflies and your rustic hut ...'

He smiled.

'There are many huts and types of fauna in Bedford Park ... and many varieties of flora.'

He fixed my eyes to ensure I had caught the satirical overtone.

'We are all butterflies or flowers to you, then?'

As I said this, I found myself unsure of this conversation. Was it an entirely casual, time-passing exercise or was it loaded with some new burden of meaning? Was this meeting truly accidental?

'Moths and flames would be more exact; the people here are moths, drawn to the flames.'

'How are your children?' I asked quickly, avoiding the ominous overtones of those flames.

'Very well, thank you. The girls perhaps fuss too much about small matters but Alfred seems strong enough. I think he may go into the City, like his father, though, I hope, with more success. I have never risen much beyond bookkeeper. It satisfies my need for order and routine and I have my other interests.'

'The butterflies and moths?'

'No, the lepidoptery is camouflage for my true interest, which is electricity. That's what the hut is for – my experiments with electricity.'

'But everybody said butterflies ... I had no idea ...'

'The true depths of this force have yet to be plumbed. That may be why it makes people nervous and why I must conceal my true interest. Butterflies are more calming to local sentiment.'

Was I being chosen as a rare initiate?

'And phosphorescence, I work with phosphorescence. It may, of course, be the same phenomenon. We live in a world of invisible connections. You do not, by the by, believe that Stepniak was the murderer of Binks?'

Now entirely at sea, I stared at him, feeling I must pin this man down, stop him flitting like a butterfly from one momentous subject to another. He wore a long black, rather worn coat and narrow striped trousers. Modest whiskers decorated his cheeks and a delicate moustache his upper lip. His figure was youthful and lean, his age only being fully apparent about the eyes, from which sprang fans of fine lines, compressed at this moment as protection against the sky's brightness.

'I do not know whether I believe or disbelieve, but how …?'

'If it is any help, I believe that Stepniak was not the culprit.'

'Then who was?'

'I don't know, but they cannot live in Bedford Park. Why go to the trouble of arranging that fatal meeting so close to one's own home? I am sure they came from elsewhere and I am equally sure they deliberately laid a trail of red herrings – the Z or N, the occult overtones …'

'Have you any idea at all who it might have been?'

He turned to face me. His eyes, I noticed for the first time, were a sharp blue.

'Have *you*?'

I paused, shocked by the emphasis.

'None whatsoever, though, on the basis of countless hints down the years, I could believe that everybody in London, myself included, was involved.'

'Binks was indeed connected. I once gave him some electrical demonstrations. He seemed very excited and spoke of contacts in the City and some spiritualists. Have you time now?'

'Time?'

'Time. Time to visit my hut and see my experiments.'

From the kitchen window, only a matter of fifty feet away, you would not have known it was there. Studiedly rustic in manner with deep, overhanging eaves, a mossy roof and rough bark dressing around the windows and door, Tremlett's hut turned its back to the house. Sunk deep into the verdancy, it appeared to have preceded the house – indeed, the whole of Bedford Park. It could have been the home of a locally cherished sorcerer or wizard, an adept of arcane practices. Any activity within was further concealed by a high, vine-laden trellis that formed a right angle along the rear and one side wall. A huge weeping ash provided an awning overhead, its leaves brushing the roof of the hut. From within the drooping branches of this tree a thick black cable curved down to follow the roof ridge before entering through a small side window.

'Electricity,' said Mr Tremlett as he struggled with the warped door, 'tells us that there is an invisible world. This is why, I imagine, Binks thought the spiritualists would be interested. It confirms their view that the solidity of things may be an illusion. The problem is ...'

The door sprang open, the vibrating wood making a shuddering, bell-like sound.

'... we have no idea what electricity is.'

A thick, oily, metallic smell emanated from the deep gloom of the interior.

'We can make it work for us ...'

There was a loud click and a row of electric lights suddenly cast a deep yellow glow on Mr Tremlett's equipment.

'... but we don't know how or why. Swans...' he gestured at the bulbs '... they are quite serviceable for now.'

'Good Lord, Tremlett, you have an entire electrical factory in here!'

'More of a menagerie, in fact. Electricity is a living thing that takes many forms, which, admittedly, may simply be variations of one form. We ourselves may be a form of electricity.'

He removed his coat to reveal a stained, sulphorously yellow waistcoat over a cream shirt with a faint green check. He turned another switch and, on the table at the centre of the hut, a strangely shaped glass tube held by large brass clamps glowed blue, then red and finally a brilliant gold.

'There is very little in the tube, air has been evacuated and replaced by a trace of gas, and yet electricity can make this near-nothingness shine like the sun.'

We stared at the pulsing, humming light in silence. It burned the retina, a floating after-image leapt into existence with every blink; nothing born of nothing. Then Tremlett began to turn a handle fixed to the table by a vice. I felt a prickling on my scalp.

'Binks was particularly impressed by this species of electricity.'

He turned the handle slightly faster.

'He felt it could be deployed as some kind of weapon.'

There was a crackling report. A bolt of lightning had leapt from a large silver sphere to a smaller one perhaps a foot away. The spark's extremities danced across the shining surfaces.

'A leap through empty space, you see. Where was that hidden in nature for so long?'

He stopped turning the handle.

'Immense power, immense power.'

'But surely the very fact that we can do these things indicates we have some knowledge of the nature of electricity.'

'A common illusion. Our science is a superficial affair. We make artificial light without having any idea what light is.'

'Surely …'

'No, we have said it is wave-like, we have affirmed it is particulate; neither seems to be wholly true. Perhaps the duality is intrinsic, ultimate, and the world at its heart is not one but two. Perhaps it extends to human affairs – you have the particle Gonne and the wave Parsons, for example.'

He smiled. I did not react to this. I was growing accustomed to my entire life being an open book – or a source of metaphor – to the hungry readers of Bedford Park.

'You sound as though you are in the vanguard of thought in these matters. Perhaps the waves should be Tremlett Waves and the particles Tremletts.'

'Thank you, but even the vanguard is still very far from the front line.'

From a metal box, he extracted a small fragment with a long pair of tweezers. It glowed bluish-green.

'And this, what do we make of this? An element that emits radiance of some kind. Is this also one with electricity and light? I think it may be.'

'I understand such radiance has health-giving properties.'

'It does, I believe. It is natural enough.'

He waved it in front of my face.

'Feel any better?'

We laughed.

'Binks,' he said, as he burrowed into a large Chinese cabinet on the top of which a vase containing dead flowers wobbled perilously, 'was very active, an energetic resident. Perhaps too energetic. The correct attitude for dwellers in Bedford Park is, I think, a certain taking for granted. One should assume one is highly intelligent and cultivated and, further, that a suburb should be built as an island designed for the highly intelligent and cultivated. This was not Binks's way, he saw this suburb as a ladder.'

He emerged from the cabinet holding a marble base from which sprang an elaborate wire contraption in the midst of which a thin screen, apparently silk, was suspended. He smiled broadly.

'You are familiar with the old trick of painting flammable material on to a screen to create, as it were, a fire picture?'

'Of course.'

'This is the same thing except I am using an electrical force to control the burning. The other phenomena I have demonstrated are widely known, this is known only to me. I did not even demonstrate it to the curious Binks.'

He stood the contraption on the table and returned to the handle of his lightning generator.

'It is certainly not widely known that electrical force can be disseminated through the air with as much efficiency as through metal wires. Laying cables under the Atlantic or wires in pipes beneath the street is quite unnecessary.'

He began to turn the handle at no more than a moderate speed, seemingly not enough to produce lightning between the globes. Nothing happened. I smiled encouragingly. Tremlett smiled confidently. Moments passed.

'Do you like Bedford Park?' he asked, as if he had entirely forgotten his demonstration.

'I do indeed.'

'Not much like America, I imagine. But doubtless you also have your suburbs in which people are encouraged to take themselves and their accomplishments for granted. The architecture would be different, of course, I imagine something more classical or perhaps some larger version of my own hut.'

He continued to turn.

'The strange thing about this particular suburb is that the residents, knowing everything, know, in fact, nothing. They know a remarkable assembly of facts and they organise these into an equally remarkable assembly of competing ideas or schema. But the ideas are as discrete, as disconnected, as the facts. They claim, from an aesthetic or spiritual or political perspective, to be seeing things from above. I suspect the only way to see things is from below; looking upward at the foundations will reveal more of the true pattern than looking downward at the elementary patterns of the streets, river, park and so forth. By looking from below we could, for example, solve the mystery of Binks's unfortunate demise.'

I was not entirely sure this meant anything at all.

'Your friend Harris,' he added, 'he looks from below.'

The thought struck me with the force of a revelation that I could not quite define. I stared at Tremlett, absentmindedly turning his handle, with nothing short of awe. Before I could ask him to elaborate, there was a sound like the snap of a trodden twig and a spark emerged at the base of his contraption. This created a pinhead-sized ball of golden flame which began, very slowly, to move across the silk screen, emitting, as it did so, a thin line of silvery smoke.

Slow as was the movement of the tiny ball, its path displayed something of the delicacy and engagement of a human sketcher. It quickly became clear that it was capable of a range of artistic effects. Three-dimensional shapes and subtle shadings appeared. A world made of scorched silk was coming into view. The ball accelerated slightly as if gaining confidence. A tree rose on the left-hand side of the screen, its branches hanging downward towards the centre. More vegetation appeared around its base, including superbly realised grass. Some human structure was emerging. After a few more moments it revealed itself as Tremlett's hut with, astoundingly, Tremlett standing at the door and another figure. It was I.

Then ... something had gone wrong. A new flame had appeared at the lower right-hand corner. This one was uncontrolled. It flared up suddenly and the entire screen was engulfed. For a moment, in lines of burning gold, Tremlett and I hung in the air before, finally, falling as black, papery ashes on to the marble base.

5

'Cal! Miss Parsons! Wonderful, wonderful ...!'

The greeting faded. Some stray thought seemed to have gripped the mind of Edward Round. We were forced to wait for the return of his attention. A Liberal member of Parliament for an obscure West Country constituency, he was neither fat nor thin but, somehow, bulky. His head was cylindrical and he lacked a neck. His superstructure thus appeared to be like the stump of a telegraph pole driven into the space between his shoulders. This structure seemed permanently affixed in the straight-ahead position, so that his whole body must move when he turned to the side.

'Hello, Edward, it is a delight to be here,' I said in an attempt to remind him of our presence.

'Good evening, Mr Round, you are looking well,' said Dora, gaily ironic.

'Am I? Ah yes, of course, come in.'

The house was number 27 Marlborough Crescent. It had a grand Dutch gable and was carefully tended inside and out with, here and there, an 'artistic' touch in the modern manner. Round and his wife, Emma, did not possess an 'eye' between them so these touches – flamboyant Morris curtains, a daringly modern vase or, in the garden, an unusually frank nymph on tiptoe plucking an apple – sat uneasily and alone in a desert of timid orthodoxy.

I had taken languid, morbid pleasure in these things many times before; on this occasion, however, I was entering the house in a state of anxiety rising to panic as I left Dora and pushed my way past a startled Round, his eyes blinking furiously and his body rotating like a gun turret as he attempted to follow my desperate lunge into the living room. I surveyed the gathering, recognising nobody and seeking only the face of Maud. She was not there. Relief flooded through me. Dora appeared at my side and regarded me, sceptical eyebrows raised, requesting a reaction, an admission.

'I'm sorry, I had to …'

'I know, but standing there looking panic stricken may attract adverse comment,' she paused, before adding, 'It is also an affront to me.'

Insensitively failing to respond, I spotted Mr Tremlett. He was standing by a sofa, his hand resting on the shoulder of his seated wife. They formed a small 'd', a line and a circle. She sat patiently with an eagerly acquiescent smile, her hands on her lap clutching a small cloth bag. Dora saw the focus of my attention and, with a dismissive wave, gave me permission to leave while she went to speak to Round's ambitious and impatient wife. Dora had told me that she always enjoyed rising to the challenge of preventing this lady looking desperately about the room in search of somebody more influential or interesting.

'Tremlett, may I have a word?'

He removed his hand from his wife's shoulder, bowed briefly in her direction and led me off into a corner.

'What you said of Harris, about seeing things from below, interested me intensely.'

He was silent, studying the room as if wishing to avoid answering.

'The future,' he said finally, 'is emerging from below. That is what all these revolutionaries are about, is it not? It is what these reading masses are about. It is what all these advertisements for cocoa and laxatives are all about. I feel it is what electricity is about, a force rising from below. It is a democratic force.'

'And what Frank is about?'

'Hilda, my dear ...'

He had decided to notice Mrs Harper. His hand raised in a frozen greeting, he left me at once. Before I could draw breath, his place by my side was taken by a pale, slender, dark woman, pretty but not healthy looking. She handed me a glass of Round's hock, a disgusting, cloying wine of which he was unjustifiably proud.

'I saw you did not have a drink, Mr Kidd, and I have sought an excuse to meet you for so long!'

'Really?'

'My name is Audrey Sims. I read widely. Now please tell me the American view.'

'Of what?'

'Of the times in which we live, of course, of the great issues on which we must opine, of the revolutions that are afoot, of art and beauty, of the other world.'

'Mrs Sims ...'

'Miss.'

'Miss Sims, I hardly know where to begin. Furthermore, I have not been in America for some years so I cannot pretend to be up to date on the American view of anything.'

'Well, tell me anything, then, anything interesting, I am so bored with all the people I have met.'

Her dress was of clinging grey silk with a black sash to exhibit the extreme slenderness of her waist and the more than adequate swell of her hips.

'What about you?'

'All that you need to know is that I am a woman, I wish to know everything. We women must prepare ourselves.'

She had a delicate mouth and, in her enthusiasm to consume the knowledge of the world, she frequently passed her tongue across her lips. It would have been a harmless pleasure to feed her with what I knew, but Dora was glancing in our direction and I needed to extricate myself.

The murmur of voices in the room suddenly rose to a loud babble and people were gathering around the door. I carefully eased my way round Miss Sims, the better to see what was happening. I suspected I knew – Maud must have arrived. I looked desperately around for Dora and saw her as if outlined in Byzantine gold against a background of dark figures. I smiled encouragingly. She did not smile back. Lost in this moment, I failed, at first, to hear what Miss Sims was saying. But then my head cleared.

'It is Mr Yeats!'

She left me to join the huddle around the door.

'Mr Yeats! You must recite "Innisfree" for us!' she cried as she forced her way through the huddle. 'Or anything else you might think is appropriate.'

'Yes, "Innisfree"!'

'Oh please, Mr Yeats!'

It was certainly Willie but was he accompanied by Maud? He was still on the threshold. She could have been behind him. Dora was looking downward, evidently feeling effaced by this new focus of my attention. The crowd by the door formed a three-quarter ellipse like iron filings round a magnet. Between the poles stood Willie, his eyes unfocused. I skirted round the edge of the crowd to be with Dora, catching a glimpse of Maud-like hair as I did so.

'Dora, darling ...'

She looked up. The crowd had parted under the pressure of Willie's sudden decision fully to enter the room. The Maud-like hair belonged to … not Maud, to nobody in particular. I was light headed with relief and I clasped Dora, feeling the length of her compact body against my side.

'It's only Willie,' I offered feebly.

'But you were terrified it might be Maud. Terrified of what exactly? Her wrath and your weakness? Terrified of me?'

'Terrified? No. Embarrassed perhaps.'

Mr Round was clapping his hands to quell the babble and make an announcement.

'Ladies and gentlemen, please, we must begin our discussion.'

There was a general settling and scraping of chairs. Willie drifted forward and attained a central seat. Mr Round put on a pair of spectacles and held aloft a sheet of paper.

'The theme of our discussion today is summarised in this quotation from *The Picture of Dorian Gray* by Mr Oscar Wilde.'

There was some shuffling and a few murmurs of consternation. Advanced as we were in Bedford Park, Wilde's crimes still disturbed a few, not least Mrs Tremlett, who had stopped smiling and was clutching her cloth bag more tightly. Mr Round squinted at the paper through his spectacles.

'The aim of life,' he quoted, 'is self-development. To realise one's nature perfectly – that is what each of us is here for.'

He waited for a reaction and, hearing none, he repeated the quotation, this time with extended pauses between each word. For minutes on end not a word was spoken. Finally, there was a sob from Miss Wynnstay, the suburb's leading spinster.

'Oh, poor Oscar!'

Most nodded and murmured in sympathy and then, once again, silence. Miss Wynnstay, clutching a handkerchief, turned to Willie.

'Mr Yeats, could you favour us with a recitation of "The Lake Isle of Innisfree"?'

Mr Round was irate. Turret-like, he rotated his body in frustration at this sudden intrusion of superfluous celebrity.

'Please, please, my dear friends, delighted as we all are to have Mr Yeats with us, this is a discussion rather than a poetry group.'

'Mr Round is right,' said Mrs Harper, 'we cannot allow mere chance to determine our agenda.'

'Well, we could,' growled an unidentifiable male person, 'allow mere chance to determine our departure.'

The gathering was cowed by the combined authority of Mr Round and Mrs Harper and, as a just detectable wave of disappointment crossed Willie's features, the gathering settled down to discuss whether or not the aim of life was to realise oneself perfectly. On balance, it was decided, after an hour or so, that it was, as long as it was accompanied by a generous provision for the poor. I paid little attention. As each minute passed, I gave thanks that Maud had still not arrived. By the end of the discussion, when Mrs Round was serving sherry and cakes, I felt the threat had lifted and sufficiently confident to discuss the matter with Willie.

'She has left,' he explained with an expression of lofty, self-indulgent fatigue, 'for Paris to see Millevoye and her offspring.'

'I see. I thought, for some reason, she had to be in London.'

'She did and now she has to be in Paris. Her life consists of one entirely imaginary obligation after another. Political concerns are a gale on a blasted heath. I feel they will wither her, though not before she has withered me. But such is my obligation, my fate. We are both in the same boat, are we not?'

'I have disembarked.'

'Really?'

'She was, I have decided, an imaginary obligation for me. Now I have something more substantial.'

I gestured at Dora, who was in conversation yet again with Mrs Round. Her head bobbed continuously, she was keeping her eyes fixed on those of Mrs Round, playing her game of preventing them straying in the search for somebody more important or interesting.

'Ah, Miss Parsons. I had rather thought she was a temporary measure, a palliation if not simply a distraction. I had not dreamed she represented your withdrawal from the contest.'

'It was no contest, Willie, not after she had met Millevoye.'

'She has been toying with us, you mean?'

The word 'toying' gave me pause. It felt too raw. It seemed to involve a judgement of Maud I was not yet ready to make, a judgement that Frank, of course, would have made at once. I still could not master women in quite that way; I persisted in believing in the superiority of their sensibilities.

'Is that what you think?'

'No,' he said firmly, 'I believe she is incapable of toying with anything. She uses her power unconsciously. She is, ultimately, innocent about the scorching effects of her beauty.'

'Perhaps all women are.'

'All women are not beautiful and none are as beautiful as Maud. But I don't know. I find it hard to attend to anything less interesting than my thoughts and my thoughts are often of Maud's beauty.'

Audrey Sims appeared between us, demanding our attention.

'Mr Yeats, Mr Kidd, I have you both. Now, please, tell me what I must know. What is happening? Where are we going?'

I introduced them to each other. Willie lapsed into a brown study while Miss Sims flicked her eyes, birdlike, between us and, finally, lost patience with our silence.

'What, in particular, do you attempt to achieve with your poetry, Mr Yeats?'

'That is not a question for my tragic generation,' he said with a touch of ethereal anger.

'I don't regard your – which is, of course, my – generation as tragic. On the contrary. Perhaps you mean your generation of men.'

'Perhaps I do. What do you think, Cal, are women as they are now not tragic?'

Alert to the fact that he was being condescending, that she was being excluded from some significant precursor to this remark, Miss Sims clicked her tongue and, beneath the grey silk, her body stiffened.

'Of course we're not,' she said. 'Besides, tragedy is not the issue here. We must not be distracted by aesthetics, by games with language and definitions. Men always use such things to drag us down. We want what you know not merely to possess it but to improve upon it.'

Dora tugged at my sleeve and, apparently noticing it for the first time, pointed at the still visible mark of her make-up – I had meant to have it removed but then retained it, sentimentally perhaps – while pursing her lips to indicate contrition but also an intimacy and a warm availability in contrast to the cool hectoring of Miss Sims.

'Willie,' she said, 'it is good to see you.'

Miss Sims, noting Dora's hand on my arm and her familiarity with Willie, stiffened further.

'I don't believe we have met.'

'Dora Parsons.'

'Audrey Sims.'

They exchanged names mechanically without their eyes meeting. I felt light headed and detached by the spectacle of their beauty and their animosity. What would it be like to kiss the determined but delicate lips of Audrey Sims? With that thought, I horrified myself. The impulses of the human male defied reason. I had been in a state of nervous anguish about Maud and, relieved of that burden, I seemed to be taking on another.

'Miss Sims,' said Willie, 'wishes to know what I am attempting to achieve with my poetry.'

Dora raised her eyebrows, clearly sensing she had been handed a weapon with which to assault Miss Sims.

'Achieve? What a question! The answer is obviously beauty.'

'There,' said Miss Sims, 'is as clear a case of a question begged as I have ever heard.'

'Beauty,' murmured Willie, 'the secret rose.'

'Miss Parsons and I must be leaving,' I said hurriedly, the fantastic thought having crossed my mind that Willie was wrong and Maud was still in London, 'we are expected ...'

Dora reluctantly submitted and I rushed her back to my house where I fell on her, pulling desperately at her clothes and then her nakedness, searching for something I did not find.

6

I returned to Soho.

'Ain't I seen you before, dearie?'

'No.'

'If you say so, sorry this place is so small.'

'I like that.'

'Give us a kiss, then, sweetheart ... Steady on, I'm not a piece of meat, you know.'

'I'm sorry. Please let me take off your clothes now.'

'Hurry, hurry. Very hot you are, ain't you? What's the matter, wifey not obliging?'

'I am not married.'

'Oh, that's it, then. There, you like my little titties? That's better, gentle like. Nice. What's your name, then?'

'I don't want to have a name, that's why I am here. And please put out that light.'

'All right, then, but most of my boys like to see their little flower. I wish it was electrical. They're really good those electrical lights and you don't have to go looking for matches.'

'Please let us not discuss electricity.'

'What do you want to talk about, then, dearie?'

'Nothing, absolutely nothing. Talking causes thinking and I am not here to think.'

'Not a word, then, dearie, not a word.'

Chapter Seven

The Consultation with Mrs Smith

I

'People are always ready to allow agonised literary men to do rather odd things and walking all night around the East End seems acceptable.'

Dora, naked, was smoking a cigarette, her head flung back, her compact body arched against the heavy cushions of my sofa. I was staring, mesmerised, at her sex and at the delicate flattening of her breasts.

'I suppose so ...'

'They are even allowed to be absurdly poor. Cal, you really must do something about that robe. The smell is not objectionable but it lends a distracting strangeness to the air in your house. It is why I smoke so much when I am here.'

'The smell cannot be fully erased. It is probably why the collecting of buffalo robes lost its appeal. But my father ...'

She disposed of her cigarette and looked intently at me for a moment.

'Yes, I know,' she said briefly, a sudden hardness in her tone, and flung her head back once more, this time closing her eyes.

We had been discussing the literary aspirations and career of one Jarvis Mulholland. He had been taken up by the Rounds and the Harpers, who felt the promotion of sound literature was a most urgent task.

'For Jarvis,' she said, returning to the subject, her eyes still closed, 'it seems to be a simple matter of not doing anything.'

'A brisk judgement from busy Dora.'

My mockery caused a shadow to cross her face and a slight shift in her posture suggested she felt less comfortable about her nakedness.

'Yes, why would one do nothing? There is so much to do in the world. Jarvis is just being idle and calling it something grand and romantic. So pompous.'

'The romantics do indeed have a lot to answer for.'

Why was I pushing her away? Dora squirmed into the cushions as if seeking concealment, prompting a wave of hopeless, angry desire.

'Anyway, it doesn't matter, he's just the right kind of failure for Hilda.'

Mulholland's success with two early novels had earned him the epithet 'promising', but then he had been overcome by a mysterious affliction of the will. Seeking a spiritual cure, he had taken to praying in Westminster Abbey, where, late one evening in Poets' Corner, he encountered Dr Albert Tebb. Tebb, though impoverished himself, said he was certain he could help the young writer. He had, he claimed, some experience with literary types.

This was the Tebb who, I realised, had rescued Calvert from drowning, at least according to Frank. He also had some unexplained connection with Horsfall, who, hearing of his involvement with a once promising young writer, had eagerly mentioned this fact to Mrs Harper; it was one of his many attempts to impress her. She was impressed, though with herself rather than Horsfall. She seized on Mulholland as a suitable case for assistance from her newly founded Society for Self-Cultivation. It would simultaneously demonstrate the society's concern for the poor and for literature. Mrs Harper felt that the ordinarily indigent were already catered for by numerous charitable bodies. Impoverished writers had, however, slipped through the net. Mulholland was to be saved.

He began to appear at various Bedford Park gatherings. The affliction of the will was all too evident. His face was crushed into an almost permanent wince and his body, though upright, seemed reluctant to remain so. Beyond the pallor and the matted hair, he was a good-looking man, a figure of romance whose very desolation seemed to attract women to his side, murmuring their concern. Some months before, his very beautiful wife had left him after two years, taking their baby, a boy for whom, Mulholland insisted, he cared nothing, a statement which the murmuring women chose not to believe.

'I don't think,' I said, still under the spell of my need to fence with Dora, 'he should be so easily dismissed as a failure or so casually used as a hobby by Hilda. His inactivity may be the conclusion to a very complicated process of introspection and insight.'

She looked at me suspiciously.

'Are you embarked on that process? Because, if you are ...'

The question was fraught with dangerous judgements. She was imagining herself in the role of Mulholland's wife.

'No, no, of course not,' I said, my combativeness instantly quelled by the threat in her voice.

Dora threw her head back once more and inhaled prodigiously from a newly lit cigarette. She released the smoke vertically in a thin stream that fanned slowly out to form a mushroom-shaped cloud in the still-robe-scented air of the room. She had begun to assess me. Passionate Dora was now accompanied by a shadowy companion, judging Dora, a Dora taking a view on my long term ... viability.

'I didn't tell you about Shepherd, did I?' she said casually. 'An affair I had. He was married.'

'Dora!'

'It's not that important but I feel you should know. But next time. I have work to do.'

She sat upright and put out her cigarette, apparently satisfied that she had crushed my rebellion with her revelation.

'You really must do something about that smell. It is not unpleasant exactly ...'

She busied herself dressing, assembling, finally, her bags, coat and hat, kissed me swiftly and left. I picked up my notebook.

The necessary activity of capitalism in all its banality conflicts with the aspirations of romanticism. Our late romantics think the revolution, once completed, will free them of the demands of mere materiality. The better world will be a quieter, idler world. It will always be Sunday in London. The pigeons will perch in peace ...

2

In the saloon of the Tabard, tiled plaques depicted blue birds, blue flowers and green tendrils from which depended green and purple grapes. There was a frame of serpents. The place was dark even by the excessively cosy and secluded standards of Bedford Park. This had the effect of subduing the conversations of the workmen with their warm pints. There was a distinct smell of labour, of sweat and masonry. These men were filling the fields around Bedford Park with houses, pubs and shops. We were being consumed by London.

Lucian Binks entered, crouching slightly as if to conceal his bulk. He nodded warily at me. I sat him at the table and bought him a drink – cider.

'Thank you, Mr Kidd, and ...'

He paused, staring at his glass.

'And I'm sorry.'

'Sorry for what?'

'For getting so upset about Paris and all that.'

He was still staring into his drink, now rotating the glass on the table so that some of the cider slopped over the edge. I put my hand on his wrist to stop the movement. He looked up, a grateful, relieved look in his face. He had taken the contact as consolation, forgiveness.

'Oh, that's all right, Lucian. Please don't mention it.'

He was here, I was sure, to borrow money, perhaps to go to Paris.

'You came a long way to visit me.'

'All across London. I never knew there was so much of it, so many people ... Makes me feel very small. My dad, he said London was what you wanted it to be – small, big, anything. He knew everything. He said he was going to teach me, but he can't now, can he? I don't know what it's all for, this big city. I get up early sometimes before anything is moving and go out to watch it all start up. Why does everybody have to move about like that? They're all going to die anyway. But they still move about.'

'Lucian ...'

He looked up as if remembering my presence. I had no idea what I was going to say.

'... your father meant a great deal to you?'

'He was all I knew really. Mum was just there doing

things – food … I don't think she knows much about London, especially after we moved here. Dad was always out there, bringing us back news and new tricks. I wanted to go out with him but he said I was too young. He took Sophie sometimes. He preferred her, always said she had prospects. He said I was sensitive.'

He stared intently at me as if demanding to know whether I agreed with his father and, with this, came the additional, unspeakable demand that I be his father.

'How is the painting going?'

'I don't know, it's all I do but I don't know if it's any good.'

'Is it all you want to do?'

'Of course. I'll have to go to Paris, though. But there's a lot to do here first, for my dad.'

'You want to find out who murdered him? The police say it was Stepniak and he's dead. Your mother suspected somebody but our little altercation meant I did not hear who it was. I've heard about so many different suspects. We'll probably never know for sure. You don't want to waste too much time chasing ghosts, Lucian.'

The humble, inward, ashamed expression vanished from his features. He sat upright, took a large draught of cider and smiled … condescendingly!

'Well, Mr Kidd, I'm sure that's very good advice. But, you see, my dad is going to tell me exactly who murdered him and exactly how to make my own way in the world. That's what I came all this way to tell you.'

'Your father is going to tell you …?'

His smile broadened.

'Could I have some more cider, Mr Kidd?'

Irate and uneasy, I bought him another half-pint. Returning to the table, I studied his features. Madness can, we were told, be detected in the physiognomy.

'Your father is dead, Lucian. Don't you understand?'

'He did magic. It's you that doesn't understand.'

'But ...'

'He could do magic because he knew there was another world, a world next to this one. He could make things move between the two worlds. There are many worlds, he said. In some he was not murdered and I am not drinking cider. That's how he did it. And he can do it now.'

'He communicates with you?'

'Not directly with me. He does it through Mrs Smith.'

'Mrs Smith?'

'She's a spiritual medium, very famous, lives by the river. The first time I went to see her she said, "I've been waiting for you. Somebody wants to speak to you very urgently." She said my dad was in the room with me, clear as day, and he wanted to talk to me specially.'

'And he talked to you?'

'She went into a trance and there he was. And don't tell me it wasn't him. He knew everything about me, about everything. And I know you were trying to find things out about him so I came here to tell you.'

'What did he say?'

'He said he was going to tell me who killed him but not yet. He told me to come and tell you that. He also told me to look after Ma and Sophie, said I was the man of the house now.'

'Lucian, a lot of these mediums have been exposed as frauds. There is no evidence.'

'There is, there's lots. I've been reading about it. Scientists say it's all true but it's difficult because people don't know what to do after they die. My da had worked it all out. He did magic and he specially wanted to talk to me, not Sophie. He says she's going all wrong because of your friend, Mr Harris.'

Frank! Always Frank. This was a conscientious fraud. But, of course, Mrs Smith was probably right about this at least. I drew a deep breath.

'Why will your father not tell you straight away who killed him?'

'He says he has his reasons. He just wanted to tell you straight away that he would tell when he was ready.'

'These frauds always play these games, Lucian. She is trying to keep you coming back for more. What does your mother say?'

He dipped his head and sighed.

'I knew you would say these things. I haven't told Ma. She'd be cross.'

'Lucian, you are being trapped. You should think about yourself, not about a past you cannot change. What about your painting? What about going to Paris? I can help you … with money.'

He looked at me suspiciously and then angrily.

'You want to get me out of the way. Maybe you don't like what she's going to tell me. Maybe you know something you don't want me to know.'

He had begun to rotate the glass so furiously that cider was spilling all over the table, splashing my sleeve.

'Calm down, Lucian, that's silly.'

'People have secrets. I know that. But there are no secrets from people on the other side. I'll show you. My da will prove it. He knows magic.'

He stood up and stared at me for a moment, searching for something more to say. Finally, he abandoned the attempt, gasped and left the Tabard, crashing into the doors as he did so. At a loss, I stared at the tiles on the wall. Curved stems rose from a pattern of blue waves. From each sprang tendrils forming spirals that interlocked with yet further stems, some culminating in grapes, some in flowers, blue and brownish red. Between each main stem a pair of blue birds faced each other with open beaks. The whole composition formed a thick, impenetrable foreground before a dead, pinkish background. Lucian was right. People do have secrets.

3

The coat, my favourite, had, with the addition of the cider, become unwearable and, I discovered, uncleanable. I ordered another from my old tailor in St James's.

'I could just replace the sleeve,' he said sadly, 'but it would never look quite the same. Dove grey, you see, always a problem. It stands out but it marks something terrible. Now black ...'

'I want dove grey.'

I was not sure it did stand out. On the streets it had a ghostly effect amid the sea of black. I could be invisible or, perhaps, a watching machine like a cinematograph camera.

London was then unseasonably hot, the air was heavy with the smell of horses and humans and with the endless, deafening banging and clattering of business. 'Why does everybody move about like that?' Lucian asked. I answered him in my mind – because it is what we do. As birds fly, as fish swim, as lions roar, humans busy themselves with projects, with building upon building until, one day soon, not an inch of space will be left on earth.

Leaving the tailor, I merged into a crowd that was so dense that many had taken to picking their way along the filthy gutters. Cab drivers cursed them for getting in the way, under their breath if they were gentlemen, at the top their voices if not. Boys cried the latest murder and waved newspapers and, above us all, giant advertising signs offered Cadbury's cocoa, Pears soap, Sandow's Embrocation and Bird's Custard. Everything must have a name attached. Towards Soho, the whores sidled and caught men's eyes while the ladies pretended not to notice. Beggars stooped and shuffled, muttering their ignored pleas. A consumptive organ grinder coughed and wound a jangling theme. A disparity of things that were one thing, London.

On the corner of Jermyn Street I noticed a familiar figure – Besant. Together with a large, florid man, she was selling a newspaper called *Justice*. She stood firm and severe, he comfortably in his large soft hat and blue suit. I hurried past, fearing recognition.

'For the trampled masses!' cried Besant, waving a paper.

Frank was in the Café Royal, seated in a red and gold armchair reading a newspaper. He did not notice me until I was standing right in front of him.

'Thank God for the telephone!' he cried, crashing his paper to his lap. 'A letter would have taken hours and this is plainly an emergency. Is it the Adorable Dora or M-A-U-D again?'

He waved me into another red and gold chair and summoned coffee.

'No, no, neither … I don't know what it is really.'

'Excellent! Hueffer is coming to your picnic and there's some other strange man, name escapes me. I tried for Wells – but, well, you know – *The Invisible Man*. I even wrote to James. It's a one-in-a-thousand chance he would come, but what fun if he did. "So, Mr Cheiro, am I given to understand that you can – ahem – by the simple expedient of studying the markings on my hand derive firm – ahem – conclusions as to my character and even make verifiable predictions about my destiny, predictions upon which I could confidently act so as to bring about the most beneficial outcome?"'

He laughed loudly enough to turn heads.

'It's not my picnic. It's hardly a picnic in fact, more of a fete or circus. There will be special arrangements for the less well off.'

'Super! Working girls, nothing like them. They can be so grateful.'

He started to sing.

'A working girl is a wonderful thing ... I could work that up into something. Get Miss Lloyd on to it. And all this in aid of the cultivation of the self. We live, my friend, in a wonderful city at a wonderful time.'

The coffee arrived, the waiter smiling at Frank's familiar exuberance. I observed a thread of vapour rising from the pot, spiralling and spreading, and thought of Dora's cigarette.

'Good lord!'

He nudged me violently with his elbow. I did not bother to look round, knowing it would be some stunner.

'Truly,' he cried, 'SEX is the gateway to life!'

A manager appeared, wringing his hands.

'Mr Harris ...'

'I know, I know, I apologise unreservedly. The world is not ready to hear these things cried out in its most respectable halls.'

'If you could ...'

'I know, I know, keep it down. It shall be kept down, well down.'

The manager backed away. Frank leaned forward.

'I have embarked on the book, the book of sex, the life force, MY life force. It will be like a great bomb that will finish off this dying world. Then there will be such wars

… Herr Nietzsche was right. The twentieth century will be the most violent. But he said after him, I say after ME!'

First Lucian, now Frank. There was madness in the air.

'I don't wish to shock you, Cal. Let us talk about quieter matters. What is this emergency?'

'Lucian – Binks's son – has been talking to Binks through a medium. He said he is going to find out who killed Binks. We met. He spilled cider over me in the Tabard.'

'The medium's name?'

'Mrs Smith.'

'I know of her. She provides dubious consolation to the working class throughout East London. This table-rapping is a further portent …'

'She knows of you also. She – or, I suppose, Binks – mentioned you as the corrupter of Sophie.'

'Did she indeed!'

Frank's voice had suddenly returned to its former levels and the manager appeared to hover near by. He moderated his tone once more.

'But this is all nonsense, Cal, you know as well as I do. The boy has been taken in – many are, she is one of the best at this game – he will go around believing for a while and then forget about it. Why should we be concerned?'

'You do not know Lucian. He is a very intense young man. He lost his temper with me when I visited his mother – who, if you recall, also had a suspect in mind – and he simply walked out on me in anger at the Tabard.'

'Youth, mere youth – it does not endure. But you are quite pale. Has this disturbed you?'

I realised I was shaking and the coffee suddenly tasted exceptionally bitter.

'It has. I feel there is violence and madness in the boy.'

'There is violence and madness in us all. But we have our new suspect. Call Inspector Grand, if he is still around, at once. The boy killed his father so that he could have his mother to himself. Oedipus. What could be more obvious? In visiting Mrs Smith he is assuaging his guilt.'

Every problem seemed to be transmuted by the power of his will into a further occasion for his combative, speculative glee. He still met the world with savage joy.

'Please concentrate, Frank. Lucian was a child at the time and certainly not capable of overpowering a grown man. He would be now, however. He is very large ...'

'Anything might be true, Cal, anything, even a boy killing his father. But I suppose you are right.'

'Of course I am.'

'Give him some money. His violent nature will be cured in an instant. Sovereigns are sovereign remedies.'

'I tried – he wants to go to Paris to paint. I offered to help but he rejected it as if insulted.'

'He'll come round when he thinks about it. This is not an emergency, it is a diversion. I must get back to my office. Give my regards to the Adorable. I think I may seek out Sophie to see if she knows of this.'

'Frank, no ...'

He had gone. The manager watched him leave and then walked over to me.

'I'm so sorry ... Mr Harris is a much-valued customer, but he can disturb the other guests. His voice – so loud!'

He had an Italian accent and what seemed to be a permanent stoop, either from curvature of the spine or fear of his clientele. The anxiety of authority was etched upon his features together with desperation to be understood.

'He has done some terrible, terrible things here. But we love him, do you understand? We love him.'

I said nothing. Leaving a large, apologetic tip, I exited into the maelstrom of Regent Street. The organ grinder had expired and a small crowd had gathered to view the corpse.

4

The next day I had an unexpected visitor.

'Who are you?'

'I'm sorry ...'

'Who are you?'

Audrey Sims was pacing about my living room, her hands clutched together, her eyes fixed on the cornice or thereabouts.

'I am Calhoun Kidd, but I suspect you wanted more than my name.'

She parted her hands, clutched her head briefly and then flung her arms into the air, the fingers outstretched.

'Well, that's the thing. It is time to want more.'

She had simply walked into my house wearing a white dress with a blue sash and a rather prim straw hat. Percy, my valet, had reeled slightly and then brought tea.

'Do you actually live in Bedford Park, Miss Sims?'

'Audrey. Yes I do, if you can call it living. Well, in fact it is more Turnham Green. Better for the shops and the station. Look, it seems to me, Calhoun, that you should have some perspective on all this ...'

She flung her arms in the air once more.

'... all this ... all this activity.'

I lit a cigarette. Dora had lured me into the smoking habit. In fact, it was more of a non-smoking habit. All the excitement and interest were derived from wanting a cigarette; smoking one is nothing, a mere collapse of the will.

'Who are you?'

She raised her chin, preparing herself to deliver a speech about the new woman, the new world. She looked healthy now, superb in fact, in her prime, the flexing of her limbs sending shudders through the flimsy material of her dress.

'I am, I am …'

One arm was in the air.

'I am …'

The arm fell.

'… Audrey Sims.'

She amazed me by falling with absurd grace on to the sofa and smiling apologetically.

'I am Audrey Sims and you are Calhoun Kidd. The rest is silence, is it not, Mr Hamlet?'

Confused, I busied myself with taking enormously long inhalations from my cigarette, a process that left me nauseous, my head seemingly full of great voids.

'Is that enough? I thought you wanted so much more. You seem …' I used this trope as an excuse to look closely at her extended body on the sofa, less compact than Dora's but possessed of, perhaps, a more aesthetic, slender grace '… to have abandoned the quest.'

'There's a time and a place for everything, don't you think, Mr Calhoun Kidd?'

She was staring at me, her mouth slightly open. There was an unrecognisable sound from the hallway. I extinguished my cigarette and stood up. Her eyes followed me. Percy entered bearing a large unaddressed envelope. I took it and sat on the sofa next to Audrey. It contained ten typewritten pages, each surmounted, in Gothic type, with the words 'The Society for Self-Cultivation, Bedford Park, London, W12'. The first page began 'Dear Resident …' There then followed an explanation, description and justification of the picnic, or festival as it had now become, the Festival of the Self. The society itself was also explained, described and justified – this part of the essay being garlanded with quotations and references to the great events of the day. The whole concluded with a stirring call to prepare a new world for the new century. This was to be, apparently, a great festival of healing. It was signed Hilda Harper.

We glanced through the pages together. I was at a loss as to how to react. Frank and I would have agreed that it was high comedy. Dora and I would have seen it as social drama. Binks and I would have discussed it as an opportunity to make contacts. The Colonel and I would have regarded it with only faintly amused contempt. Maud and I would take it at face value, as a sign of a new world. But Audrey?

'The trouble is ...' she said, placing the pages on a table as carefully as if they were made of porcelain. She said nothing more and stared, instead, at the ceiling. I was overcome by the sensation that I should end this pause by seizing and kissing her.

'What is the trouble?'

She stood up, this time pensively rather than triumphantly.

'Well, it's just a fair, isn't it? We had those in the country all the time. My parents would take us along to bask in the deference of the farmhands and show the correct deference to the landowners. And everybody walked around on the grass doing nothing in particular. It made them happy that it was the same as last year and would be the same next year. Fairs aren't about making new worlds, they're about keeping old ones.'

This was the first I had heard of her background and the first time I had seen her in anything other than a condition of ecstatic, demanding curiosity.

'But we can decide to make them about whatever we want, can't we?'

'Who is "we"? The people will come expecting the same old fair whatever "we" call it.'

Her pensive mood fell away; she clenched her fists and stamped her foot.

'Oh, it's all so pointless if the people are content with their lot! The new world will consist of nothing more than a change of manners in Bedford Park, W12.'

'Your parents …'

'My parents are content! Very content, thank you! They are in the middle, so much better than being at the top or the bottom.'

There was a catch in her voice as she said this. I rose and put my hands on her shoulders. There was another sound from outside, perhaps more festival literature. Audrey spun round in shock at the contact of my hands. Her eyes were full of tears. There was a pause and then she leaned against me.

'Oh, Cal, I want so much to know.'

There was another sound and I saw – or, rather, felt – a movement at the window.

'Cal, can you help me? You come from elsewhere, from America where everything is new and fresh.'

There was more movement at the window.

'Audrey, one moment, I must …'

I left her swaying and went to the front door. I opened it to see a figure walking quickly down the street. It was Dora. She had a habit of knocking at the window, a stupid habit … as if the door was not quite good enough.

Chapter Eight
The Festival of Healing

I

Percy did not come in on weekends and I was obliged to answer the door myself. The knocking was furious, impatient, its tempo accelerating. I opened the door, pulling Frank, still clutching the knocker, into the hallway. Outside stood a tall young man with a ruddy face, blond hair, a blonder moustache and an abstracted expression.

'Cal,' said Frank, recovering himself, 'this is Hueffer, pronounced Hoofer. He is the great hope of English letters, an ASTOUNDING talent.'

He clutched the man's arm, forcing him forward like a carnival huckster offering a reluctant human freak or a prodigious boxer to a sceptical crowd.

'You cannot hope to understand our modern age unless you first understand Hueffer, pronounced Hoofer.'

Frank looked up at Hueffer with an encouraging grin and Hueffer looked down at him – the difference in height was extreme – with an expression of slow, ponderous bewilderment. He was wearing a pale, greenish tweed suit that presented to the oncoming world an enormous acreage of waistcoat. On his feet were mighty brown brogues and on his head a crumpled brown hat. There was something of the farm about him, and yet, also, something intimidating, a mighty self-possession.

'Delighted to meet you, Mr Hueffer.'

He offered me a soft, fleshy hand with an air of both apology and condescension.

'No, no, no, you must call him Fordie, everybody calls him Fordie. Isn't that right, Fordie?'

I glanced at him, noting with shock the pale blueness of his eyes; the pupils appeared completely flat. Even now that he was looking directly at me, he seemed to be gazing into the far distance. He bowed fractionally.

'Fordie will suffice,' he said, adding speculatively, 'Perhaps we set too much store by names. I certainly have at least one too many.'

There was an awkward pause, as if the remark had been too profound or too intimate for this stage of the conversation.

'Well then, come in, gentlemen, I have all the ingredients for martinis. Did you see much activity when you passed the Green?'

'Activity!' cried Fordie as if suddenly woken. 'Good Lord yes! It is like the preparations for the last trump! They are all assembling to be gathered up. This is the way the world ends – on Acton Green.'

'Yes, we'll gather at the river,' sang Frank. 'Come on, Fordie, let's get you inside!'

In the living room, Frank regarded the assembled martini materials sceptically.

'Almost right but for the absence of olives; lemons are not the same. Lemons are provincial.'

'An oversight. I forgot them in St James's and olives were not to be had in Turnham Green.'

Fordie drew in a shuddering breath, almost a sob.

'"Olives were not to be had in Turnham Green", how appallingly sad that sounds. How monstrously sad. Entire lives condemned to lemons. *Middlemarch*! Hah!'

He had been examining the piles of books around my room and had now swooped on one and was holding it aloft with a finger and thumb as if fearing contagion.

'Fordie, like me,' explained Frank as he made the martinis, 'lives in literature, but, unlike me, he has no other ambitions. The written word is the end of all his striving. This has proved unwelcome news to Mrs Ford, but then so much is unwelcome to Elsa, is it not, Fordie?'

'I fear so.'

'There is, however,' Frank whispered to me, 'a certain Violet Hunt involved. What a name! Hunt!'

'You don't like *Middlemarch*?' I said, alarmed that a literary rug was being pulled from beneath my feet. Fordie just shrugged massively, sat down and did not respond. Frank now had three martinis on a tray.

'The beautiful, the beautiful river ...' he sang as he delivered the drinks, adding, confidingly to me, 'Eliot is probably insufficiently French for him.'

'I thought it was universally agreed to be a masterpiece.'

'"Was" is the *mot juste*. Everything has now changed. It is nearly the twentieth century. Violence, terrible violence is coming. Yesterday's masterpiece is today's absurdity.'

Fordie was now reading Swinburne intently.

'You like Swinburne?' I enquired hopefully.

'Yes, nice man in his way and some real genius.'

'He met them all as a child,' explained Frank. 'Lucky with his father, unlike us. Connections, you see, ready made. What we could have done with real connections, eh, Cal?'

There was real regret in this. Frank was struggling to sell the *Saturday Review*; the bullets of anger fired at him daily may, finally, have been penetrating the armour of his confidence. Was that a new desperation in his eyes? Barking the news of Fordie's high gifts perhaps reminded Frank of the deficiencies of his own.

Having finished his drink, Fordie slammed the Swinburne shut and stood up quickly. Too quickly – he swayed dangerously.

'Splendid! Splendid! Let's have another of those martinis. Now tell me about this gathering, Mr Kidd, then tell me about being American and finally explain, with copious quotations, what you see in *Middlemarch*. I will then explain to you the French nineteenth century.'

I could think of nothing to say. The arctic gale of the martini had done its work and I could not form the stray words in my mind into sentences. Fordie looked down and, noting my confusion, his body seemed to collapse and his face was swept by a great sadness. He sat down at my side.

'I am so sorry, Mr Kidd, I am a posturing fool and, here in your house, it is unforgivable. I always feel I must make an impression, put my stamp on things. It is a curse.'

'Pah! No curse involved,' said Frank. 'Making an impression is what we all must do. We live in an age in which no man can rely on mere talent, it is all in the pushing forward.'

Fordie winced at his words and murmured, 'The pushing forward ...' His face had become that of a rural simpleton, bewildered once more.

'Fordie,' continued Frank, 'is modern in literature but not yet in life. I am drawing him on, as I have drawn you, Cal.'

This remark, combined with the martini, plunged me back into the contemplation of all my present crises. I was swept by a wave of foreboding, formed from anxiety about what must turn out to be my loss of Dora, the ambiguous influence of Frank on my life, the alarming sadness of

Fordie, my own lack of purpose and talent and the potential cataclysm of Lucian Binks. These things clung to me like so much crumpled and stained clothing. Perhaps it was time to go home to Chicago.

'This is a remarkable place, this Bedford Park,' said Fordie, his face and body having largely recovered from his attack of remorse. 'Peter Kropotkin is very keen, he thinks it may be the cradle of the revolution. One would have expected that to be Hackney or Walthamstow, but apparently not, it is here that history is being nursed into being. The thing about Bedford Park is it wants to be somewhere else, somewhere better, but condescends to be here as if wishing to be of service.'

'I am not sure what you mean.'

'Spot on, Fordie!' cried Frank. 'The revolution will wash over us all. Then the place will look like the Raft of the Medusa, your Hildas and your Tremletts clinging on for dear life.'

My head still clouded by my more personal forebodings, I served the second round of drinks. Frank, naturally, sensed my anxiety and chose to exploit it.

'How is the Adorable? I refer, Fordie, to Cal's paramour.'

'She is well, I think, but ...'

'Cal had something of a *crise* on the matter of Maud Gonne, the saviour of Ireland, but that has passed, the wounds of rejection having been healed by the lips of Dora the Adorable.'

'Capital,' murmured Fordie, 'Maud is gone. I am delighted to hear it. There you see a name that, for the moment, has some practical purpose. Unlike Madox, what am I to do with Madox?'

'Incidentally, Cal,' said Frank, for once ignoring Fordie, 'did you hear the latest of Maud? A spiritual marriage to

Willie in Dublin. Very exciting, a turning point in contemporary literature.'

'I thought she was still in France. What is a spiritual marriage?'

'A union of souls involving no physical impropriety whatsoever. Not what Willie had in mind, I imagine, but I'm sure it is better than nothing. In fact, much better if further frustration continues to stimulate his poetry.'

'Willie?' queried Fordie.

'Yeats.'

'Ah, of course, Yeats, Yeats, Yeats ... He would need a union of souls of some sort.'

He plucked another book – Hardy – from a nearby table and began to read. He seemed at once so absorbed that I felt I could seize the opportunity to explain to Frank the circumstances leading to the probable loss of Dora. I had to tell somebody and somebody was always Frank. I embarked on the story, whispering to avoid distracting Fordie from *Wessex Tales*. This took some time as Frank demanded a wealth of detail, about Audrey in particular.

'I was simply attempting to console her,' I explained.

'Cal, Cal, but this is wonderful news. Darling Audrey. Move on, move on, how can we men do otherwise? It is our nature, is it not, Fordie? I was saying it is the nature of men to seduce many women.'

Fordie raised his gaze from Hardy.

'It is our nature to finish conversations, which is why we must seduce women. The sex act has to be got out of the way, though, of course, it never really is.'

'I see your point,' said Frank with a mock-thoughtful look, 'so after "How do you do?" comes the sex act and then she responds, "Very well indeed, sir". Sound as ever, Fordie.'

Fordie responded by slamming this latest book shut,

muttering, 'What on earth are we to make of this?' He then stood up, swaying now so much this time that no part of the room seemed quite safe. He sought somewhere to put down the book, but abandoned the attempt and simply dropped it on the floor. The dull thud hung in the air.

'Enough! Enough! Let us go to the festival! Let us cultivate our selves! God knows, nobody else can be expected to do it for us.'

2

In the hallway we cannoned into each other like three billiard balls as we struggled to leave. Frank, throughout, hummed one of his music-hall songs and, finally attaining the street, he marched boldly northward away from the Green. Feeling too light headed and impatient to correct him, I simply steered Fordie in the right direction.

'You have romantic problems, I gather,' he said, suddenly, now that Frank was out of the way, intent and confiding, 'I wish I could help. I can tell you stories but I can't help. I don't think anybody ever can when romance is involved.'

'Aren't stories helpful?'

'No.'

We walked on in silence for a few moments, the noise from the Green growing louder.

'Wouldn't it be wonderful if ...?' I began, only to be interrupted by the reappearance of Frank. He was panting slightly and, behind him, two young girls were trying to keep up, their skirts and their hats preventing them matching the pace of Frank's muscular stride. One was pretty, one was not, as was the way of these things.

'These two charmers set me in the right direction – more than I can say for my SO-CALLED friends!'

The girls, laughing, caught up.

'These, ladies, are two very important men, but they know nothing ... OF LIFE!'

The last two words were said in such a way and with such a lubricious swoop of his entire body in the direction of the girls that they at once came to mean that life and the sex act were one and the same thing. This – and probably, such was the swoop, the feel of Frank's hot breath on their faces – made the girls laugh even more.

'Fresh cunt,' Frank whispered in my ear, 'fresh courage.'

Satisfied his conquests were all but complete, Frank, no longer, to me at least, an object of pity, took one on each arm and the three walked briskly ahead of us.

'Frank has sexual problems,' said Fordie, 'in the way people are said to have drink problems – an excess which, to him, is an insufficiency. I can see you are troubled, Cal – if I may.'

'I am troubled, but, if I am honest, I am troubled because I am not troubled enough. I thought I was passionate about one woman to the exclusion of all others, but, in an instant, that passion was transferred to another. I seem to be morally deficient.'

'You are, so am I. Morality exists to make us aware of our deficiencies. But you are the more deficient because you said it. Society is founded on the assiduous evasion of such truths, even among close friends. Wilde failed in this.'

'That is rather a bleak way to organise society.'

'It is the only way. It would be a good deal bleaker if we all spent our time confessing our iniquities.'

'Frank would not agree.'

'Frank may not be as modern as he thinks. His views are socially romantic.'

'He was practical enough about Wilde. He says he had

a yacht waiting for him to take him to France, but Wilde would not flee the verdict.'

'Crossing the Channel in a yacht in flight from one's persecutors seems quite romantic to me.'

The festival had been under way for more than an hour and, already, the Green was crowded. Tents had been erected, mostly small with pyramid-shaped tops and fluttering pennants. Two much larger, slightly grubby tents, draped with bunting, ran along the embankment by the railway line, concealing the spot where, all those years ago, I found the remains of Binks. The light was unusually livid, giving the scene, as Fordie had suggested, an ominous, end-of-the-world aspect. Frank and the two girls had already dashed across The Avenue and disappeared into the crowd, which seemed to be, judging by the caps of the men and the cheap bonnets of the women, more Turnham Green than Bedford Park, exactly as Hilda Harper would have wanted. The hubbub of voices, the snatches of songs and laughter and the faint sound of a small band suggested the event was already a kind of success – though as a village fete, as Audrey would say, not as the festival of healing to which Hilda aspired.

Fordie paused to absorb the scene, his flat blue eyes drifting slowly across the crowd.

'England,' he finally announced, 'England ... These same people ... They have been here for hundreds, thousands of years, gathering ... England. Do you have things like this in America, Cal?'

'Gatherings, certainly, usually religious.'

'Ah. Perhaps that is what this really is. Religion is not really about belief, more about belonging to something, as these people belong to England with its weak sunshine, its flags and mud. But it is ending, I fear ...'

With that, Fordie strode purposefully on. Uncertain whether to follow, I foolishly smiled and bowed to a short, freckled man in glasses who was staring at me. His skin suggested youth but his girth and his fussy manner middle age. His hair was cropped in the manner of a monk's tonsure. His lips were strangely moist and there was a fleck of spittle at the corner of his mouth.

'Sir, sir,' he said breathlessly, holding his arms out, palms splayed to discourage any attempt at escape, 'my name is Pollock and I would very much like to interest you in our little display. It is without question,' he gestured imperiously around the Green, 'the most modern thing you will find today and, I dare to say, the most important. Believe me, sir, you will come to look back on this encounter with gratitude and elation, with, in fact, joy. Come, come, I will show you.'

I glanced about me. Fordie had vanished and there was no sign of Frank. I resigned myself to the attentions of Pollock. He took my arm and drew me towards one of the smaller but newer tents. The sign at its entrance said 'Positivism: The Way of the Future'.

'There! Your life, sir, is about to be tremendously enhanced. Positivism, the creed of the new world!'

I hesitated. The martinis were a poor preparation for reasoned discussion of the new world and my former elation had just begun to turn sour. The fine thread of an incipient headache now ran across my right eyebrow and my mouth was very dry.

'Come, come! I feel you are a man who will understand at once. You have a look of great wisdom and discrimination about you.'

I succumbed and found myself inside the tent, amid that strange odour of canvas, mud and grass. There was a very old but very upright man seated at a table. He had long, thin hair through which his scalp shone, he wore one of the brown Rational Hats favoured by the *Daily Mail* and he seemed to be scratching his teeth.

'And this is none other than Mr Richard Congreve, a great, great man who has advanced understanding of the ideas of Monsieur Comte more effectively than any other.'

'Monsieur …?' I enquired.

'Comte.'

'Mr Congreve, may I introduce … I do not appear to know your name, sir, an oversight on my part.'

'Kidd, Calhoun Kidd.'

'Ah, an American,' said Congreve, 'wonderful! Of course. We have high hopes of opening churches in America. We have several very successful ones here in England.'

'Churches?' I said, gesturing at various pamphlets on the table proclaiming the death of all gods.

'Churches of Humanity, Mr Kidd, Churches of Humanity. Humanity is the only rational faith. We have one in Lamb's Conduit Street. You should visit it some time. You will learn a very great deal about the true nature of the world.'

'There are three stages of human knowledge,' explained Pollock, 'theological, metaphysical and positive. We have at last driven the clouds of theology and metaphysics from our minds and attained the clear blue sky of the positive.'

'Why, then, do you need a church?'

'To celebrate that very fact!'

Pollock was plainly a man too easily exasperated. The fleck of spittle had grown and was about to detach itself from his mouth. Congreve stirred and seemed about to speak again.

'It does not seem a very firm grounding for worship.'

'On the contrary, Mr Kidd,' said Pollock, 'we worship our own competence, our ability to see only that which is there before our eyes.'

'In my experience, what is before our eyes is just a buzzing confusion, a constant shifting. Surely to see only that is to see nothing.'

'Everything,' announced Congreve, 'is relative, and only that is absolute.'

Pollock put his palms together and bowed.

'Ah, the words of Monsieur Comte himself. Do you not see, Mr Kidd? Only that is absolute.'

'I still don't see ...'

Pollock was now shifting from foot to foot and grinding his right fist into his left palm.

'Mr Kidd, you are privileged, privileged to be ...'

'What on earth are YOU doing HERE with these madmen?'

Frank had materialised inside the Positivist tent. Pollock stared in horror at the dark force that had sprung into being before him.

'Oh, Comte!' said Frank, picking up a pamphlet, 'fresh Comte, fresh courage! Well, he was probably right, but, if he was, there's no point in thinking about it further. IS THERE?'

The last two words were boomed at Pollock's face from a distance of no more than six inches. Comte's earnest emissary took two steps back.

'Sir, sir, this is a place for rational enquiry! I demand that you moderate your tone.'

Frank ignored this and pushed Pollock aside, the better to address himself to the old man.

'I bet you're Congreve. It must be difficult to feel POSITIVE AT YOUR AGE! Where does Positivism get you when the limbs stiffen, eh?'

Congreve continued to scratch his teeth, though a slight closing of the eyes betrayed annoyance. Frank abandoned him.

'Come on, Cal, I've Stead. There's a lot more Positivism there than you will find in this tent.'

Pollock became agitated.

'Sir, sir, Mr Kidd, do take some pamphlets before you go. I detect in you an enquiring mind.'

'Meaning, I suppose, I don't have an enquiring mind,' said Frank. 'Well, sonny, I've enquired into more cunts than Comtes and learned a lot more from THAT, I can tell you.'

The spittle drop finally detached itself from the point of Pollock's chin and landed, remarkably, on the toe of his boot as if reluctant to leave its master. Frank spun away from him and, in one movement, grabbed my arm and swung me, stumbling slightly, out of the tent. His muscular strength was a constant wonder.

'Raft of the Medusa,' he snarled, 'clinging on for dear life.'

As we departed, I heard Congreve announce once more, 'Everything is relative, and only that is absolute.'

3

Stead had been standing watching this Positivist drama from a few yards outside the tent. He was dressed absurdly in a yellow jacket with thin, pale green stripes and grey, checked trousers. He had a cigar in his mouth and his hands in his trouser pockets.

'That looked like damned good fun!' he said with relish as Frank seized him with his free hand and led us both in the direction of a tent where drink was available.

'Cal,' Frank said as we marched, arms locked, 'as you know, this man is the second-greatest journalist of the day.

He is wrong about Gladstone, wrong about spiritualism, wrong about the Empire and quite wrong to deny gentlemen access to young working-class girls. He is also lower class, damnably religious and he has been abominably rude about me. We have made up our differences, temporarily, and the benign fate that watches over him has decreed that we should meet here today. I have told him all about you but he wishes to know more. There's always more to know as far as Stead is concerned. He is a man preoccupied with EXPOSURE!'

'You're from Chicago, I gather,' said Stead. 'Infernal place. I was at the Great Exposition there in '93. Wrote a book – *If Christ Came to Chicago*, you should read it. It had to be written and I was the man chosen to do it.'

'Ha!' cried Frank, still filled with the anger induced by the Positivists, 'if Christ came to London he'd be told to go back where he came from.'

'But Chicago is not all like that, any more than London is,' I protested.

'Oh, he's done London vice,' said Frank, 'he did child prostitution in the *Pall Mall Gazette* – "The Maiden Tribute of Modern Babylon". Wonderful title, made me feel quite ... aroused. It made him absurdly famous. He just moved on to Chicago vice. It's what we journalists do – different place, same story, always the same story.'

'I got three months in prison for that story,' said Stead proudly, 'stone and iron, stone and iron. But I learned, that was the thing, I learned. It was the greatest good fortune of my life.'

'And you dealt with Dilke.'

'I did indeed. Dealt pretty thoroughly with him.'

'And Parnell ...'

Stead looked uneasy.

'This man is a marvel,' said Frank, 'a dynamo. Wrong, of course, and very opposed to the sex act, but energy, pure energy.'

'The telegraph and printing press,' explained Stead, 'have turned this nation into a vast agora in which whoever has a penny for a paper has a vote. I am the beneficiary of that astounding transformation. An editor is the uncrowned king of an educated democracy ...'

'You see,' said Frank, 'here we differ ...'

'... we aid man in his ascent of that infinite spiral traced by the finger of God between the universe and the ideal.'

'Good Lord! You should not forget, Stead, that you created that damned half-penny weekly with the Besant harridan. Closed in months and quite right too.'

Frank seemed to have forgotten the number of times he had damned the man in my presence. He had what Frank could only pretend to have – moral purpose. Frank chased tales of kissing and fighting or, in more serious publications, provoked literary outrage. He was driven by the moment; Stead was driven by the cause. They shared an obsession with the masses and with the future.

We had arrived at a tent reeking of beer. Barrels were kept in place by wedges on a table covered with horribly stained white linen. Beneath the spigots, buckets caught the spillage, which was evidently prodigious as the serving women were as drunk as their customers. Beneath the warm canvas the smell of beer was mingled with an even more pungent form of the thick, heavy odour of grass and mud, here further mingled with the rank whiff of cheap tobacco and the damp, fleshy stench of unwashed humanity. The husbands and fathers of the poor eyed us suspiciously but then backed away deferentially as Frank pushed us towards the table. Some touched the peaks of their caps. Stead, strangely, shook the hand of each man he passed, his left hand grasping each forearm as he did so. Their eyes moved up and down to take in his strange clothes. Finally, Frank stood before the serving women, staring in apparent wonder at such extreme variations on the basic form of the female. Stead, next to him, now had one hand in his pocket and one holding his cigar at an upward angle by his face.

'Salt of the earth,' he said, 'salt of the earth. The very stuff of humanity. These people are our project, Harris!'

Frank groaned.

'Three pints of your best, ladies!' he cried, having finally recovered from the spectacle of the serving women's mighty bosoms.

For a moment, I thought that all four of these women – who looked like four identical twins – were going to refuse him. Their arms were folded and their expressions seemed angry, perhaps offended by this intrusion of gentlefolk. Then one smiled and, astonishingly, curtsied.

'Of course, sir, an honour!'

With a special flourish for each, she filled four heavy glasses with warm beer. Clutching these, we made our way out of the tent. Deference once more accorded us a parting throng. Stead nodded to each man as if they were already old friends.

'Have you had English beer?' enquired Frank.

'Yes, of course, I didn't like it.'

'Takes application,' said Stead.

'I wonder what YOUR FRIENDS the Positivists have to say about beer.'

'Frank, they are not my friends.'

'Positivists are such fools,' said Stead. 'I have hard evidence that they don't know what they are talking about. I am speaking of spiritual encounters. You must read *Borderland*, my journal. I have extended the art of the interview of the famous and the important – an art I, as you must know, invented – to include the dead. They must be heard.'

'They are,' said Frank, laughing and slapping Stead on the back, 'loquacious to an extraordinary degree.'

'Speaking of occult matters,' I said, 'do you know of a Mrs Smith?'

'I do,' said Stead cautiously, 'why?'

'Later, later,' said Frank. 'Cal is to have his palm read by Cheiro.'

'Ah, the great Cheiro!' said Stead. 'He gave me a reading once. He does many prominent people. I found it most interesting and wonderfully accurate. He warned me of death by water, though he did admit it was a commoner result than actual cases of drowning would seem to justify.'

'Perhaps, Cal,' said Frank, 'you could ask him about the Adorable and dearest Audrey, perhaps even M-A-U-D herself.'

Embarrassed, I turned the discussion to generalities.

'Is cheirology that specific? I was under the impression it was more a matter of outlines, or probabilities.'

Stead looked at me and laughed.

'It's as specific as you allow it to be. I have learned from my own contact with the spirit world that asking the right question is more than half the battle. Gladstone was very insistent on that point.'

'Gladstone just died.'

'That probably explains his insistence. The discovery that one has survived death often provokes a certain vehemence.'

'I can see that,' said Frank. 'One might well feel strongly about things following one's recent demise.'

The beer, mercifully, was clearing my head of the pain and my mouth of its aridity. A warm wave of gratitude prompted me to drink the whole pint in a couple of gulps. Stead noticed this and slapped me on the back.

'Steady there. I think, Cal, you and I are to be firm friends.'

The warm wave of gratitude was followed by a warm wave of well-being. Now I felt I could see clearly enough what was before my eyes. The three of us, newly at ease with each other, fell into silent contemplation of the whole expanse of the Green and the festival. Over by one of the large tents beneath the railway embankment a brass band was playing 'Hearts of Oak', the sound reaching us as a thinnish treble that was just able to penetrate the thunderous hubbub of the crowd. A train was passing above; pale faces stared from the carriages at the astonishing spectacle laid out before them. Behind us, outside the beer tent, a scuffle had broken out, cheered on by the men, disapproved of by the women. The fight seemed appropriate, a necessary part of the holiday, people simply being people. Hawkers cried the virtues of their stolen wares and boys raced to fetch drinks or carry messages or just to run, as boys do. There were sudden roars and applause from the games of skittles or from the drench-a-wench contraption. Three doves, stark white against the trees, fluttered out of a conjuror's hat and, near by, Turnham Green's own Marie Lloyd sudden launched into 'A Little of What You Fancy' with a repertoire of pouts, licked lips, proffered breasts and thrust hips. Where was Fordie? Where, come to that, were Frank's two girls? I decided not to break the silence of the moment by asking what he did with them.

The thought brought me back to my crises, to my inability to be in my world as Frank was in his. I glanced at him. Perhaps he was past his best, perhaps his future place in London society was now uncertain, but at least he had a place. There he stood, four square, his beer in one hand and one of Stead's cigars in the other. He was at one with his world, a Positivist in all but name, planted as firmly in his materiality as Stead was in his spirit world. Next to their solidity, I was translucent, my edges were blurred. Suddenly, loathing my weakness and determined to escape its clutches, I took our three heavy glasses over to the beer tent to be refilled. The working men nudged each other as I passed and the serving women winked. I could not master them like Stead nor ignore them like Frank. Returning, I found the two of them gazing in wonder at a point in the centre of the crowd's densest mass. Looming over his immediate neighbours was Fordie. Before him a deferential vacancy had appeared, an empty space. He was addressing this vacancy with enormous enthusiasm, making expansive gestures over the heads of the crowd and even pointing at the heart of the void, nodding vigorously and apparently saying, 'You, you, you!'

4

'What or whom is he talking to?' asked Frank.

'And what,' wondered Stead, 'is he so exercised about?'

'Perhaps he has gone mad,' I suggested, 'and has taken to addressing the Void.'

'Nietzsche would approve,' said Frank, 'but does not the Void simply grow bored and move on?'

Fordie was now nodding even more vigorously, apparently in agreement with what the Void had to say.

'We must investigate,' said Frank, 'or rescue him. It would be a tragedy if the great white hope of English letters were to be consigned to a bedlam.'

He led us into the crowd. Deference in respect of gentlemen was little use in this mass. People were pressed against us on all sides. Our progress, seen from above, would have been a response to random external forces rather than a sign of a distinct plan. I feared falling and being trampled; my boots were slithering on the ever more compacted surface of mud and crushed grass. Finally, as if by fate rather than intention, we were by Fordie's side. In front of him, we now saw, was not the Void but a man of a little below medium height. He wore high boots from which rose tweed plus-fours. His upper body was encased in a tight reefer jacket. There was a white silk cravat at the neck and he had a closely barbered beard. Every aspect of him seemed to come to a neatly defined point.

Fordie made the introductions.

'Stead, Kidd, Harris,' he said, 'Conrad.'

'Gentlemen,' said Conrad, 'it is a great pleasure to meet you, a great pleasure! Your friend, Ford, has already informed me of your existence.'

He took each of us by the hand, murmuring, 'Joseph Conrad, a great pleasure' to each of us.

'*The Nigger of the "Narcissus"*!' cried Frank when it came to his turn. '*Almayer's Folly*! I knew I had heard that name.'

'The *Evening News*!' cried Conrad. 'The *Fortnightly Review*! Your name has also crossed my path.'

He had an accent, curious and, to me at least, indefinable.

'When,' I asked, 'did you first meet Fordie?'

'Fordie? You call him Fordie, splendid.'

He laughed extravagantly.

'We met for the very first time here about a quarter of an hour ago and immediately became firm friends. He has just been telling me how I should write my novels. If I follow his instructions, apparently, then I shall be the man to lead England into a modern golden age. It is most exciting.'

'Forgive me, Mr Conrad,' said Stead, 'but I am not sure I can place your accent.'

'Polish, I suppose, Polish and maritime and also Russian. I have been at sea for some time.'

Stead glanced at me.

'Death by water, eh!'

'Death? No, I am alive here and now.'

'Conrad and I,' said Fordie, 'are to meet to discuss a collaboration.'

Frank put his arm round Conrad, a gesture which caused a flicker of irritation to cross Fordie's face and a beam of amazement to cross Conrad's.

'We should celebrate this encounter,' he said. 'Let's find some champagne!'

We made our way through the crowd towards the larger, more respectable tents.

'The popular mind,' observed Conrad as we passed a fortune teller, 'is incapable of scepticism, it is a prey to charlatans and the politics of extremity.'

'But surely,' said Stead, 'it is also capable of great wisdom.'

'Wisdom? No. Impossible There is no evidence of such thing.'

Fordie, plainly impatient with these airy generalities, returned to his lecture on the condition of the English novel and Conrad returned to his nods and smiles. Finally we were in the hot interior of a tent that appeared to be the festival's headquarters. Here wine was available, though not, to Frank's annoyance, champagne. Around us, voices, quieter and calmer than those outside, discussed the success of the festival. In one corner I noticed Hilda Harper explaining her projects to an enthralled group of about twenty young women. Frank noticed too and, apparently without thinking, took two paces in that direction, but then recovered his sense of immediate priorities and hastened off to return with four glasses of red wine on a tray. Fordie picked up a glass while continuing to lecture Conrad, who nodded and smiled and then bowed extravagantly in gratitude for the wine. Suddenly he looked not Polish or Russian but, somehow, oriental, though still a sailor. The situation left the three of us at a loss since Fordie's entire mind was on Conrad and he would plainly brook no interruption. Conrad seemed happy to accept this.

'Stead,' I said, 'tell me more about your spiritualist adventures. Many years ago, Frank and I had a rather peculiar experience among the faithful.'

Stead planted himself in what I now knew was his holding-forth position.

'Spiritualism is science, not faith. We are conducting a hard-headed investigation of the world seeking not belief but knowledge. Facts, hard facts, are what we are after and we have found plenty. It is only a matter of time before our evidence will bring down the roof of ordinary science and admit the clear light of day. The spirits are as real,' he dug into the ground with the toe of his boot, 'as this mud.'

He held forth for some time, explaining the ways in which the spirits might be contacted and telling stories of his own experiences interviewing the dead. Our group had now become two lectures delivered with equal conviction and volume. Into one ear floated the names of Turgenev, Maupassant, Balzac and James, into the other drifted the names of Blavatsky, Besant, the Fox sisters, Podmore, Crookes and William, the other James. I finished my glass of wine and found myself craving more. I slipped away, passing through this more delicately perfumed crowd to the table full of glasses and bottles. I poured myself a glass and paused. I was weary and reluctant to rejoin our group. I needed the refreshment, the warmer complications, of femininity. Happily, Hilda's talk was over and the young women were breaking up, talking excitedly in a turmoil of skirts, blouses and lustrous hair. The sight overcame me with a crushing wave of desire and I was obliged to steady myself until it passed. Suddenly, and quite without warning, I found Dora at my side.

'Cal, how nice to see you here.'

5

'Dora!'

'How is Miss Sims? You seemed so close that day I saw you together.'

'You must know that was not what you thought. She was very upset. I have not had an opportunity to explain myself.'

Dora studied me for a long and almost unbearable moment and then seemed to decide something.

'Let me explain you, then. You are a weak man, Cal. I knew that from the moment I met you. You do not seem to see, from moment to moment, the significance of your actions, nor even the possibility that they may have significance. You are blown from side to side like a falling leaf. I found it attractive, touching. It seemed to signify sensitivity and gentleness and I felt I could guide you safely to the ground. But when I saw you with Audrey Sims, I realised you were merely one more kind of fool, just another leaf fated to fall.'

She drew herself up.

'I cannot persist after such an insight; even if affection were to return, it would be tainted. And, I should point out, your teeth are unpleasantly blackened by all that red wine.'

She waited, apparently for my reply, but I could say nothing, overwhelmed, as I was, by alcohol and desire, shame and incapacity. I was a falling leaf, a graceful but hopeless thing. How could I argue? How could I do other than cry, 'Catch me! Catch me!' Finally, realising I was to offer nothing in return, Dora clicked her tongue, sighed and left, the hem of her skirt, damp and muddy, swinging heavily in her wake. Her swaying hips were there but lost to me. This was intolerable, my existence was intolerable. I drained the glass and fetched another. I drained that also and left the tent.

I stumbled for a few moments and then found myself confronted by four familiar figures, blurred as if seen through frosted glass.

'Wonderful, Cal,' said Edward Round, 'is it not quite wonderful, a triumph for Hilda?'

'It wasn't just Hilda,' said his wife, Emma, with some annoyance, 'there were others involved, Edward.'

'Yes, yes, but she was the guiding light.'

'If you say so, Edward.'

'You must get your palm read, Mr Kidd,' said Mrs Tremlett, placing her hand confidingly on my arm. 'That Cheiro is just extraordinary. He told me all kinds of things about myself and he knew about Tremmy's electricity.'

She looked excited, even transported, by the idea of this exotic wisdom. Tremlett himself was aloof.

'And he told me,' said Emma Round proudly, 'I would live into my nineties.'

'I do not doubt it,' said Edward.

'Come on, Mr Kidd,' Mrs Tremlett was now tugging at my arm, 'let me take you over there.'

Stung out of character by Dora's words, I found I was now reluctant to fall like a leaf or to be jostled by this crowd. With an effort, I formed a sentence.

'I am somewhat sceptical of these matters, popular though they are.'

'That doesn't matter, you can at least play it as a nice game.'

'There is something in it,' said Tremlett. 'We know individuality is expressed through the markings on the skin of the hands. In India they already have an Anthropometric Bureau which identifies criminals through fingerprints. If individuality, why not destiny?'

'What did Cheiro tell you, Mrs Tremlett?' I asked, wearily, weakly, sinking into the pressure of involvement, a falling leaf once more.

She laughed, placing one hand over her mouth.

'Oh, I couldn't possibly say. It was very ...' her voice dropped to a whisper '... intimate. But I am sure he is a great seer. He has predicted the date of the Queen's death, though I cannot, for the moment, remember what it was.'

A wave of defiance swept through me – what did Dora know? I might be a prophet of these times, it was history itself that was the falling leaf. I was one with the age. I succumbed to Mrs Tremlett's tugging and, followed by the other three, I was led to the palmist's tent.

'Cal, this is Count Louis Hamon,' said Mrs Tremlett excitedly, 'or Cheiro as he is better known. Count, this is Mr Calhoun Kidd from America.'

A man with an irrefutably Irish face and a greenish tweed suit turned to greet me. The skin was smooth, the lips tight and the eyes sharp, though, I judged, by some artifice rather than by nature.

'An American! Wonderful. There is no country in the world where the study of character is more indulged than in the United States of America. I have given lessons in my art to hundreds of Americans in New York, Boston and Chicago. Your celebrated writer Mark Twain was most impressed by my insights. Sit down, Mr Kidd, I note at once from your unusually long and thin fingers that you err too much on the side of ideality and refinement. I would hazard a guess that you are here because you fled a practical, business career in America. Very wise; your best qualities would be useless in any such position.'

I was too defiant to feel surprised and yet too compliant to resist the focus of his determination. Indeed, in my present mood, compliance felt like a heroic act, a grand repudiation.

'You are quite right. I left Chicago in fact.'

I sat down opposite Cheiro. The intervening table was covered in lace, the pattern of which involved roses, unicorns and crescent moons. For a long moment, he studied my face and then seemed to be examining the whole upper half of my body.

'You have, I note, a fondness for dove grey. You wish to stand out without playing too clear a role. You don't want to disappear but neither do you wish fully to appear.'

He said this with a very slight smile. He took my hands and, at once, looked concerned.

'I see from your second finger you are prone to melancholy, though it is, I am happy to observe, straight. A long fourth finger indicates subtlety in the choice of language. Your thumb, I fear, is too "tied-in", suggesting a timid personality. But, never fear, it is better than a thumb that stands too far out from the hand – all who have this are extremists.'

'All?'

'All. Show me a bomb-throwing anarchist or any radical and I will show you a man with a stand-out thumb.'

'Remarkable. I shall be on the lookout.'

'I note the Line of Head is lighter on your right hand,

suggesting you have not made the most of your intellectual inheritance.'

'I suppose that is true. All too true. But, as from today, I shall.'

The touch of Cheiro, at first ticklish, had begun to burn my skin. With each word he brushed my fingers or my palm, leaving a fine thread of fire. He repeatedly looked up to note my reactions.

'Your Line of Fate is unclear. It does suggest a fatal contact with water, though I should not set too much store by that. It occurs far more often than actual incidents of drowning. I suspect you are a man who finds himself being pushed and pulled by others. I am troubled by the rising of your Line of Heart on the Mount of Saturn. This means you are selfish in romance. You will long for the object of your desires, but show little tenderness or devotion when you are successful. These small, extra lines show inconstancy. You are unlikely to have children judging by your flat Mount of Venus.'

He continued to study my hands, but had now fallen silent. Finally, his brown eyes fixed steadily on mine.

'You are a troubled man, Mr Kidd. You live an indefinite life and you are unlikely to attain satisfaction either in yourself or through procreation. You cannot, to be brief, ever hope to understand or master your life.'

Now I was on the raft, clinging on for dear life. My four companions stood frozen behind me.

'I have never heard such a reading,' said Emma Round in a loud whisper.

'That,' I said slowly, 'is a most appalling diagnosis. From what you say it appears I can do nothing about it.'

'That is not the issue. The issue is: do you want to do anything about it? What I have described is your nature.

Your nature is such as it is, your nature wants to be thus. Going against your nature may seem superficially desirable, but it could cause discomfort, unease, perhaps actual disease. The cost may be higher than you bargained for.'

My defiance faded, my grand historical posture drooped in the face of my nature, embarrassment. Shame swept over me and I cursed myself for unthinkingly allowing the Tremletts and the Round to hear all this. The accuracy – the 'intimacy', as Mrs Tremlett would say – of his insights was enough to give substance to his withering judgement. I was exposed in all my feebleness and indecision. I was dragged out of my uncaring condition and, once more, I was plunged into the maelstrom of all my present woes and, once more, I was overcome by the feeling that it was time to return to Chicago, or rather to flee to Chicago from this city that demanded one's very soul. London was enfolding me, watching me, choking me. The healing festival had become a trap from which I could not escape. I needed to conquer this embarrassment, this exposure, by putting Cheiro in his place. A petulant urge to defend myself sprang up in my breast.

'Where do you get this nonsense? I believe you are a fraud!'

'From India mainly,' he said suavely, 'in particular from a strange book I was shown made of human skin. It was ancient but the ink used burned bright red. There are many such treasures in Hindustan, but all are so jealously guarded by the Brahmans that money, art, or power will never release such pledges of the past.'

'Oh, this is preposterous. I don't doubt that this is some obscure story made up by Wilkie Collins. Doubtless a murder is involved.'

'Several.'

With that, I rose and turned to see the two couples staring at me; three displayed a kind of fear, the fourth, Mr Tremlett, was smiling slightly.

'Have you seen Harris?' I asked him. 'I need to hear at least one sane voice.'

'Sane?' Tremlett smiled.

6

Frustrated and my face burning, I pushed past them all, striding furiously out into the mud and flags, the unknowable, unreadable chaos of modern England.

The light, still livid, had become sinister, the brilliant sun blackening all it touched with deep shadows. From the west, a dark, slate-coloured and ominously exact line of high cloud was advancing towards London like the wrath of God. I walked rapidly, skirting the edge of the dense and now, to me, sickening mass of people. Some instinct told me that determined movement was the way to escape the cauldron of my present mind. I increased my pace, wishing to make myself sweat and pant, to exhale the manifold absurdities of my position, the ill-favoured trajectory of the years that brought me from my father's conservatory to this manic and, for me, ill-favoured festival of implausible meanings and dubious purposes. I was now outside the festival itself and heading diagonally across the Green towards the embankment. There was no one here, the local population had been entirely sucked in by the gravitational mass of the dark melee of healing. Reaching the embankment, I finally paused, my blood racing. Nothing had happened, I told myself, nothing; the world was unchanged. But I knew this was just my frantic mind, seeking a place to hide – from what? I glanced back at the crowd. It suddenly seemed to be no more than an unthinking phenomenon of nature, a particulate mass blindly following laws of which it knew nothing. Nothing matters, said Frank, nothing and anything might be true.

There was a murmuring in my head which, as my heart steadied, I gradually realised was a real, very deep male voice, cajoling and soothing. It must be the voice of incipient madness. Resigned to lunacy, I began to walk slowly in a large circle. I noticed at once that the volume of the voice changed. It was not in my head, it was out there in the world of livid light. I could not, at first, imagine where it was coming from, everything seemed to be in plain sight, there was nowhere for this murmurer to conceal himself. There was a curious indentation in the embankment. I looked inside and saw nothing but then noticed there was a curvature which created a small inner space concealed from the road and houses. Light headed, I took a step forward and peered into this green, humid hollow.

There was an ivory-coloured, crumpled conical shape covered in black and red markings. I stared in wonder for several moments before recognising the buffalo robe. Bewildered, I concentrated on the darkness where the head of the wearer should be. It was Frank, of course. Kneeling before him was one of the girls – the plain one – into whose mouth he was forcing his sex. He looked at me, apparently unsurprised by my sudden appearance, and winked and wrapped the robe round the kneeling girl.

I gasped, turned and ran, appalled by the sheer literalness of what I had just seen, its horrible obviousness. Twenty yards along the embankment, I slowed to a steady walk. To be seen running would make people think I had found something terrible, another body perhaps, whereas, in fact, I had only found Frank. Now I no longer wanted to escape the people, I wanted to be safely back among them, lost once again in their concerns. Beyond the enclosed world of strangers lay only this grotesque bestiary. I strode along the embankment until I reached the first large tent. Stepping over its raking ropes, I entered with the aim of finding a drink, which, I told myself, I now needed or had earned.

Audrey Sims and Hilda Harper were standing inside, both looking alarmed by the spectacle of Fordie, who was introducing himself and Conrad as if they were the oldest of friends and self-evidently the most important men in England.

'Mrs Harper, Miss Sims,' Conrad was saying, 'I must congratulate you on the most extraordinary festival, a great delight and, I am sure, consolation to all involved and a credit to the curious idyll that is Bedford Park. It is the most … the most fabulous place, a place of fables, and I speak as a man who has seen many places of fables around the world. It is, perhaps, like certain islands of Java or off the coast of western Africa. But an island certainly. Yes, most definitely an island.'

Audrey looked at a loss, perhaps dubious about the suggestion that this idyllic suburb had anything in common with an island occupied by savages, but Mrs Harper basked in Conrad's insinuating flattery, his words dazzling her in some way she plainly found impossible to define or resist. She groped for a response. A few meaningless syllables issued from her lips while Audrey, seemingly with relief, settled her gaze on me and, smiling, dipped her head coquettishly. The gesture was tainted in my mind by the recent spectacle of Frank and the plain girl.

'It is an extraordinary place,' said Mrs Harper, 'you are quite right, Mr Conrad. We once had, for example, a murder, you know, one Binks, done to death most hideously – just here, in fact.' She gestured towards the back of the tent. 'It was a great mystery until the police announced the murderer was Stepniak, the Russian revolutionist.'

'Really,' said Conrad, 'how extraordinary. But people will kill each other even in the most comfortable of climates. They seem to have no choice in the matter. I believe I have heard of this Stepniak. Did he not also murder the chief of police in St Petersburg?'

'The very man,' I said, relieved at being provided with a distraction, 'though there is some dispute about whether he was the murderer of Binks. The police think so and, as he is dead, that appears to be the end of the matter, though not if Stead has his way.'

'Dead?'

'Hit by a train on the level crossing.'

Fordie's eyebrows rose and Conrad emitted a brief bark of a laugh.

'Too perfect, too perfect!'

'We must continue this conversation,' said Mrs Harper eagerly, plainly feeling she had finally moulded this encounter into something to her liking. 'Stay here for a few moments, I have a speech to make.'

She made her way to the low stage at the back of the tent. There was a small table on which a large brass handbell had been placed. Mrs Harper grasped its mahogany handle and rang violently, bringing a startled silence to the small crowd.

'My lords, ladies and gentlemen, it is time to speak of the wider meaning of these proceedings, time to reflect on what has been done here today ...'

I noticed, for the first time, Jarvis Mulholland, gaunt, unwell, and Albert Tebb standing near the stage. They were watching Mrs Harper intently. I remembered, suddenly, that the modest task of saving Mulholland from himself was the spark that lit today's conflagration.

Frank appeared at the entrance to the tent, still wearing the robe; deep creases left by the folds caused it to project at strange angles from his body. In my mind, Mrs Harper's words were, at once, reduced to a background hum. He winked at me conspiratorially.

At once I had an idea, an idea that filled me with joy, with a gleeful anticipation of the immediate future. I tugged on Fordie's sleeve. He turned slowly and directed his bewildered gaze at me, his mouth opening slightly beneath his blond moustache.

'Fordie, a word, if I may.'

'Very well,' he said, and lumbered after me as I drew him away from the stage. A step from the entrance, he looked back on the scene.

'England, England … the blurred impasto of history.'

'Fordie,' I said, 'I have some writing of my own.'

'Writing? About what?'

'About many things. London, people. It is for myself and nobody has read it. I wish to know its worth. Would you be so good …?'

'As to look at it. Certainly, but I must be free to be as frank as I like.'

I was flooded with relief and excitement. A new future of opportunity and purpose appeared before my inward gaze.

'Of course you must be frank. I am not looking for empty flattery. I wish genuinely to know its value. You are the man for the job.'

'Am I? Am I? It depends on the job, I suppose.'

'I say, is that Conrad?'

Mulholland had appeared at Fordie's side.

'I'd dearly like to meet him, Mr Ford.'

The ghostly Tebb was standing just behind the salvaged author, a pale familiar.

'I suppose it can be arranged,' said Fordie, sighing. 'I will be with you in a moment.'

Disappointed with this intrusion that had turned me into just one more literary supplicant, but euphoric at Fordie's acceptance of the task of assessing my notebooks, I made myself listen to what remained of Mrs Harper's speech, an act, I felt, of some considerable magnanimity.

'... a new world,' she was saying, 'arising, phoenix-like, from the ashes of the old. That, no less, is what we have in mind. This is an age of infinite promise, an age in which we can take the manufacturing crafts and skills so recently acquired and use them for the great project of saving the human self from the crushing oppression of mere industry and profit, of bringing the learning and sensibilities of the few to the many. Nothing can stop us if we have but the will. And here today we have demonstrated the will with this great festival on this little local green ...'

'It remains a great sadness to me,' whispered Fordie with studied inconsequence, 'that no olives were to be had in Turnham Green.'

I laughed somewhat too loudly, not so much at the remark, but in celebration of my new connection with this ruddy, blond giant.

'Here in this golden suburb we have made a start, this is the golden dawn ...'

An ecstasy hung, like mist, in the air of the tent. We were being renewed, reborn in the cold waters of Mrs Harper's eloquence. I had rising Fordie to replace declining Frank. Or perhaps Stead.

'... upon the great task that will fill the years to come with purpose and enterprise.'

'So you can arrange such a meeting?'

Mulholland was becoming imploring but Fordie appeared not to understand.

'And so, my lords, ladies and gentlemen …'

There was a soft cry from a woman standing near the entrance to the tent. She had been pushed aside by a bulky, awkward figure in crumpled trousers. There was something indistinct about the features of this man. As he approached, I realised it was the indistinctness of unformed youth. He was making his way towards me, pushing yet more people out of the way until, finally, he placed a hand on Fordie's mighty waistcoat and, with a violent shove, removed this final obstruction. He thrust his face close to mine and grasped my lapels.

'There you are, Mr Kidd! My dad, he told me, through Mrs Smith, he told me who did it, who killed him.'

'Lucian, I …'

'He told me it was you!'

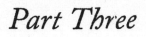

Part Three

Chapter Nine
The Bioscope

I

I was recording everything in my notebook as the spectacle unfolded before our eyes.

A small girl in a white dress carrying a stick emerges from a wood. She is followed by her mother, who wears a large hat. They embrace. Then her father appears in a light suit and straw hat. He carries something which he drops in order to pick up the girl and kiss her cheek. Now two people in shorts, white shirts and large hats are walking away from us. They have a dog. The little girl and her mother now advance towards us. They sit on a low stone wall and a man appears who offers to sell the mother containers. She refuses, the man moves away but then darts forward to snatch her purse. She fights back. The father runs up and attacks this villain. A fight ensues in which the villain is defeated and driven off.

'What is this one called?' whispered Hilda Harper.

'"The Adventures of Dollie".'

'Do you ... like it?'

'Well, it is quite different from the first one.'

'What was that one called?'

'"Arrival of Emigrants, Ellis Island".'

'You probably preferred that, it was about your country, after all.'

*

There is a covered wagon, a woman lying on the ground and a white horse. The woman rises and moves things around the fire. She lies down again. The villain rushes up to her and speaks. The woman tends his injuries, bandaging one arm. He gesticulates. She tries to calm him, but he knocks her down and leaves. Now we are back with the father and his little girl. They are playing toy tennis. The mother reappears and the father leaves with her. The girl is alone. The villain seizes her and carries her off. The mother returns and then the father; they look around, seeking their daughter. A woman in a dark dress appears. She leads the mother away. Another man appears and leaves with the father. The villain is carrying the child while a man scythes. After the villain has disappeared, the father and the other man reappear. The scyther joins them and they run up the hillside where we seem to be standing. Now we are back with the villain's woman, who has been loading things into the covered wagon. The villain appears with the child. The woman seizes her. The villain takes her back and puts her in a barrel. He puts the lid on the barrel.

'Oh,' said Hilda Harper, 'is that really happening?'

The father appears with the two other men. The villain speaks. The men look around, the father throws things out of the wagon. Finding nothing, they leave. The villain and the woman reload the wagon, this time with the barrel containing the child. The wagon moves off. We see an empty road lined with trees. The wagon appears, pulled by two horses. Now it is crossing a river. The barrel falls into the water and floats away. It is approaching a waterfall. It falls. Now we see it racing farther down the river. We see a man fishing. He wears shorts, a white shirt and a hat. He has caught the barrel and is reeling it in. He struggles with it. The father runs up to him. They pull the barrel onshore, the father removes the lid and spreads his arms. He pulls the little girl out and hugs her. The mother appears. She grasps the little girl and hugs her while the fisherman looks on.

A man walked past and sprayed us all with a heavy scent, patchouli probably. It compounded rather than suppressed the smells of food – oranges and peanuts in particular – sweat, urine and tobacco. People were cursing, laughing and talking. One woman had brought a bag full of potatoes to peel. She dropped them into a bucket of water and left the skins on the floor. Children were shouting loudly in Yiddish, explaining, I presumed, the story to their illiterate parents.

'Fancy that little girl in a barrel!' said one woman, two rows in front of us. 'Just fancy! Terrible thing to do to the little one.'

'I don't think she was really in there,' said her companion, a muscular man with a large moustache and two oranges in his lap. 'What I think is it's some kind of magic trick.'

'Lordy, what are you talking about, you old fool? She was in there. I saw her. You saw her, bright and clear as those oranges. We all saw her, what more do you want?'

'But it's just a picture and pictures can be made to lie.'

'You saw it bloody happening with your own eyes! Up there! How can that be a lie?'

Tremlett leaned across Mrs Harper.

'We have made the real more real than the real itself,' he whispered. 'Electricity again, you see. It takes fifty feet of film running through the projector to make one minute of what we see. Think of that. Making the real is hard work but it can be done.'

There is a flickering and we are travelling down a street in San Francisco. It is 19 April 1906, the day after the earthquake. We seem to be seated high up in a motor car. People, carriages and motors are swarming about the street as if this is a normal day. But their movements are not quite normal. They are rather frenetic and large discussion groups have formed in the middle of the street. In fact, the people seem to have taken possession of the street, forcing the carriages and motors to weave about to avoid hitting them. The buildings on either side have all collapsed. Here a wall still stands, there a complete building, but for a jagged rent in its side ...

'Oh dear, oh dear,' said Miss Wynnstay, 'what is this dreadful place called? I forget ...'

'San Francisco,' said Mr Round, evidently proud of his cosmopolitan wisdom.

'No, no, I mean this place, this room.'

'The Bioscope,' said Tremlett. 'It means life viewer, I suppose.'

'Did many die?' asked Mrs Harper.

'Above three thousand,' said Mr Round.

The motor is still driving us down the ruined streets. Occasionally it stops and we gaze around. Destruction has made everywhere the same. Chaos is more uniform than order – as, again, the anarchists intended. I wonder who we are to be seeing this. This gazing eye that sees for us all must have been something like a person in San Francisco on 19 April 1906. It is only people that saw in this way. Or perhaps it is only me.

*

There was a general roar and a crackling as peanut shells were crushed by the feet of people standing up and starting to leave. The Bedford Park group all seemed confused by this and did not immediately understand what they were supposed to do.

'Miss Wynnstay,' said Emma Round, 'I think we are supposed to leave now. Would you like to take my arm?'

Mrs Harper rose. Once this action would have been majestic, but, since her husband died, much of her grandeur had slipped away and she had become forgetful. Mr Horsfall had long since given up on or lost interest in her. Tremlett – ever more forbidding, ever more ominous, with the passing of the years – loomed unexpectedly.

'Electricity,' I said, feeling I must resist his futuristic vision in perspective, 'cannot hope to contain the power of an earthquake.'

'But, in a way, it has. It has reduced it to this harmless entertainment. It has made all our stories so simple.'

I considered his face. He was smiling serenely, evidently pleased with this response.

'But the earthquake has not been reduced at all, we have just seen a rather poor reproduction of its after-effects.'

'Can it be true,' he said, 'that photographing a thing does not change that thing at all? It cannot be said, surely, that it remains entirely the same.'

We emerged on to Bishopsgate. This was not so different from San Francisco. Here also the motors, carriages and hansoms were forced to avoid the crowds that spilled from the pavements and formed motionless knots in the street. The buildings were standing, of course, but, as I half-closed my eyes, they melted a little, becoming formless, dissolving blocks. A reeling, fully loaded omnibus passed and Mr Round offered us all oranges.

'It seems to be the done thing at these events,' he explained.

'No thank you,' said Tremlett.

'I fear you have a point,' I said, 'things really are changing.'

'You *fear?*'

The world is becoming Tremlett's electric dream and, somehow, the prospect seems connected to my own litany of afflictions. My spells of light-headedness are increasing and my forgetfulness is growing worse. I have been feeling disembodied, transparent, as if becoming a character projected on to a screen, a being made of light. Like the little girl in a white dress, I am engaged in adventures that are not happening to me. But the girl of light will outlive the girl of flesh and blood ... Perhaps this is death's first breath ...

I complained about this to Fordie.

'You have in you the death wish,' he said, 'it is too soon. It is really an affliction of the will.'

He prescribed, of course, Albert Tebb.

2

'Colcutt,' said Frank.

'Who?'

'Colcutt, Colcutt! Thomas Edward, Savoy also. Renaissance twaddle.'

He was striding ahead of me, compact and irate. I walked more slowly with age, Frank accelerated. We were on Shaftesbury Avenue, the flank of the Palace Theatre was now on our left. The building had an elephantine air of groundless confidence and Renaissance nostalgia that oppressed my spirits.

I crashed into Frank, who had stopped and turned to face me.

'What possible bearing,' he said, hands on his hips, 'could the architect of the theatre have on the dancer within?'

Frank was, by then, more truculent than humorous.

'Oh, I don't know,' I replied, trying for a lighter tone, 'perhaps the dance of the stones ... How can we tell?'

'Pah!'

He turned and continued his rush towards the crowd gathered in Cambridge Circus. Everybody wanted to see the dancer called Maud but none more enthusiastically than Frank. The moment I caught up, he took my arm and started dragging me through the press of people. Always they take my arm, they lead me.

'Harris!' said a man with hooded eyes. 'Damnable!'

'He coarsens every possible occasion,' agreed the woman at his side, a slender black aigrette leaping from her head like an exclamation mark.

These were not the sort of people I expected to see at the licentiously advanced entertainment promised by Frank. The crowd was implausibly respectable. Once inside, Frank was offering me one of two large, prearranged glasses of champagne.

'What kind of dancer is this Maud ...?'

Frank drank half his glass and brightened at once.

'Allan, Maud Allan. She is a GREAT dancer! Isadora was but the precursor. They both come from San Francisco as it happens. Real name Durrant. She changed it after her brother was hanged for the murder of two women.'

'I might have known.'

'She is said to have sapphic tendencies.' Frank smacked his lips. 'The Cult of the Clitoris. These are different times, Cal, different times. Oscar could have just waited ... Now, dammit, even I would have relations with him were he to ask.'

He drank the remainder of his champagne, swayed and collided with a large-chested man whose coat seemed several sizes too small.

'Bloody Harris,' he said after a moment's pause, 'you still look like a damned lion tamer. You should be in white tights and trunks.'

The man emitted a swift, barked laugh and looked around for signs of general approval. Frank wilted. There was a pause – the man was waiting genially for the riposte that would complete his triumph but it failed to arrive. I realised Frank knew him but had forgotten his name, the shock of which had dulled his wit, blunted his aggression. I had felt pity for Frank before – not least when he was subjected to the snobbery of Mrs Clayton's set and occasionally when despair flashed across his features as he perceived the marks, social and physical, of his own decline – but this was a new species of pity. I saw that, for a moment, he did not know who he was or was supposed to be and my soul quietly grieved, as much, I at once realised, for myself as for Frank.

'You, sir,' cried Frank, partially recovering, 'are a philistine. You should be expelled from the premises before you can besmirch the performance with your caddish gaze.'

'I suppose you're here for the art and beauty, Harris, rather than the exposed flesh, the curious writhings. I fear your reputation betrays you there.'

Frank grasped my arm and whispered, 'I am become a laughing stock. Everybody has read those cursed books.' He then turned back to his tormentor.

'You, sir, are a man of the past. Are you telling us ...' he gestured to the crowds in the foyer and raised his voice to its most magnificent boom '... that you never writhe, that your flesh is never exposed? A new world is coming, sir, when such things will be commonplaces of polite discourse.'

There was a sudden grandeur in his defeated absurdity. The thrust of his chest and his chin seemed to be the prows of ships boldly ploughing into the future while, on the shore, sceptical, disdainful faces looked on. They knew that there was no future, that the voyage was simple folly, and, worst of all, they knew this prophet was a fraud. But still he braced himself – absurd and magnificent – against the wind. O Captain! my Captain!

The man waved his hand and moved on. Frank's stance relaxed and he seemed, for a moment, lost.

'More champagne,' he muttered, and dragged me to the bar, much to the amusement of the crowd. Frank, tamer of lions, had become a clown in the London circus.

After two more glasses, we struggled to our seats in the third row of the stalls.

'Barely twenty feet from the stage,' whispered Frank.

'I wonder why they are all here,' I gestured at the genteel crowd, 'and with their wives ...'

'It is art, my friend, art teaching us to be honest. I led the way in this ... this frankness ... they follow, contemptuous of their leader. I will show them. There is a good deal more frankness to come.'

I found it easier to gaze upwards at Colcutt's Renaissance flummery. I did not wish to meet any eyes and feel the withering judgement of so many men and women who would find the role of Frank Harris's companion contemptible. Still he fought on – more frankness to come! – ever more fiercely resolved to avenge himself on a society that, he believed, had conspired against him from the moment he had proved that kissing and fighting were all the people wanted. For years now he had outflanked his critics simply by knowing more than they ever would. It is hard to despise a man with any confidence when he can quote hundreds of lines of Shakespeare or Milton to make his case – even if, in retrospect, the lines are discovered to be entirely irrelevant.

'Dammit!'

A very large, extravagantly hatted women had seated herself in front of Frank. He became angry and flustered. I put my hand on his arm, fearing an assault on the hat, and suggested we change places. As we did so, Frank was unable to resist making our reasons clear. The woman and her companion looked round and sneered with satisfaction.

Finally, the lights dimmed and the curtain rose to reveal a darkened, empty stage. A sinister, discordant overture floated from the pit, causing some murmuring and movement in the audience.

'They are out of tune!' whispered the large-hatted woman.

'It is German music,' explained her husband, 'very much the thing, I gather.'

Various characters in ancient costumes were now milling about the stage, apparently in deep conversation. Occasionally one shouted something in, I assumed, Hebrew. The music was taking on a more conventional form as it approached some sort of climax. Then the crowd on the stage hushed and parted to reveal a single crouched figure. The orchestra once again resorted to discordancy, rising to a deafening crash as the figure rose slowly.

It was Maud Allan. She was wearing strings of pearls, a transparent, slit skirt and apparently nothing else. The audience gasped as she flung her head back and her arms in the air, causing her body to arch forward, exposing every line, every cleft. She stepped slowly forward to the very edge of the stage.

I glanced at Frank; his mouth was curved downwards in a grimace of vengeful lust. He had spent his life in the company of or in pursuit of naked female bodies. There was nothing new here except the public display amid this respectable crowd. He smacked his lips at the evident signs of embarrassment as Maud held her pose, giving the audience nothing else to look at until, finally, she launched herself into a frenzied dance that took her from one corner of the stage to another, falling into poses of lust, dread, horror, ecstasy and even virginal, springtime joy as she crowned herself with a ringlet of flowers.

There came a pause when, in the interests of narrative, the drama settled down to some routine exposition in the midst of which King Herod appeared, monstrously fat.

'Not unlike,' whispered Frank, 'our own dear monarch.'

Herod began a tedious mime of law-giving and courier despatching. Salome was nowhere to be seen and Frank began squirming uncomfortably. He flung his head back and yawned ostentatiously. A thought struck him and he sprang forward, clutched my arm and thrust his face close to mine.

'Why did Pound punch you?'

At a party in Bedford Park, a repellent American named Ezra Pound had punched me in the face, knocking me unconscious.

'Gently, my good friend, gently,' Stead murmured as I came to, 'you have had a bit of a shock.'

'He rose on tiptoe as the blow landed,' said Mr Round.

'Rose on tiptoe,' said Dora, 'and fell like an autumn leaf.'

This might, I reflected, be the first time I knew something about a famous public event that Frank did not.

'You don't know?'

'No idea whatsoever.'

'It was because I told him I had conquered Maud and he took this to be an affront to English poetry. Willie should have got there first.'

'But, but, but ...' Frank could not speak, not, I realised, because of Pound's belief in the primacy of Yeats's lust, but because, out of absent-mindedness and embarrassment, I had not told Frank of Maud's submission.

'She had abandoned politics because of MacBride,' I said irrelevantly, 'and I suppose that made me no longer quite so unacceptable.'

Frank recovered enough to say, 'Well, it did until you actually did it! I expect you were a terrible disappointment.'

He started to laugh. At first, he stifled the noise, but then abandoned the attempt and roared forth, a full bass boom that filled the theatre and startled the dancers on stage so much that the action came to a complete halt. I looked desperately around. We were stuck in the middle of a row so there was no easy or dignified escape. Angry voices were being raised. I slumped into my seat, powerless. Frank laughed louder and louder and then, evidently irritated that I was not joining in, he started prodding his elbow into my ribs. I turned, and he looked at me through the laughter with an expression I had never seen before – knowing, wry, resigned, an expression that somehow demanded a public celebration of our companionship. Unable to resist, I began laughing, softly at first but then rising to a choking, spluttering climax as I saw men in uniform hastening to evict us from the theatre.

3

On 12 December 1891 Miss Julia A. Ames died. Stead had met her the year before – a professional connection since Miss Ames was attached to a newspaper in Chicago. The blow of bereavement fell heavily on her friend Ellen and, for months, she feared life was no longer worth living. Amid the very depths of her despair, Ellen was awoken one night be a bright light in her bedroom. Julia was standing by her bed, dressed as she had been in life. She radiated peace and joy. Slowly the vision faded and Ellen was comforted. Her friend had gone to the other side. Stead subsequently met Ellen and, hearing the story of Julia's return, he offered to communicate with her through his preferred method of automatic writing. At once the method was successful.

'When I left you, darling,' began the first letter from Julia to Ellen, 'you thought I was gone from you for ever, or at least till you also passed over. But I was never so near to you as after I had, what you called, died.'

Stead plunges through life – and death. He wishes to improve, inspire, to know. He is all that I am not, but, perhaps, would wish to be. For Frank the world must be recast, reformed, remodelled, battered if necessary into a shape more flattering to Frank. For Stead – the Chief, as his followers and family call him – recasting etc. is still required, but he does not seek flattery, rather an end to his own impatience. He is very angry with this age, with its ignorance and corruption, and he sees too clearly how this anger might be assuaged. Too clearly, because how could the world he wants could ever be brought into being? The wanting is a lust like Frank's; both are kept alive, alert and purposeful by lust. Is it indolence that keeps me from embracing such purposes? Is it incredulity? Is it this fading unto death?

Whatever once surged through Frank surges still, even in defeat. It will surge to the last. Nothing surges through me but a vague sense of error, of wrong roads taken. My past is an empty prairie; Frank's is the Rockies.

'His Nostromo,' said Jarvis Mulholland, 'was absurd – impenetrable, tedious, futile.'

Stead emitted a brief snort. Mulholland ignored him.

'Who could care about such a character? And the politics of some nasty, barbarous, South American state – well, it's just suffocating. How can he expect this book to sell?'

He was lecturing us in the faded green saloon of his club. Beneath his inflated, though still just youthful, physiognomy and immense girth sprang two tiny legs that had avoided the consequences of the last decade's feasting. Dr Tebb's ministrations had been all too effective.

'And gloomy! I don't think we are helpless creatures buffeted about by uncaring nature and, more to the point, I don't believe there are many people out there who do. Who feels buffeted? I don't! And then there's glum old Hardy.'

In a monstrous checked suit that had shocked the doorman almost to the point of refusing him admittance, Stead, ageless but for the grizzled beard, chuckled quietly behind the thick clouds of blue-grey smoke emitted by his mighty Havana.

'Let me ask you this – what, exactly, is wrong with the age in which we live?'

At this, Stead's chuckle turned to a shout of laughter. Mulholland gave him a disdainful glare.

'Well, what? The condition of the poor is improving daily, we have telephones and electricity and motor cars have replaced filthy horses. Far from being buffeted by nature, we are buffeting her, the old hag.'

A further shout – from the billiards players in the adjoining room – interrupted his syrupy flow.

'We have peace, our navy is unchallenged, the empire is intact. Great heavens, this is close to paradise! We need stories that raise our eyes to the miracle of the present age.'

He plucked his glass of Madeira from a heavy Moroccan table on which also rested a copy of his latest work – *The*

Onrushing Tide – and, manoeuvring his corpulence, he sank, squeaking slightly, deeper into the thick folds of the old leather armchair. To augment the Madeira, he took a cube of Turkish Delight from an ornate dish.

'I make no apology,' he continued through his chewing, waving an obese hand, 'none whatsoever, for my success. My books are not made worse by their popularity. I do not regard sales as a badge of failure and disgrace. This is the age of the people and sales mean the people have spoken and spoken clearly. *Vox populi, vox dei*. We have made our own great democracy of the people's wishes, whims, desires, faith ...'

'Whims and faith,' said Stead, 'whims and faith. By Jove, that's a good headline for a piece on the condition of the people.'

'And reason, don't forget the people's reason. You must not condescend, turning them into a superstitious mob. They have their wisdom and their reasons.'

He was now chewing on a second thick cube of jelly; it gave his speech a glutinous texture. A film of sugar had coated his lips.

'In *Nostromo*,' I suggested, 'Conrad says the people are incapable of scepticism ...'

'There! What did I tell you? He understands nothing, nothing of the people and their wisdom.'

'Writes damned well, though,' said Stead mischievously.

'Pah!'

A mighty chain formed asymmetric golden catenaries across the figured velvet of Mulholland's waistcoat. A substantial anchor could have been suspended therefrom, though, in fact, the chain was attached only to a rather small and delicate timepiece given to him by his publisher on the occasion of the stupendous sales of his first novel, *Irish Love*, a book which was, to my horror, based on some tales I had told him of Maud Gonne. His explosive 'Pah!' had caused the heavy chain to pull the tiny watch from his pocket.

'And what about that Shepherd's Bush showground, that White City? My God, if that is not what the people want, I don't know what is! If that is not TRUTH, I don't know what is! Conrad would wish to fling us back into a new dark age. We, the people, have the modern Olympics in West London!'

His prodigious paunch, the freakish creation of less than ten years of publishing success and, among other foodstuffs, Turkish Delight, was a perfect sphere, a planet of flesh. The cadaverous seed that was the young Mulholland had become the world entire.

'Do you think you would feel such enthusiasm for the people had you not sold so many books?'

Stead was determined to wring what comedy and intellectual substance he could from the occasion. Mulholland grunted – 'Damned thing!' – and replaced his watch in its pocket, restoring the lesser catenary, before responding.

The lecture restarted, but his voice had become little more than a buzzing in my ears. Stead, meanwhile, nodded but did not speak. He was, perhaps, overcome by one of those waves of sadness that had afflicted him since December when his boy, Willie, died. The death of a child – one died oneself precisely to prevent such a horror.

My tribute to Mulholland was almost paid. He had dedicated *The Onrushing Tide* to me – 'For Calhoun Kidd, the great listener' – and this celebratory lunch – there had already been a gigantic party at the Savoy – was to mark my special role in his creation.

'Utopia,' I murmured. It was a thought that had only accidentally been voiced. I was increasingly prone to such acts of solipsistic idleness or inattention.

'Call it that if you must, Cal, my friend, my dear old friend. Doubtless that noisy mediocrity Wells would design Utopia for you while that swine Shaw sniggered in the corner.'

'And Hardy wept,' suggested Stead.

'Indeed!' Mulholland guffawed. 'And Hardy wept. But Utopia is an end, I am all about means, about measurable attainments.'

'Would we need the Samurai?' I enquired.

'Samurai?'

Not for the first time I found myself suspecting that Mulholland had not read most of the authors he so vigorously condemned.

'The voluntary aristocrats Wells suggests will be needed to govern Utopia.'

'Aristocrats! We will need no such creatures. Democracy pure and simple is the solution ...'

In spite of his dedication, I never really listened to Mulholland. He was like the soft roar of London traffic or waves breaking on a beach – a dull, ever-present bass drone that must be made of many different things but was always the same thing. This was why his marriage to Audrey Sims was so perfectly judged. She kept asking the same question and he kept giving the same answer.

The thought of Audrey as the wife of a fat Mulholland made me feel very old, opening up an abyss of time at the far side of which was Hilda's festival, Audrey in her grey silk dress and an emaciated Mulholland accompanied by Dr Albert Tebb. The festival was never, sadly, repeated after the police had been forced to intervene in a violent confrontation among the working people. My sensation of immense age and deep time was intensified by this mausoleum of a room with paint that seemed to have been applied some centuries ago, carpets faded to a bluish beige and monstrous curtains of once green velvet that looked as though a single blow would dissolve their enfeebled fabric into choking clouds of dust. The nineteenth century clung on in this room like an old dowager clinging to life while, in the streets outside, the twentieth hummed and conspired to destroy her, to let in the light on the old London that so feared windows that let in the life of the ordinary day.

Or perhaps I was just old *tout court*. At fifty-seven one had the choice – one was either in one's prime or one was almost sixty. One made the choice daily. Some days I strutted the streets straight backed and immaculate, giving and receiving interested glances; other days I wandered vaguely, my shoulders hunched, oppressed by an awareness that my shirt was not quite right, that there was an oddity in the hang of my trousers suggestive of incipient senility.

There was a pause in Mulholland's flow; he seemed to have run out of ways of saying what he always said. Groping towards the surface of my melancholy, I remembered something I must say.

'Stead, we shall meet ...'

'At Stanford's, yes,' he said, taking pleasure in the reference to an arrangement that did not include our fat friend. Purposefully I rose to my feet, causing momentary dizziness, and took *The Onrushing Tide* from the Moroccan table.

'Jarvis, I must be leaving you now. The honour you have done me ...'

'Don't mention it, Cal, don't mention it, richly deserved. The least I could do.'

The last wave of his hand, though apparently a gracious dismissal of my gratitude, also served as a dismissal of me as an entity no longer of interest or importance.

4

In Westminster Square by the statue of Palmerston, I found a cabman to drop me at the corner of Chiswick High Road and Turnham Green Terrace. The evening was cool and clear, a short walk would wash away the many confusions of the day. Mulholland was a confusion. He reminded me that age brings with it connections one could not avoid but would not choose. Acquaintances hardened into dependants as surely as their opinions hardened into dogma. There was no such thing as a single man.

The competing glows of gas and electricity lined the streets and there was a roar of voices, some raised in song, from a nearby pub. Couples gazed into the windows of the closed shops in the Terrace and, in the alley, at the end of which Pinker the agent used to live, a boy and a girl kissed and fumbled.

Some years before, seeking relief from the memory of Lucian's accusation, I had engaged Stead to contact Binks through his then preferred method of automatic writing.

'The hand inert, the mind passive,' explained Stead as he took up a pencil and then rested his hands on his desk on either side of a small pile of blank sheets of paper.

'Should I …?'

'Please, sit down quietly.'

We sat in silence, Stead bowed over the paper, his hands inert. I attempted to picture forces coming into the room, the figure of Binks himself, but I knew well enough that nothing other than my own mind was at work. After five minutes or so, Stead began to write in the curiously crabbed manner of a left-handed man. Long moments passed to the sound of his scratching. Finally, he sighed and relaxed.

I passed the station and stared bleakly to my left at the darkened Green and the railway embankment, humped against a sky lightened by the cold glow of a half-moon. Here had lain Binks. Alive, he drew me in; dead, he drew me in still farther.

Stead handed me the paper. He had only covered one sheet. The hand was small and exact, unlike his own. It took me some moments to make out any words other than 'I am here'. I glanced at Stead, seeking help.

'It is from Frederick,' he explained, 'a guide; he often comes to me on these occasions.'

The trees were no longer the bare saplings they were when I first saw Bedford Park and the houses now seemed sunk in the vegetation which marked the bricks and the woodwork with stains and streaks. Were we not, like these bricks, nature's own? Not once we started talking and making a second world that would sit pompously on the first, a world of iron, iron in everything.

I looked again at the paper. This time it could be deciphered. There were many words of greeting to Stead and fragments of news about others, primarily one Julia. I scanned this rapidly until I came to the word 'Binks'.

'I have encountered Binks,' wrote Frederick, 'he looked shocked, pale and angry. In their first years on this side it is easy to spot those who have died violently.'

My footsteps echoed off the walls of the empty street. I sucked greedily at the cool air. It rushed between my clenched teeth and down to brush, feather-like, the tubes and hollows of my lungs, staining red blood redder still. At least there was, for the moment, this, the sensations of my brief continuance. A cat appeared on the pavement before me and, affronted at finding a human abroad in its world, turned and stepped silently away.

'Binks was at first unclear about the manner of his demise. He seemed ...' illegible word here '... and incredulous. But all he would say about his attacker was that it was a man he knew well, too well.'

What was the last thing my father said to me, face to face? 'You are my son, but I am not your mother.'

'*Your father dead*,' curt Kurt had cabled.

He had seemed old when I left him in that sweating room but he had survived another twenty years. I returned to dispose of his affairs. In Chicago there were men directing company matters – gruff, calculating men, bureaucratic versions of the Dell, Ford and Reece who had lured Frank to the West. I had known nothing of them, having believed that my father had continued to control his own and his company's affairs. They told me at some length of my father's disapproval of my continued absence and of his sadness. They played successfully, in short, on a son's residual guilt. I let them have the business at an absurd price, having been shamed out of demanding more.

Chicago itself was a dream city, as grim as London, as dirty as London, harsher than London in its day-to-day encounters, but still, somehow, not as real as London. I wandered the streets seeking some anchorage in the safe haven of memory, but even the Fremont House Hotel provided no purchase on this seabed. The whole place was little more than a painted backdrop, the stage set of my distant past. I had become a strutting, fretting actor in my own memory. The calculating men – in fact, everybody I met – quickly detected my detachment. They treated me like a simple-minded tourist, distracting me during the negotiations by showing me the new wonders of the city, buildings that proclaimed the taming of this lakeside settlement but failed to mask the stockyard smell.

The night before I left Chicago, two of the men who had so brazenly defrauded me took me to dinner. In the midst of consuming their blackened and bloodied steaks, one winked at the other before turning to address me.

'Cal, in London do you often encounter a fellow called Calvert? Thin, weasel type, miserable son of a bitch.'

'I did, how on earth …?'

They smiled at each other.

'Well, I guess it's OK to tell you now that the Colonel has joined the choir invisible. Calvert was his spy, checking on you. Bad choice, of course, he even tried to kill himself and the word was that he killed somebody else.'

The Colonel had meant that my mother could have kept me in Chicago, but he could not. I wonder if he was right. Women stabilise, cling … anchor. They prevent unnecessary, inconvenient movement, movement caused by tides, waves and currents and, therefore, chance, nature's whim or the despotic demands of stronger-minded people, of, for example, Frank. Frank could not be anchored. He fed on women but did not submit to their stabilising demands. And on me he placed demands not in words but in actions. 'Why are you not like me?' he said with his every act, and he said it insistently enough to make me feel I should, indeed, be like him, but not so insistently that he could make me entirely abandon my … well, my nature.

I had wandered. I was at the point where The Avenue turned into Southfield Road. I decided to walk down Southfield, turn left into Alban's Avenue, left into Speldhurst Road, right into Fielding Road, crossing The Avenue, and finally right into Woodstock, my road. I visualised this route as if I were a bird or birdman, from high above.

I wanted to be anchored, I wanted Maud. I still do, I think, in spite of what I said to myself and others, in spite of her evident lack of utility as an anchor. Ireland was not her true love, for 'true' would imply that Maud was subject to forces beyond her control and that would be unthinkable.

One day, doubtless, there would be an explanation, a complete account. The future, into which Frank's violence rushed us, would unwrinkle all our brows. Perhaps when we saw all, all would seem good. The clouds would clear, the glass brighten, the words become legible. Our natures will lie before us in plain view, like a map. Will it be a map of London or Chicago, a confusion or a grid? No matter, it will be a map by which we can navigate.

"'Perhaps,'" said Frederick through Stead, "'I showed him too many tricks.'"

I turned right into Woodstock Road and increased my pace, feeling the need to increase the rate at which my head was cleared. Ahead of me, a boy was running away into the darkness. Here was my home, the Binks house. All was still well in spite of everything.

5

'Mr Kidd, forgive the intrusion.'

The stooped figure of a man had emerged from the darkness of the bushes in my garden. He wore a black homburg – too large for his thin face and his short stature – which he now raised in greeting.

'I have been waiting for some time, no hardship for me, of course. Waiting was always my calling.'

The face partially emerged from the gloom to reveal a great, grey moustache.

'And it was most urgent that I speak to you. So many developments to report.'

'I'm sorry, I have no idea who you are.'

He replaced his hat and shuffled from foot to foot as if dancing.

'Oh yes you do, oh yes you do! And I certainly know who you are, Mr Calhoun Kidd.'

I stared hard at the face, noticing a fine map of lines and, in spite of the depredations of age, a certain youthful and very theatrical insolence.

'Mind you, we didn't meet for long, a rather brief encounter, in fact, not so very far from here. It was a very long time ago, twenty years or thereabouts; it stuck in my mind, perhaps not in yours.'

He raised his chin. It was the defiance of his class, a challenge to his social superior. The movement was also enough to reveal his whole face and that, combined with the tone of his voice, was enough.

'Inspector Grand!'

'Well done, sir! Yes, that is me, though not, strictly, Inspector any more. I am retired from the force, thank God, twentieth-century policing is very taxing.'

He paused. The theatricality faded.

'I have felt it necessary, Mr Kidd, to tell you something of great ... significance.'

A few moments later he was seated in my living room, still wearing his coat and his hat in his lap. He had declined my offer of a drink and he sat on the very edge of the chair, both indications that he did not intend to stay long, though he paused for an unconscionably long time before finally speaking.

'Some time ago one Lucian Binks came to tell me that he had ascertained, through the offices of a medium named Mrs Smith, that you had killed his father ...'

'But ...'

He raised his hand.

'Bear with me, Mr Kidd. As he had no evidence other than the word of Mrs Smith – a fraud, I can assure you – I dismissed the idea and clung to my old certainty that Stepniak was the guilty party. However, something this Lucian said stuck in my mind.'

Again he fell silent, this time agonisingly.

'He said his mother had always been of the view that another party was involved, a gentleman who had seduced his sister when she was but a child. As I say, this stuck in my mind but I took no action until I was visited by an old gentleman name of Orr. He had once worked for Mr Frank Harris at the *Fortnightly Review* and bore him a considerable grudge – the causes of which need not concern us here. Mr Orr insisted that Mr Harris was the murderer and, to cut a long story short, he was.'

'What!'

'Yes, there is no doubt about it. Further investigations revealed conclusive evidence.'

'But why did you not arrest him?'

At this, Grand seemed to shrink before my eyes. Suddenly he was a broken man.

'I did confront him with the facts and he confessed – he had little choice. He then offered me an enormous sum of money to suppress this information. To my shame, I accepted. I am not a rich man, Mr Kidd. I have obligations. I have not long to go now and I feel I could go some way to easing my conscience by telling you. Perhaps this is foolishness.'

'But why did he do it?'

'I asked him that, of course, but, to be honest, I could not understand his answer.'

Chapter Ten

Flip-Flap

I

'Canadian. Butter. Sculptures. Three words I never thought I would hear in one sentence or, at least, not in that order.'

Peter the anarchist fingered his beard as he spoke.

'They're very good,' said Mrs Round, 'though not instantly recognisable.'

'Perfectly recognisable,' said Fordie, 'so long as you consider them as sculptures OF butter rather than sculptures made of butter representing something else. They are, in a nutshell, recognisable as butter.'

'I really hadn't thought of that ...'

'Nobody has. Yet.'

Fordie raised his eyes to the sky and shuffled his farmer's feet.

'The Franco-British Exhibition ...' he began.

Peter snorted.

'More imperial nonsense,' he said. 'Do you realise they have even imported natives with their villages from Senegal and Ceylon. And, with supreme condescension, the Irish are represented by Ballymaclinton, a fictional village, and by one hundred and fifty "colleens", doubtless with Harris in mind.'

'They are all gratifyingly clean,' said Mr Round, 'surprisingly so. The press has remarked on that fact.'

Mrs Round winced in expectation of a tirade from Peter directed at her husband.

'A fictional village,' Fordie mused, his eyes still fixed on the empyrean, 'like Bedford Park, I suppose. There too people were planted to be stared at by the masses who would return to their own homes thanking God they did not have to endure such privations.'

'Oh, Mr Hueffer, for goodness sake! Do not be so foolish.'

Hilda Harper was struggling to conceal her outrage behind a mask of urbanity. She had, in her imagination, remarried, not a man but a suburb.

'The difference is, surely, that the Senegalese and the Irish would wish to live in Bedford Park, whereas ...'

Peter, now circling our group, emitted a shout of laughter.

'Whereas,' he said witheringly, 'we would not wish to live anywhere but Bedford Park! We are so amazingly ... special!'

'Well,' responded Hilda triumphantly, 'indeed we are. Our understanding contains their lives, theirs cannot contain ours.'

But Fordie had moved on.

'Franco-British is a sound idea. These are two nations could each do with more of the other. I should like to write a French novel ...'

Peter sighed and shrugged and then started as Fordie emitted a surprisingly high-pitched shriek.

'... What on earth is THAT?'

Having lowered his eyes from the sky, he had encountered a bizarre, moving object at the far end of the showground. Two cars were rising into the sky; each was fixed to a tapering metal arm, the structure forming a giant, closing V shape.

'It is the Flip-Flap.'

Tremlett had appeared as if he had been waiting for this

moment. Suffused with the complacency of progress, he placed himself in front of our little group.

'The fare is sixpence and it takes three minutes and twenty seconds for the cars to complete their full semi-circular progress. Each arm is one hundred and fifty feet in length and each car can carry forty-eight passengers, raising them to a total height of two hundred feet. It is an excellent piece of engineering.'

Fordie stared at him, aghast. He was struggling to find the right words. Two, finally, emerged, as if from some cavern deep beneath his waistcoat.

'But,' he said, 'why?'

'Why?' said Tremlett, baffled. 'You might as well ask why the Eiffel Tower, which this, in some ways, resembles – note the structure of the arms. And you seem to approve of the French whenever I hear you speak.'

'The Eiffel Tower is a contemplative object. You can stare peacefully from the top and consider your moment in time. This is a version for people who cannot contemplate and must be forever in motion. At its heart, if I understand it correctly, is a simple movement from one place to another, an exercise in futility. Dear me, Tremlett, surely you can grasp the difference.'

Peter, still circling our group, was clutching his head. Tremlett, anger and amusement now warring on his face, was about to speak, but our anarchist interrupted his orbit to intervene.

'The marathon race is a simple movement from one place to another, but you all seem enthusiastic about that. Or have you now changed your mind, Fordie?'

The two cars, as Tremlett called them, were now slowly passing as the V briefly became, from our perspective, a single tower.

'Perhaps, Peter,' said Fordie, 'we can discern the distinction in the nomenclature. The marathon is named after a heroic moment in classical history, a moment that still informs our lives and which inspires superhuman effort. This thing is called the Flip-Flap and it inspires nothing.'

'Oh, come now,' said Peter, producing a programme, 'surely the historic nature of this race has been compromised by the sponsorship of ...' he leafed through the programme '... OXO! "Let the experience of Britain's healthiest sons teach you the value of OXO as a strengthener." And WAWKPHAR, a military foot powder – "Strengthen the Feet! Free samples available to competitors in the dressing room." Depravity! The corruption of commerce!'

'WAWKPHAR?' said Mrs Harper, bewildered.

Unperturbed, Fordie returned his gaze to the heavens.

'You are not sceptical enough, dear Peter. Those things do not work, that is the point. The runners are, therefore, on equal terms with their Greek forebears. A marathon is a marathon and nobility is nobility with or without OXO.'

'Do you suppose it has begun?' said Mrs Round. 'They were starting from Windsor.'

A hand, claw-like, clutched my upper arm.

'It HAS begun. I spoke to Conan Doyle, he is here for the *Mail*. They are already approaching Slough. There is concern about the heat. All were examined by doctors, but a death or two would be normal. Several are expected.'

It was Frank, a crazed gleam in his eye and sweat pouring down his face; a few drops were blackish from his hair dye and some had dried to form streaks.

'Ah, Harris, have you examined the colleens yet?' said Peter.

Frank spun round, in confusion rather than anger. He was still gripping my arm, now to anchor himself rather than announce his presence. In the act of spinning, he seemed to forget Peter's sneer and spun back to whisper urgently to me.

'Put your money on Tom Longboat, a certain winner, a Red Indian, he runs like the wind. His training has been kept secret, the use of some drug ... Conan Doyle tells me he went straight into the lead. I had some dealings with Indians in my time. No one can touch them at open running.'

Mrs Round, frustrated by his whispering, tugged at Frank's sleeve.

'How long will they be, Mr Harris?'

'Another two hours at least.'

'Oh dear, perhaps we ought to take our places in the stadium.'

Murmurings of assent passed around the group and they began to move.

'TWO HOURS, I SAID!' Frank shouted after them, but they paid no attention and continued to shuffle nervously towards the stadium. Frank wanted to walk around the White City and insisted I join him. We plunged into the fantastic blazing white forms.

2

'Inspector Grand called on me,' I announced as we plunged.

Frank stopped. I was expecting an outburst or some subtle squirming to free himself from what was to come. But, far from shocking or deflating him, this statement seemed to inject a high, bright, serene energy into his frame. He straightened his back, he puffed out his chest, then, quite literally, *rose* to the occasion.

'He did, did he? And what did HE have to say for himself?'

I took a deep breath.

'He said you killed Binks and bribed him to keep quiet about it. He said the evidence was conclusive. Why, Frank?'

He stopped and stared at the Flip-Flap: the two cars, having exchanged places, were now on the ground.

'I wished to make a point.'

'What point and to whom? To me?'

'To myself. I wished to prove to myself the true meaning of ACTION! I mean what I say, Cal, when I speak of this century of violence. We will, soon enough, be killing each other, killing ourselves. I wanted to be sure I could do it.'

'But why Binks?'

'Because he needed to be killed. He was like verminous, muddy water flowing about the place, polluting everything. If I could not kill him, who could I kill when the time came? I, above all men, must be fully prepared.'

'He was a father, Frank, and a husband.'

'Good God, man, what has that got to do with it? Everybody is SOMETHING and SOMEBODY must be killed! And you have no claim on high principle. I know all about your whoring, your tarts. Why you should pay for it with your looks I can't imagine.'

I felt my face grow pale in shock. I wanted to run away, to hide.

'You had me followed?'

'Occasionally. But I often had men talk to the Soho girls to find out if they had had any famous visitors. The dove-grey American came up quite often. Not quite as pure as you seem, eh? Perhaps you should have worn black. But I don't care about that. I knew you were what the French would call *un grand timide*. You would only ever go so far. No follow-through.'

I could not bear this talk of my frailties. Shame, like blood, was rushing through my veins, making my temples throb and my face burn. I had to drag the conversation back to Binks.

'But did you have a *reason* to kill him?'

'REASON! I had a million reasons and none. He was a pest, a plotter, and I saw that he was about to drag you into one of his plots. Oh yes, plenty of reasons. I could have chosen others to kill. The point was the killing of a victim who had to be appropriate; there are many such. I just had to be ready. We ALL have to be ready. The violence is at hand. Look at where we are now, at what we have become.'

He gestured at the brilliant white buildings around us.

'They're not real buildings, not built to last, just to make a bit of a show. Like the cinematograph. It's what happens now. We decorate things, apply make-up – like your tarts, look for a while and then turn away. It's all coming to an end on a painted stage. Bedford Park was a painted stage, but now they can't even be bothered with bricks, the fools, the damnable fools.'

His own make-up in the form of hair dye was also not built to last. His face, though triumphant in expression, was taking on an alarmingly exotic aspect. Movement was difficult amid the crowds but Frank, having explained himself to his satisfaction, decided to plunge on, pausing every so often to gaze in wonder at some perilously young girl, much to the consternation of her companions or parents.

We stopped to watch the people climbing eagerly into the Swan Boats.

'I have spoken, now it is your turn. What was it like … with Maud? Was there something horribly wrong? You have said nothing.'

I knew he had been containing himself for days, ever since our eviction from the Palace Theatre, but I had no answer prepared. What *was* it like?

'There is nothing really to say.'

'Oh, surely ...'

A child eating something brushed against me, leaving a dark line of purple sugar on my sleeve. I examined this for a moment. The White City was fictional, Bedford Park was fictional, I too was fictional. Our purity did not survive first contact with the world and we became as real as – no more real than – a stained sleeve. The murder of Binks suddenly seemed a trivial thing, an almost invisible mote in the great eye of London, and I felt Frank had bought my silence with his knowledge of my whoring.

He was breathing heavily and sweating ever more profusely at my side. I saw him among these colourful, joyous crowds. Why did he talk of violence, why was it 'all over'? Why should it not be just beginning? These teeming London souls seemed happy enough, happier than we had been in Bedford Park, happier, perhaps, than any crowd there had ever been. They organised and improved the world. They *engineered* and then their leaders built them these Hindu temples, these Swan Boats, as rewards. And their fat, funny king said everything was all right. They could even look at Ceylonese or Irish villages, here in Shepherd's Bush, and be consoled by the thought that their own hardships were as nothing. Perhaps there should have been a Chicago village. And they were all watched over by the Flip-Flap, the mechanical god of the happy masses, the machine that raised them up so they could look down. Finally, I returned to the matter of Maud.

'When I said "nothing", I was being very precise.'

It was not, I knew, enough and, realising I needed a ruse to distract him from this line of thought, I turned to face him. To my horror, his face had now become zebra-like; the lines of dried hair dye would have made him look perfectly at home in the Senegalese village.

'Frank, we must do something.'

'Nothing, now something, what is the matter with you? Have I lured you into ACTION? Do you want to KILL somebody?'

'No. Your face ...'

He touched his cheek with his fingertip and was startled to see it had turned entirely black. He rubbed it on one of the blazing white walls near by, leaving a dirty grey cloud. I grasped his arm – a novelty in the course of our friendship – and pulled him away, searching desperately for some kind of washroom. After some rapid walking, I noticed the one undecorated door at the back of a Hindu temple which contained a display of French cheese and wine and German sausage. The door led to a dank, cistern-like space with a row of basins. The floors were stained and the walls cracked. The undersides of these structures revealed the truth of Frank's words – these buildings were not made to last.

I extracted two handkerchiefs, one from my pocket and one from Frank's, soaked them and began to rub at his face. He stood there as I did so, obedient as a naughty little boy. Things, I saw, were going to get much worse before they got better. The lines smeared as I wetted and rubbed them. Frank was no longer a zebra, he was a music-hall Negro. I rubbed and rinsed but the density and distribution of the dye only seemed to increase. I felt myself becoming angry and frenzied. At this rate, I would miss the end of the marathon – or I would have to abandon Frank.

'Nothing?' he said suddenly. 'Maud was nothing?'

I paused, my left hand still holding his chin. I wanted to scream at him, perhaps even to punch him as Pound had punched me. Then I noticed that the expression on his face was not that of Frank the lustful gossip, but rather that of

Frank the genuinely puzzled. I had slipped through the net he cast over the world. The Ca. that loved Maud and distracted himself with Dora and sundry tarts had suddenly become something he could not understand. I sighed, my shoulders sagged and my hands dropped to my side.

'Another time, Frank, another time.'

'You need,' said a voice behind us, 'a surfactant.'

'Tremlett!' I gasped.

He reached past us and picked up a white bar I had not noticed from one of the basins.

'Soap is a surfactant. I saw there was a crisis over by the Swan Boats so I followed you in the expectation of being of some assistance.'

We stared at this figure of sudden authority in dismay. Now we were both naughty little boys.

'Let me see what I can do.'

He worked up a dense lather between his hands and then smeared it over Frank's face. The whiteness was immediately streaked with brown and grey.

'Please rinse that off.'

Frank obeyed and, at once, it became clear that a surfactant was exactly what we had needed. Tremlett lathered and applied once more. Frank rinsed and emerged as, more or less, his true self.

'I think that is enough. We could go on but with ever diminishing returns. Also I gather the runners have passed Pinner.'

'Pinner!' cried Frank, now quite restored. 'Closer than I thought. I'll wager Longboat is still in the lead.'

'You would lose,' said Tremlett with a superior smile. 'He dropped out at Ruislip utterly exhausted. The drug employed in training was strychnine. I suppose it may have worked in lower doses. Johnny Hayes is now in the lead – your compatriot, Cal. It would be a great event if he wins, the Americans have been so bitter about the British at these games. They refused to dip their flag before the King at the opening ceremony.'

'A necessary gesture,' I said, slightly surprised to find myself being an American for the day, 'forced upon us by history. And, anyway, we think you cheat.'

A temporary patriotism was, I supposed, in the spirit of the Olympics and these were great distractions from the horrors exposed by Frank.

'Of course we do,' said Frank, suddenly revitalised, 'we have an Empire, what choice do we have but to cheat? You can't play fair and expect to rule the world. We will find a way of defeating this Hayes, trust me on that. I must speak to Conan Doyle. Fred Appleby must now surely win.'

'A victory,' said Tremlett, 'would be more important to the Americans. Having exchanged rural for urban life, they feel the need to fight the ensuing fatness with fitness.'

'Oh, for God's sake,' said Frank, 'enough of this.'

With that, he led us back out into the dazzling whiteness and strode rapidly, risking further zebra stripes, in the direction of the stadium.

'Cal, my friend,' said Tremlett as we both tried to give the impression of strolling while keeping up with Frank's headlong rush, 'I am so sorry you missed my demonstration as a result of that American poet's violent intervention.'

'Demonstration?'

'Of unusual effects of static electricity.'

'I am sorry too, though I was at least experiencing unusual effects of poetry.'

Tremlett declined to smile.

'Static current, you see, is evidence of the astonishing ubiquity of this force, evidence that it forms the very core of materiality. We do not have to make this power, it is just there, everywhere, all the time.'

We had reached the strangely naked structure of the stadium. Seen from above, it formed a vast, grey oval in the White City, an infective corpuscle that would one day colour this site to match the rest of London.

'Electricity binds everything together; this concrete, this steel, these bodies, our very brains are electric ...'

Frank had vanished into the gloomy echoing interior. For no good reason, panic tightened my throat.

'... we will find, soon enough, that all forces are one ...'

'Tremlett, we have lost Frank. Have you any idea where we are going?'

I imagined he was seeking another victim; perhaps he would return, armed, to murder me. Tremlett woke from his electrical reverie and smiled condescendingly.

'Of course,' he said, 'we are in the royal enclosure. This way.'

Through the gloom he led me to a metal staircase at the foot of which stood a policeman. Tremlett nodded to him and, to my amazement, he saluted.

'You are known here?'

'Services to the military. Electricity will transform war, perhaps even making killing unnecessary.'

'Killing unnecessary? Frank would disagree.'

I had spoken rashly but Tremlett merely nodded and led me up the staircase. We emerged into sudden sunlight and heat that seemed to be made more intensive by the great oval bowl of the stadium. I could see, at first, nothing, but the noise was tremendous, hard and unyielding. Through this, Tremlett's voice gradually became audible.

'... seven hundred feet by three hundred feet, ample room for javelin throwing. Cycle track, cinder track, grass track, swimming pool greater than three hundred feet in length, seating for sixty-eight thousand, standing room for another twenty-three thousand. And, today, full, I believe, for the marathon. And all being captured by cinematography. The Pathé Brothers are using eighty miles of film a day. Welcome to the new world, Cal, the British world.'

'It is a world of games?'

'Of sport rather. Sport is the electricity of the human realm, it combines all other forces.'

As my eyes adjusted to the glare I saw a man falling headlong into the pool; a diving competition was in progress and there seemed to be much activity elsewhere in the stadium. For some reason, I had come to think the marathon was the only event of the day.

I followed Tremlett into a long, rectangular box with properly cushioned seats. A further, inner box contained the royal party. Frank was here; he leapt to his feet.

'Appleby has given up! The fool Hefferon – the next possible winner – took a glass of champagne from an admirer and collapsed with cramp soon afterwards. Men will die, I tell you!'

His hair had lost its lion tamer's lustre because of the drainage of dye, but still there were streaks, mostly smeared. He had evidently been trying to control the striping.

'Who is now in the lead?' I asked, not that there was any name I would recognise.

'We don't know! The reporting back to the stadium seems to have failed in some way. The board is out of date.' He pointed to a vast scoreboard of names and numbers at the far end of the stadium.

Mr and Mrs Round, bright red in the heat, were watching the unfolding events in what looked like a state of panic. Fordie, also reddened but in a way that seemed to be justified by his straw-like hair, was seated, vastly immobile and alone amid a line of empty seats closest to the royal box. There was no sign of Hilda Harper, nor of Peter.

Fearing I might be subjected to more of Tremlett's pedagogy, I made my way over to Fordie. Frank followed. We became again the trio that had once set out for Hilda's fair, Frank and I now in decline, Fordie on the rise with his new journal and, apparently, a new love.

'I'm sorry about Pound,' he said the moment I sat down. 'He will be an important man if he can control his impulses and the usual arrogance of the young and gifted. I think this can be arranged.'

Frank laughed.

'If you are bewildered by that remark, Cal, then it is because you have failed to notice that Fordie now owns literature. It came quite cheap, I gather.'

The remark wounded me with the remembrance of Fordie's stiff note of rejection of the writings I had sent him. It had arrived in a cream envelope that was difficult to open; I cut myself in the process. The paper inside was equally thick and unyielding – like the damned buffalo robe, not so much folded as bent. It sprang open to reveal a single line

'Seek not your satisfaction in the garden of literature. Ford.'

I could not write and now, according to Pound as he ranted prior to punching me, I could not read.

'Next to nothing,' said Fordie, nodding seriously.

'Ah, yes, nothing,' said Frank, winking at me, 'we have been discussing nothing, a surprisingly fruitful subject.'

There seemed to be a new commotion in the stadium. More people were pouring in, filling every empty space, and, from the dark cavern a hundred yards or so to our

251

right from which the runners were due to emerge, great boomings could be heard.

'They must be close,' said Frank, 'and, good God, we have no idea who will first appear. I have been unable to find Conan Doyle this last half-hour.'

Fordie stirred at the mention of the name.

'A pity,' he said, 'since we have all become such excellent studies in scarlet.'

He began to laugh, a ponderous heaving of the waist-coated frontage combined with a haw-haw emission from beneath his moustache.

'Very good, Fordie,' said Frank, trying to dispose of the distraction of Fordie's increasingly noisy self-satisfaction. Mr Round had heard the joke and was trying to explain it to his wife.

Our group having become so inward looking, we had failed to notice what I now noticed – that the games in the centre of the stadium had ceased and the athletes had gathered along the length of the track between the runners' entrance and the royal box. Hilda Harper appeared in our box, staggering as if she had completed the race herself.

'They are coming, they are coming!' she cried before lowering herself gently into a seat. Peter, anarchically uncon-cerned, had strolled in behind her, a tiny black cigar in his mouth.

'The race,' he observed with satisfaction, 'seems to have descended into disorder.'

Officials, one clutching a mighty megaphone, and, Frank gleefully informed me, a doctor had gathered around the entrance. There was a huge roar as a group appeared, two men supporting a third.

'Longboat!' cried Frank. 'It is a false alarm, he was brought here by motor car.'

Longboat crashed to the ground as the men released him.

Then nothing further happened. As if to urge on the event the band struck up 'See the Conquering Hero Come'.

'What if they have all failed?' asked Peter. 'What then?'

'Surely that is unlikely,' said Mr Round, 'is it not, Mr Harris?'

'Pah! Impossible!'

Then another false alarm. A clown walked through the entrance wearing gigantic red shorts, a white shirt and a white cloth wrapped round his head. His absurd legs, like twisted twigs, made it clear he could be no athelete, as did his drunken gait as he turned in precisely the wrong direction on the track. Officials tried to correct him but he pushed them away as if he felt he was being deceived. The crowd roared with laughter.

Frank, however, was flicking the pages of his programme.

'Number nineteen!' he cried. 'It is the Italian Pietri, Dorando Pietri!'

The crowd had realised the same thing. This was no clown. They fell silent and then roared as Pietri, now moving in the right direction, stumbled and swayed like a man in a dream, surrounded by men in suits determined not to wake him. He fell, crumpling as if every bone in his body had become disconnected from every other. It was hopeless; there was still some distance to go to the finishing line and there was nothing in Pietri's body that suggested the possibility of further movement. The men, sweating in their thick suits, formed a desperate cluster around him and raised him to his feet. Some last pulsations of muscular force stiffened his legs enough to propel him forward. His feet could not seem to point in the right direction and his gait became a protracted stumble, his mind forcing him forward at war with his body, which wanted to turn in ever smaller circles before finally expiring. Again he fell, a sinking ship, again he was raised.

'Surely all this assistance will invalidate the result,' said Tremlett.

'Oh, but the glory of it!' said Hilda Harper, her gaze fixed on Pietri, her hands flat against her cheeks, her eyes blazing with the shock of sudden passion.

'The glory indeed,' murmured Fordie.

'And now,' growled Frank, 'he needs to die a Roman death. Die, Dorando!'

Another runner had entered the stadium, Johnny Hayes, the stars and stripes emblazoned on his chest. Old Europe was dying on the last straight while young America pounded healthily onwards.

My mind, meanwhile, had withdrawn from the scene. I was watching the drama as if from some distant future, perhaps watching a few miles of the Pathé Brothers film in the Bioscope. Pietri's race had been run and, like every other race, it had been trivialised by time. Born at Windsor, his childhood had passed in Slough and Langley Marsh. At Uxbridge he had attained manhood. Ickenham, Ruislip and Pinner witnessed his golden years, but, by Harrow, his decline had begun. At Willesden Junction his body began its agonising repudiation, though his soul drove it onward to the White City, where men in suits, officials, tugged and pushed to deny him his final rest at the end of his great semicircular voyage. As the man with the megaphone and the doctor at last scooped poor Dorando across the finishing line, just before Hayes could catch up, I knew London was exhausted and I must, somehow, return to America.

Dorando Pietri was disqualified and the gold medal went to Hayes. However, moved by the spectacle, the passion of the crowd and the encouragement of Conan Doyle, Queen Alexandra awarded a special silver cup to the brave Italian. Tremlett's head was right but Hilda's newly discovered heart was vindicated.

I left the stadium with Frank and we wandered aimlessly among the temples as the low sun softened their whiteness with warm summer gold. The crowds were leaving – no Swan Boat, no native village, no exotic foodstuff could hope to compete with the sensational climax of the marathon – and, after about half an hour, we found ourselves almost alone in the White City of the West.

We barely spoke. Something was, indeed, over. Frank seemed dazed, his face newly streaked with dye, and my mind was in turmoil. America was now inevitable but my idleness stood in the way. How would it all be arranged? Where would I go? What would I do? For some reason I could not get beyond the long list of petty tasks that would need to be completed – disposal of the house, shipping of my goods, packing of the robe, the farewells and explanations and false promises of my return. Maud was lost to all common feeling and ritual, but Dora …

America still lived in my imagination as the coarse, simple place that I had fled to discover the smooth complications of London. But this city had teased me, sending me down false trails, offering me great hopes, golden visions, and then snatching them away. Or had it all been my doing, my undoing? Or had Frank been the puppet master behind the painted stage?

I would miss him, even now I knew him to be a murderer. I had known before. He told me he had killed a man while out on the Western ranges. Now, with the sudden signs of his decline, the scorn of London society and the increasing youthfulness of the objects of his desire, I sensed a desperation. I owed him much and perhaps now was the time to repay. He was no longer my guide, now I might be his. If he were left alone in this city, I could see his decline into lunacy or further criminality.

After we had walked in silence for twenty minutes or so, Frank grasped my arm.

'The Flip-Flap,' he said, 'it is still working!'

I looked up to see the two arms returning to the horizontal.

'Come, come, we must try it! You go to that end, I will go to the other and we will cross in the middle.'

In spite of my languor, I could see that it was something that had to be done. We parted to board our opposing cars. I was one of only half a dozen people in mine. We sat, mutely, smelling the metal and oil, waiting for the machinery to take us on the semicircular ride. The air was darkening around us.

The Flip-Flap started with a jolt and a great clanking sound that made us all look at each other nervously, as if considering the company in which we might encounter death. Free of the ground, the car swayed and, at once, I feared an onset of seasickness, not something from which I had ever suffered, but, perhaps, in the air, I would.

The ground was steadily dropping away and we were rising above the domes and spires of the people's white dreams. I began to see beyond the showground to the farther rooftops – glowing gold to the east, but dark and shadowed to the west, the chimney pots silhouetted by the sunset that now flooded the western sky with lurid colour. A little higher and the landscape began to form a plan of sorts, the streets appearing between the houses, narrowing in to the centre of the city or splaying outwards to the fields beyond. I tried to make out Bedford Park to the southwest but it was now too enfolded by London's dark embrace.

Higher still and I thought I could just make out Big Ben and the Abbey and, beyond, perhaps, St Paul's. But the view was smudged by smoke and a darkening glare. Then there was a sudden flash of red and gold and the Thames sprang into view, cutting through the city eastward to the sea. I could see two steamers, their paths diverging, two silver trails forming pale arcs as they sailed away. Endlessly, in one motion, we depart from each other ...

The car swayed once more as we neared the summit of the arc. I could see the other car approaching, also swaying and appearing, from this perspective, to be about to collide with us. It seemed empty, but, as it drew nearer, I made out one solitary passenger, Frank, immobile. He did not even seem to be admiring the view. As he drew nearer, I could see he was staring downwards. Finally, just as we crossed, the sun caught his features, streaked and lost in some dark reverie. The intensity of the light destroyed all depth. He had become a silhouette, a cardboard cutout, half a man, a photograph, a memory.

I closed Notebook 78 and rang for my whisky.

Mid-Atlantic, 1912

A tide of voices leaves me gasping on the shore; it has 'all'
been a dream. Too fearful of the bitter cold to move, I pat
the deck with my fingertips to find my notebook – number
ninety. The damp gloss of the wood gives way to its dry,
matt cover. I draw it to me and write a few lines.

'You are very important to us.'
 Dora. The golden threads in the air.
 How did Binks push that cigarette through that coin?

I had fallen asleep in a port-side chair wrapped in a heavy
blanket. Ever since that incident at lunch with Stead, I
have been treated as an invalid, subjected to stern warnings about the cold, but I feel it is mistake to be indoors
on such a voyage, I would be missing something. Four
days out – according to Stead, we are a few hundred miles
south-east of the Grand Banks; how he loves saying those
words! 'Grand Banks!' The chest puffed, the beard almost
horizontal. He keeps proclaiming that we are aboard the
largest moving object ever made! How he trusted the sanity
of this vessel, this voyage. Dear Stead, for all his elderly
mysticism and grandeur, still has the soul of the editor of
the *Pall Mall Gazette*.
Wednesday morning, they say, Wednesday morning, I shall

set my foot on American soil again. Not Chicago, not yet, perhaps not ever; New York will do for me or westward where people, it is said, go to be reborn or, perhaps, in my case, to land, the leaf finally fallen. But on the soil of the New World!

'Rose on tiptoe and fell like an autumn leaf,' Dora had said.

And Maud ...

Pound, the betrayer, told Willie, who, thereafter, tortured me with extravagant *politesse* or whatever the Irish call it. Knowing I must, still I could not leave London. The years passed ...

I was in the lobby at Morley's. Something made me turn. Maud was standing before a mirror, a pagan goddess in her heavy, figured jacket and her favourite hat crowned with bird wings.

'A bird,' Frank used to say, 'stooping on its prey had miscalculated its trajectory and collided with her head. The surgeons were at a loss and, in desperation, she called upon her milliner ...'

She did not know I was watching. Her feet in black jewelled slippers were making curious movements.

I had asked Stead why it should be so cold in April. He laughed at my ignorance.

'The Great Circle Route, the Riemann Circle, the shortest distance between two points on the surface of a sphere. It means we must head north, almost clipping Greenland before we follow the south-westward line of the eastern seaboard.'

He loves the language of engineering, navigation and control.

'A semicircle, then?'

I find myself on a maritime Flip-Flap – two semicircles; I will have completed the Great Circle. Stead looked exasperated.

'It may look thus on a two-dimensional projection, but it cannot be a semicircle unless we travel halfway round the world, the Riemann Circle, you see ...'

I let him explain his wisdom to himself. My mind wandered as it always does these days.

She caught my eye in the mirror. Any embarrassment was concealed by the mask-like pride in her face.

'I am discovered dancing,' she said, 'it has happened before.'

'Dancing?'

'A tinker shuffle I picked up in a village in Donegal.'

I looked at her, stunned by her cool regard. Stead had written she was one of the most beautiful women in the world. He dissembled. Every man knew she was the most beautiful. That meant she was Helen of Troy, she belonged to history, not to any man. Make me immortal with a kiss ...

Stead, the beloved Chief, has decided to spend the voyage nursing and educating me. He has not declined, as I have, into absent-mindedness, forgetting, a sense of failure and missed opportunities, fading into a photograph. The list grew in my mind each night.

Why had I let Fordie extinguish my literary ambitions with one sentence? Why had I not spent my time with Stead rather than Frank? Why had I let Dora go without a fight? Why had I not pursued a career with Frank's periodicals?

When being kinder to myself, I thought of myself as a victim, one of the necessary adjuncts to any history. I blamed either London, the great eye, or Bedford Park, the enchanted suburb, for my inertia. Or, perhaps, my father and his spy Calvert. Had he blackened my name about town? I would never know. Calvert finally succeeded in killing himself by hanging, in Regent's Park.

Stead does not make lists, nor, I suspect, does he lie awake. The tonic of purpose courses through him, tightening his muscles, brightening his mind. In some quarters he has made himself ridiculous with his pursuit of the dead – his critics said a once great force for good had declined into superstition and delusion.

It was not that ridiculous. In the midst of Ireland and empire, good works, the poor, Tremlett's electricity, Fordie's literature, Hilda's culture, Frank's women, Peter's anarchism and Mulholland's optimism, Stead's spiritualism was not unusual. The age demanded answers of one kind or another.

'We shall know the answer soon enough,' Stead had said, 'all earthly things will be made clear on the other side.'

Having assured the Morley's clerk that her enormous dog – a Dane called Dagda – would damage neither carpets nor furniture, we went up to the room. Dagda, with the air of a dog who has seen it all before, lay down on the rug, his great jaw resting on his front paws and his eyes looking upwards, pleading with us to complete our business so he could be back out amid the smells of the street.

'Nothing?' Dora had said. 'Nothing – is that all there is to be said?'

Frank, predictably but to my dismay, had ensured that my description of the fulfilment of passion with Maud had been thoroughly published.

'In essence, yes.'

Wry triumph crossed her features, quickly replaced by piteous resignation, tinged with the pleasure of revenge.

'Poor Cal, after all that ...'

'I think I misunderstood the whole sex game. Perhaps Frank is right to treat every woman as nothing more than a stepping stone to the next, the language of love being a kind of fiction.'

Dora stiffened.

'Nellie has not proved to be a stepping stone.'

She spoke censoriously. There did seem to be a Harris household forming. Having regarded Nellie O'Hara as just one of a crowd, I had been startled to discover she was still at Frank's side, like Maud's Dagda, waiting for the sordid business of his dalliances to be over so they could get on with their lives together. The Irish have a way with men.

As she loosed her clothes, she told me of her vision of Ireland's Queen.

'I was returning from Mayo triumphant. I had stopped a famine and saved many lives ...'

Her hat was unpinned, her jacket fell to the floor.

'I look out of the window of the train across a dark bog and there was this beautiful woman with dark hair blown in the wind. I knew it was Cathleen Ni Houlihan.'

The shoes, stockings and skirt gone.

'She was stepping from stone to stone over the treacherous surface and the little white stones shone, marking a path behind her, then faded into darkness.'

Her nakedness slowly emerging as an afterthought.

'I heard a voice say, "You are one of the little stones on which the feet of the Queen have rested on her way to freedom."

'The sadness of the night took hold of me and I cried; it seemed so lonely just to be one of those little stones left behind on the path.'

This was enough for Willie – he made theatre out of Queen Cathleen and her demands for a blood sacrifice for the freedom of Ireland. Violence clung to Maud. Mr Yeats had been horrified by her enthusiasm for war at that first meeting when his son said the troubling of his life began.

Maud, as she intended me to conclude, was not merely a stepping stone, she was the Queen herself, as, indeed, she was in that damned play.

Naked, she lay on the bed and her feet rehearsed that shuffle again.

The ship, creaking and shivering, churns on to the cold horizon, now just beginning to be warmed by the first colours of sunset.

Frank had often brought up the subject of Nellie's red-gold hair and vase-like hips and I had, from time to time, noticed that he had done so more often and for longer than with any previous hair and hips. He was clinging to her and Nellie was clinging to Frank because that is what she did. People said she made him, if anything, worse, more of a rascal, a cad, a bounder, and no less of a seducer. It was because she believed in him, in what he was – in his destiny and in his part in hers.

The realisation that Nellie could be with Frank to the end came as a shock. My unattached condition had always been justified – perversely perhaps – by Frank's cavalier infidelities. There was, I thought, heroism in not being trapped by a woman, even if out of weakness. With Frank trapped, I was undermined, not a heroic bachelor, a lonely old man. And, dear God, he was now editor of a ladies' journal called *Hearth and Home*. I had been mistaken about his decline; the man was simply settling down.

'Come to America with me.'

I was kneeling at Dora's feet. She had, at my desperate request, come to my house in Bedford Park.

'Why on earth should I do that?'

'Because we are in love.'

As part of my rebellion against English ways, I had cut back the bushes in front of my bay window. Dora was thus haloed by her still-golden hair.

'You were in love with Maud and then you betrayed me with Audrey.'

Maud belonged to the world, she was more statue than woman, and Audrey was a ridiculous widow – Mulholland having, by all accounts, exploded, some even spoke of spontaneous combustion, after which she wrapped herself in a blanket of self-pity so capacious that it contained, finally, much of west London.

'The first my delusion, the second yours. There was nothing between us – in both cases, ultimately. You did not deny you were in love with me.'

She turned to gaze out of the window and then left without saying a word.

Maud growled suddenly and then laughed at the shocked expression on my face.

'Oh, Cal, you are so easily scared! The Comte de Cremont claimed to have been a tiger in a previous incarnation and would insist that I was his tigress mother. I do miss Paris ...'

I undressed slowly, watched by Dagda. Maud seemed absorbed in her memories.

Dora's silence was enough to convince me that this was just the start of a campaign of persuasion. I wrote to her at length, inventing American plans to give substance to my avowals. I forced meetings upon her. She remained non-committal until, one day, at lunch.

'What is America like? I mean, I know you speak of it, but what is it like just day by day?'

I started at this sudden expression of at least a passing interest.

'It is like … everything … whatever you want it to be. There are cities and wilderness …'

She seemed to wake as I lay beside her.

'My prince of Tir na nOg, the fairy land to the West …'

It had been no more than idle curiosity. I fought on to get her to sail with me, but she saw the entire project as one risk – America – laid upon another – me. I was, I realised, for the first and last time in my life, broken hearted.

'Cal, are you still here?'

Stead looms over me.

Maud said no more and, afterwards, I hurriedly dressed and left. Dagda leapt on the bed after me.

Stead helps me rise from my chair, a boy runs past us towards the bow, already eager for the first glimpse of what was to come.

'It is time to dress for dinner. Only a few more nights at sea, we must exhaust every possible topic.'

He rubs his hands and then stares upwards in the direction of travel.

'America is waiting for us both, Cal, America! It is the future.'

Appendix

Bedford Park is fiction but it is constructed around a few historical truths, most notably:

Frank Harris's adventures in America certainly have some truth, though his own obfuscations make it difficult to be sure in detail. His romantic and journalistic careers are more or less true.

W.B. Yeats did first meet Maud Gonne when she visited the Yeats home in Bedford Park – and she was wearing slippers. The rest of the details about Maud's life are also true.

Peter Kropotkin was in London at the time I describe, though my version is an invention.

Stepniak was a murderer and a resident of Bedford Park. He did die on a level crossing.

Madame Blavatsky and Annie Besant were as I describe them, though the ritual is an invention.

Oscar Wilde, Ford Madox Hueffer (Ford) and Joseph Conrad are as they seem to have been and there was a Dr Albert Tebb offering cures to the literati.

The Bioscope was in Bishopsgate and the behaviour of the audience is accurate. The films described are genuine.

Maud Allan was real, as was the marathon runner Dorando Pietri. The Flip-Flap, the White City Exhibition and the Olympics are accurately described.

Biographical facts about W.T. Stead are true and he did indeed sail on the Titanic. He was not among the survivors.

Calhoun Kidd only existed as a name – that of a passing American in a story by G.K. Chesterton entitled *The Strange Crime of Dr Boulnois*.

blog and newsletter

For literary discussion, author insight,
book news, exclusive content,
recipes and giveaways, visit the
Weidenfeld & Nicolson blog and
sign up for the newsletter at:

www.wnblog.co.uk

For breaking news, reviews and exclusive competitions
Follow us 🐦 @wnbooks
Find us 📘 facebook.com/WNfiction

Bryan Appleyard is an award-winning special features writer and columnist for the *Sunday Times*. He is the author of several books, including *The Brain is Wider than the Sky: Why Simple Solutions Don't Work in a Complex World*, *How to Live Forever or Die Trying: On the New Immortality* and *Brave New Worlds: Genetics and the Human Experience*. He lives in London.

Praise for Bedford Park

'A witty and erudite historical novel, set mostly in London in the late-Victorian and Edwardian eras ... It is also a brilliantly lively, often very funny reconstruction of a lost world of artistic endeavour and social idealism through which Appleyard's American abroad wanders in a fruitless search for his true self.'

Nick Rennison, *Sunday Times*

'Appleyard has created this novel, set in the West London suburb of Bedford Park, around the lives of noted Edwardians ... Beautifully written.'

Daily Mail

'Nothing in Bryan Appleyard's *Bedford Park* betrays the fact that it is his first period novel: not its deft characterisations, its virtuoso dialogue, its dry and economical wit, or its choice of a narrator and material quite outside the author's own experience ... Excellent fiction.'

Timothy Mo, *Spectator*

Also by Bryan Appleyard

The Culture Club: Crisis in the Arts

Richard Rogers: A Biography

The Pleasures of Peace: Art and Imagination in
Post-War Britain

Understanding the Present: Science and the Soul of
Modern Man

The First Church of the New Millennium: A Novel

Brave New Worlds: Genetics and the Human Experience

Aliens: Why They Are Here

How to Live Forever or Die Trying: On the New
Immortality

The Brain is Wider than the Sky: Why Simple Solutions
Don't Work in a Complex World